Lucy is a professional medical writer from the UK, with a PhD in cell biology (and has got used to saying "no, not that kind of doctor" to anyone who asks). She enjoys talking about science and horses, listening to 1980s soft rock music (Jon Bon Jovi, call me?), and binge-reading uplifting, happily-ever-after stories. *The Hot Henry Effect* is Lucy's first novel and was as much a surprise to her as to anyone who knows her, but now that creative writing has turned out to be a lot more fun than it was in GCSE English (sorry about that, Mrs Caswell), hopefully the first of many.

www.lucychalice.com

instagram.com/lucychalice.author
x.com/LucyChalice
tiktok.com/@Lucychalice
facebook.com/LucyChalice

T0253072

THE HOT HENRY EFFECT

LUCY CHALICE

One More Chapter
a division of HarperCollins*Publishers* Ltd
1 London Bridge Street
London SE1 9GF
www.harpercollins.co.uk
HarperCollins*Publishers*
Macken House, 39/40 Mayor Street Upper,
Dublin 1, D01 C9W8, Ireland

This paperback edition 2024

1

First published in Great Britain in ebook format
by HarperCollins*Publishers* 2024
Copyright © Lucy Chalice 2024
Lucy Chalice asserts the moral right to be identified
as the author of this work

A catalogue record of this book is available from the British Library

ISBN: 978-0-00-864619-6

Printed and bound in the UK using 100% Renewable Electricity
by CPI Group (UK) Ltd

MIX
Paper | Supporting
responsible forestry
FSC™ C007454
www.fsc.org

This book contains FSC™ certified paper and other controlled
sources to ensure responsible forest management.

For more information visit: www.harpercollins.co.uk/green

For my daughter, the best small human I ever did know. Keep being unapologetically you.

Playlist

Style - Taylor Swift

favorite crime - Olivia Rodrigo

Stay - Gracie Abrams

Late Night Talking - Harry Styles

My Silver Lining - First Aid Kit

Looking at Me - Sabrina Carpenter

Fallin For You - Colbie Caillat

I Know Places - Taylor Swift

My Love - Florence + The Machine

Dial Drunk - Noah Kahan

Can't Help Falling in Love - Haley Reinhart

Heart of Glass - Blondie

Quit - Cashmere Cat, Ariana Grande

Lie Like This - Julia Michaels

July - Noah Cyrus

Nonsense - Sabrina Carpenter

Only Love Can Hurt Like This - Paloma Faith

You Are In Love - Taylor Swift

Love U Like That - Lauv

ceilings - Lizzy McAlpine

Kiss Me - Sixpence None The Richer

Radio - Lana Del Rey

Dandelions - Ruth B.

Chapter One

The ridiculous swooning had started almost the instant he set foot in our laboratory. A wave of fluttering eyelashes, a gust of breathy sighs. Astute, intelligent scientists reduced to simpering wrecks. I felt like an extra in the screen adaptation of *Pride and Prejudice* rather than a doctoral student at one of the most acclaimed academic institutions in the world.

And it irritated me to the core.

"Bloody hell, Henry, stop touching the tip of the pipette to the top of the bottle, or you'll get all the cultures infected," I complained, slightly more acerbically than I had intended.

"Sorry," he mumbled, head bent against the glass partition. A faint blush coloured his cheeks and even though he didn't look in my direction, I could see from his perfectly formed profile that he seemed a bit wounded.

Damn it. Must. Be. More. Tolerant.

Tongue poking out in concentration, he tried again. His hand flailing the Gilson pipette wildly around the cell culture hood like he was conducting some kind of scientific semaphore, attempting to locate a fresh new tip from the sterilised box in the corner and suck up the required amount of bright pink growth media.

I couldn't help the impatient little huff that escaped from my lips, and he glanced over distractedly, splattering the once pristine stainless steel base of the cabinet, and completely missing the wells of the ninety six-well plate he was aiming for. I really tried to stop the eye roll, but my eyeballs seemed to be rotating reflexively these days.

"Just try again, with less exaggerated arm movements and you'll be fine," I said in a falsely bright and positive voice that was not well received, judging by the creased brow and slightly pouty look behind the goggles. I wondered if this was his version of Zoolander's "Blue Steel" and had to suppress a snigger from escaping.

It was easy to see why our research group had suddenly become a hive of female activity. I wasn't totally oblivious. Even Prof. Hart from genomics (who was fifty-seven years old and happily married to the dean of the medical school) would waft about in Henry's presence, clutching her pearls and sighing theatrically. In the last month, oestrogen levels had become worryingly high, and we had had an influx of undergrad and postgrad applications to work in our group, ninety-nine per cent of which were female. And, while I was all for encouraging women into STEM research, transferring laboratories or selecting a career just to stare at some guy's pretty face did not seem to be an appropriate or sustainable motivation.

In his defence, Henry Fraser did look like a cover model for GQ magazine; blue-grey eyes, impressively symmetrical bone structure, wavy chocolate brown hair, and at well over six feet tall he cut an impressive figure. Also, amazingly, he seemed blissfully unaware of the effect he had on anyone female. Or male actually; the dead faint that Ben, my undergrad research student, had performed when I introduced them would have made a Regency debutante's mother proud.

But the man was hopeless with a pipette, and at this moment in time I was attempting to teach him the intricacies of cell culture, whilst also frantically trying to finish my final few experiments in order to complete the last chapter of my doctorate here at Oxford. At least Henry's was only a short stint in our lab, just a few months for me to train him before he returned to his engineering PhD in the States.

He flashed a triumphant smile as he finally managed to get the full one hundred and fifty microlitres of growth media into the first well on this plate, and I responded with a double thumbs up and an attempting-to-be-supportive expression, which was probably more akin to a bulldog chewing a wasp.

"Good work, Henry, just ninety-five more to go," I crooned sarcastically.

"Motivational speaking is not your forte, Clara," he muttered, flicking the used tip off the pipette and dropping it into the plastic beaker he was using for waste. Hesitantly he went in for a new one, hand shaking madly causing the tip box to rattle musically as if he was trying to incite a flamenco dance-off.

As his mentor, I could not fault him as a student. Quietly polite, thoughtful and staggeringly intelligent. In fact, the unwavering attention and focus that he gave my every word, studiously copying out my protocols and seeking me out to ask detailed questions on the minutiae of every procedure, was to be commended. I couldn't recall a time when our dingy little office had ever been so well visited, what with Henry regularly dropping off coffees and pastries for me, stopping in for little chats, and then the constant stream of groupies who thought that I was the keeper of his diary, and could maybe guide them on the way into his heart, or his bed (some were more blatant than others), it was like Piccadilly Circus most days.

Staring out of the window, I let my mind wander just a little, the lure of this late summer afternoon providing an enticing distraction to those of us stuck inside. The hum of the strip lights and the astringent, antiseptic laboratory aroma triggering memories of many long and tedious hours spent in pursuit of my research. The constant second-guessing and attempts to do something important, something worthy of publication. And I was so nearly there, so close to getting my thesis written up and finished, after which I was convinced that a whole world of new and exciting opportunities was waiting for me. I just had to get through the viva first. The mere prospect of attending the trickiest exit interview in the world had my heartrate spiking and palms sweating, the multitude of horror stories told to every graduate student the world over flashing through my mind. But I could bloody well do this, I had to, and it was about time I said goodbye to the self-doubt and fear of rejection that had plagued me since I was a child.

"Shit." Henry's voice brought me back to the present day with a sweary little bump.

The tip of the pipette was now aimlessly sinking to the bottom of the container of growth media and Henry was attempting to fish it out, wholly unsuccessfully.

"It's alright, Henry, just leave it in there," I said, closing my eyes briefly, having already decided to write this bottle off and pour it down the sink after our session, convinced that it would have all kinds of funky organisms growing in it come the morning.

"If you're sure…" he replied, turning his whole body to look at me and catching the edge of the bottle with the cuffed sleeve of his university regulation bright blue lab coat, and sending the almost full container teetering precariously. On instinct, I shot my gloved hand into the hood, desperately trying to avert the impending doom of flooding all the plates that we had spent two hours painstakingly seeding with stem cells. But just as I thought I'd saved it, our hands collided, and I watched in dismay as the bottle was flung against the back of the cabinet, and a pink tsunami engulfed all in its path.

"Shit," he said again, eyes wide with horror behind the slightly battered and scratched laboratory goggles he was wearing.

"Indeed."

I wasn't sure how I was staying so calm. Ahead lay an entire afternoon and evening of clean up and decontamination of the cell culture suite before starting all over again on growth and expansion of my diminishing source of bone marrow stem cells, setting my experiments back at least another two weeks.

"I am so sorry," Henry whispered, trying to shrink away to somewhere deep inside the recesses of his lab coat.

"It's ok." A surge of pity and compassion warmed behind my ribs at his distraught face, so I added gently, "Don't worry, we can sort it out."

I have no doubt that some of my fellow graduate students would have considered this turn of events to be a disaster of truly epic proportions. One that heralded the point of no return. The time at which to permanently eject hapless Henry from the lab, while simultaneously lamenting the loss of the cells and crying into a cup of strong tea with Morrissey playing on full blast in the background, all due to the inevitable delay to their thesis completion. And, while I was tempted to theatrically throw my hands up in defeat and run off a string of expletives about what a complete and utter ball ache this was, I didn't actually have it in me to do any of these things. Because, in spite of my initial misgivings and annoyance at having to babysit an engineering student, Henry had grown on me in the last few weeks, and I had begrudgingly begun to like him. Indeed, no one was more surprised than me when we formed an unlikely friendship.

Initially, I had assumed that he was going to be an arrogant prick, a player, a cad, adept at using his handsome face and charm to manipulate those around him. But I couldn't have been more wrong. Even with my almost constant barrage of snarky comments and little digs, his patient kindness and dry humour had proven unexpectedly disarming, so much so that I spent more and more of my time in his company trying not to smile. Plus, while he was undoubtedly dedicated to his own research, he was also hugely generous with his time and insights, often approaching things from such a different perspective that I was beginning to feel as if I was the one getting the most benefit from our mentorship. Although I tried never to let it show just how much value I placed on being with him – even someone as nice as Henry didn't need to have their ego stroked too much.

He also had this particular expression, one he was wearing at this moment, one that he used if he needed me to stay late or help with something, one that he could use to devastating effect. It was hard to discern; a soft light in his eyes, a slight tilt of his lips, open and hopeful, indulgent and encouraging, shy and secretive, all at once. And, despite my best intentions, I seemed to fall for it every single time.

"Shall we clear this up, then perhaps you can buy me a drink and we can work on some theory in the pub?" I suggested quietly, any lingering anger or resentment completely dissolving away as he huffed a sad little sigh.

"Sounds like a good plan," he replied with a dejected nod.

Handing me a spray bottle of seventy percent ethanol, he picked up a full roll of blue paper towel and started to mop up the disaster that was now dripping onto his plastic over-shoe. We worked in comfortable silence for a few minutes, scooping all the mess into the clinical waste bin and systematically taking apart, cleaning and disinfecting all of the equipment.

In general, Henry wasn't a massive talker, particularly in large groups, preferring to let others be the centre of attention, and we had become quite content to just be quiet in each other's company. It was refreshing not to have someone else's opinions foisted onto me all the time, and I also knew that when he did eventually speak, he would have considered what he was going to say very carefully and weighed up the merits of the topic thoroughly, and would not just spout the regular drivel or postgrad posturing I was usually subjected to.

With both our heads close together inside the laminar flow hood, Henry turned to me nonchalantly and said, in a deadpan voice, "What did one stem cell say to the other when it stood on its foot?"

"What?"

"Ouch, that's mitosis."

I snorted with laughter. "That's a really dreadful joke, Henry."

"Yeah, but I know that you're going to pass it off as your own when you see Jo later," he said, a small smile playing over his features.

"I might do," I answered with a non-committal shrug, thinking how my best friend Jo would definitely snigger too. "How many engineers does it take to change a lightbulb?"

"None, that's a maintenance issue."

"Hey, you stole my punchline!" I threw a balled-up piece of sodden blue paper at his head, and it stuck to his goggles with a satisfyingly wet thud.

"Have I got something on my face?" he asked, his tone utterly serious.

"Nope, no, nothing at all."

"Are you sure? Not something around here?" His hand was waving around the blue splat that was now dripping and sliding down the plastic lens. "Because you can't stop staring at me."

"Maybe a little something, but generally I think it's a huge visual improvement on your face."

"Ah, in that case I'll leave it where it is," he said, grinning widely. And my heart stuttered, just a little bit. Christ, Clara, get a grip, they're just his teeth, and lips. And dimples.

"I might have to record this as a cell culture health and safety violation, where's the logbook?" Henry carried on, as he peeled the blue sludge off his plastic glasses and wiped his face.

"I definitely know somewhere that we can put the logbook, Henry, somewhere that the sun doesn't shine, even from you…" I muttered darkly, eliciting a soft chuckle from him.

"I know what will cheer you up – let's listen to some music!" he said brightly.

"Urgh, not your best of Bon Jovi playlist again, Henry," I groaned, trying to hide a smile.

"Jon Bon Jovi is a god amongst men, Clara, the sooner you accept this, the better," Henry replied, fishing out his phone and linking it to the speaker on the back wall of the lab.

Soon the room was filled with the upbeat tones of 1980s soft rock, and I couldn't help tunelessly singing along using the mop handle as a microphone, with Henry right there next to me on air guitar. And even though I knew that it was going to be a very long day of cleaning, that I'd lost pretty much an entire batch of irreplaceable stem cells, and my thesis completion date had likely been delayed yet again, I suddenly didn't feel so bad about it after all.

Chapter Two

Seven years later

I slung my heels in the cavernous recesses of my handbag and hoisted the laptop case strap over my shoulder, glancing in the mirror by the door. Dark grey pencil skirt, check. Cream blouse, business-like but not frumpy, check. Mad blonde wavy hair tamed into sleek tresses, check. Make-up applied, full coverage without being slutty, check. Satisfied that I looked like a composed professional, I opened the front door of my little Victorian terraced house in Headington, ready to go and face whatever fresh hell my boss would undoubtedly throw at me today.

It was a cold, crisp January morning and the bright atrium of our office building shone with winter sunshine, a busy hive of pharmaceutical professionals going about their usual morning routines. Judy called over her customary welcome in her cheery and lilting voice, the hint of an Irish accent still evident, as I swapped my trainers for heels and leant against the reception desk.

"Morning, Judy. Good weekend?"

"Ah, you know, quiet one with the grandchildren," she replied, her face lighting up at their mention.

"Lovely." I smiled in return.

"How about you, Clara?"

"Working as always, I did manage to read some of that book you lent me though."

"Oooh, that hunky highlander really sent my heartrate running, Peter thought I was having a funny turn!" she laughed, fanning herself dramatically before we were interrupted by the main phone line ringing and, after a quick wink in my direction, she schooled her features, answering with a clipped and thoroughly professional greeting.

Judy loved a good raunchy romance novel and had started handing them to me when she'd finished them, commenting that, with my perpetually single status, I needed a little 'spice of an evening'. I couldn't say that I entirely disagreed.

Smiling and shaking my head slightly, I grabbed a coffee on the way up to my office, and had barely unpacked my laptop before my boss, the company's Chief Medical Officer, Richard Holmes, strode in, hair sticking up where he had clearly been running ragged fingers through its thinning ends, his comb-over flopping forwards, moustache twitching.

"Morning, morning. You've not forgotten about that presentation, have you?" His Etonian accent and slight accusatory tone managing to set my teeth on edge.

"Good morning. No, I have not forgotten. Is the meeting still at 2pm?" I enquired with a modicum of forced civility.

"Yes, yes. Very good. I want to see it before you present it, send me the slides, will you?"

As his tall, stooped figure disappeared out into the hallway again, not at all unlike a pantomime villain muttering evilly to himself, I shouted my reply, "I sent it to you last week, Richard."

Leaning back in my chair and taking a deep breath, I stared blankly at my computer screen for a minute. Thinking again that it was about time I started looking for a new job, I'd worked too hard and struggled too long to spend my time with a cartoon bad guy giving me orders.

"Woolgathering, Dr Clancy? Or just planning our evil boss' downfall?" Simmy enquired, entering our shared office like a brightly coloured whirlwind and dumping a chocolate croissant on my desk with a flourish. "I thought you might need this."

"Thanks, Simmy. Good weekend?"

"Trying to visit my overbearing mother-in-law without killing her. Ferrying reluctant children to various parties and events, wiping runny noses and mediating in fight-to-the-death sibling rivalry contests. The usual, you?" she replied, sitting heavily in her chair, splashing black coffee on her desk, narrowly missing her keyboard.

"Not much. Reviewing next year's clinical trial plan for study 128, and finalising the symposium slides for the San Francisco trip in a couple of weeks." I took a slurp of coffee and tucked into the croissant while I waited for my emails to load up.

"Pfft. As a middle-aged mother of three and married to an accountant, I want to live my life vicariously through you, my attractive and single colleague. Yet you repeatedly let me down with such work-related banality," she huffed, while hastily mopping the coffee up with a baby wipe pulled from an enormous stash that she kept in her handbag.

Simmy watched a lot of romance films (with a penchant for Bollywood classics), and hoped one day that a very handsome, spangly waist-coated man would sweep in (preferably with an entourage of equally spangly waist-coated men and beautiful, demure, silk-clad women), grab my hand and whisk me off in a stunningly choreographed dance scene.

"What about Bhavin's accountant friend, you've met him a couple of times now, haven't you?"

Urgh, Hugh. He was a fairly persistent suitor, someone who I'd met up with because Bhavin, Simmy's husband, had gone to such great lengths to organise a date for us. That, and I was an unbelievable people pleaser. So, we'd been on four dates, which had culminated last week in a highly unsatisfactory doorstep snog. He had made very weird snorty throaty sounds, slobbered on my face, and seemed incapable of kissing without smacking his lips noisily. Off. Putting. This was all followed up by a whiny request to meet his mother.

"I've called it off with Hugh," I said evasively.

"What? Why?"

"Well, several reasons, not least because he reminds me of that famously weaselly Tory politician, lives with his mother in Henley-on-Thames, and uses those weird sock suspender things to stop him having wrinkly ankles," I said, eyebrow raised. I left out the throat-clearing noises during kissing, because no one needed that image in their head.

"Oh, Clara, he's not that bad!"

No, he wasn't *that* bad, granted. There had been worse in my fairly disastrous recent dating history. There was Paul who'd actually attempted to sneakily steal items from my (dirty) laundry basket on our third date, while I was downstairs trying to cook a soufflé. When I set off the smoke alarm and he came charging into the kitchen and pulled my knickers out of his back pocket to waft the smoke away, I swiftly kicked him out (after I retrieved my best silk and lace pants), got a Chinese takeaway for one and watched *Fifty Shades of Grey*. Then there was Guy, who proclaimed his undying love for me and actually lay down on the road behind my car in an attempt to stop me leaving when I turned down his marriage proposal. On. Date. Number. One.

No, in the grand scheme of things, Hugh was actually the best of a fairly bad bunch. He was considerate and confident, had a good job and seemed to know what he wanted in his life (including very specific requirements for a spouse, which he'd laid out for me in an excruciatingly detailed diatribe on date number two). But therein lay the issue: I had a hard time in believing that anyone was ever genuinely interested in me, at least not for the long-term, so I usually ended things fairly early on, before feelings became an issue and I was inevitably let down. This crippling fear of rejection had persisted since my father had left when I was a child, holding me back from ever really opening up to anyone. My best friend, Jo, had regularly accused me of indulging in histrionics, usually in response to my drunken monologues that centred around me having a heart composed of shards of broken glass, and being entirely incapable of loving anyone. Dramatic, moi? Not at all.

"Sorry to disappoint you, but I think I'm staying single from now on." Of late, I had much preferred to curl up with a cup of tea and my tabby cat, Spencer, whilst reading about a (preferably kilted) book boyfriend, who I could send to the charity shop as soon as I had grown tired of him. I whispered to her in mock horror, "I've turned into a spinster cat lady!"

"Not yet, but that is the path you are heading down," she agreed. "Alright, perhaps Hugh isn't the answer, but there must be someone?"

"Nope, and that's fine by me. I'd rather spend time with fantasy men who I don't have to try to impress. And Spencer, because he only judges me based on the cat food I buy."

"What about … there's always … fine, I have nothing…" she trailed off lamely, shrugging her shoulders, and then pouted. "Not all men are hopeless, Clara."

Just as I took another bite of croissant, flaky pastry dropping on my top, a looming figure appeared over my desk, and I gave an impromptu shriek and proceeded to choke on my breakfast as a firm fist thumped me on my back, while I simultaneously clutched a hand to my chest in shock.

"For crying out loud, Clara, don't be so dramatic. I'll work on those slides and send them back to you. Just to let you know that Claus Baumann called, and he is coming after all, so the whole day has had to be rearranged and the meeting's been brought forward to 10am to accommodate his schedule." Richard glowered. "Get to the conference room on time."

And then he was gone again.

Claus Baumann was the company CEO, Swiss, and looked a bit like a corporate Father Christmas, but decidedly less jolly. And not at all philanthropic. We were hosting a full day of meetings and a tour of the offices and manufacturing plant for potential stakeholders in our cardiovascular portfolio, including investors, collaborators and even potential acquisitions, and everyone involved (including me) had been prepped on our role in the proceedings and warned not to screw up.

"He's like some silent, sneaky Dick Dastardly. I wish he'd focus on catching that pigeon rather than creeping about in our office," I muttered.

Simmy sniggered, while I sent the slides over to him yet again. Now I just had to wait for the inevitable slating that they would almost definitely receive.

A sense of dread and crushing anxiety was filling my thoracic cavity as I called the lift to the conference room floor. Richard hadn't sent me any comments on my slides and had been entirely incommunicado since he'd left my office at ten past nine. It was now approximately three minutes to ten and I had left it as long as I dared, hoping that he would send them back to me ahead of time, but no, and now I knew with absolute certainty that I was going to be the last person in the room. This was a disaster in lots of ways, but not least because my presentation on our clinical trial portfolio and publication plan was second on the list, after a brief introduction provided by Claus, so no time at all to prepare. I was just going to have to wing it. My least favourite style of presenting key information to a highly important and influential audience.

"You're looking lovely this morning, Clara." A silky voice dripped in my ear, the sudden appearance of another person making me jump.

"Err, thanks Dominic. Get up to anything good at the weekend?" I enquired casually, trying to step away to regain some personal space.

"Oh, you know, this and that. You?" he asked, as a group of people came down the corridor, squeezing us closer again, until I was now almost pressed up against the lift doors.

"Work. Again. Ha-ha!" I was still getting to know Dominic since his relatively recent appointment into the cardiovascular marketing team here at Pharmavoltis, and hadn't made my mind up entirely about him yet. We had been part of a number of collaborative projects together and he had been pleasant enough, if a tad smarmy, but I'd always found myself getting a bit awkward (ok, more awkward than normal) whenever we were alone together, and I couldn't put my finger on exactly what it was that bothered me.

"Are you going to the collaborator meeting?" Dominic said, his gaze fixed on a point somewhere below my chin and above my waist, which I didn't want to think about too much and was definitely a bit sleazy. But as I was finding it difficult to look directly into his wandering eyes without feeling a little kernel of unease popping into my brain, would I be taking the stance of burying my head in the sand and completely ignoring this? Absolutely and categorically yes, I bloody would. An excellent piece of work on inter-colleague relations there, Clara.

"Yes." I turned slightly away from him and furiously pressed the button again, where the hell was the lift?

"Oh good, me too. I've just come from there, I had to nip back to my office and pick up some more glossy brochures to wow them with." He smirked and waved the shiny sales materials in front of my face. "There are so many of them in there, including Claus."

Staring intently at the polished metal of the lift door, arms folded protectively, I took a moment to consider the reflection of Dominic Graham, in all his smug, slightly self-satisfied glory. He was good looking, I supposed, in a slick, suave way, and he seemed well liked judging by other people's reactions to him, so I had decided from the outset to keep any misgivings I had about him to myself, striving for a thoroughly professional relationship. The only person I'd told was Simmy, who agreed that there was something a bit off with him, and reassured me that she was also keeping a close eye, so that if he ever stepped out of line, she'd lop off a ball or two. It was nice to know she had my back.

Finally, the ding of the doors opening resounded through the air, and in my urgency to get inside and not be late for the meeting, I almost trampled the poor girl exiting the lift carrying an enormous stack of files. Only then did I realise that I was now trapped in a confined space with Dominic, who was staring straight at me with his best police mug shot expression. Trying for a polite and distant smile, and pretending to read emails on my phone, we rode down to the basement in silence. I was a stalwart of avoidance techniques, keeping my eyes trained downwards and resolutely refusing to even look at my colleague, even though his gaze felt like it was slithering all over me.

After what felt like four years in the fiery pits of hell, the doors efficiently slid open, the lobby beyond suspiciously quiet, confirming my fears that everyone invited to the meeting was probably already inside the conference room across the hall.

"This way, come on, you don't want to show up late, do you?" Dominic placed a clammy hand on the small of my back and gently pushed me towards the doors to meeting room one, the largest in the building. "Oh, and by the way, you've got something on your chest."

The way he said it made me wonder if my entire bosom was on show, including spangly nipple tassels waving in the wind. But when I looked down, I was as dismayed to see a large smear of chocolate in a prominent position on my right breast. Dabbing it with my hand just enlarged the cocoa-based blemish, which had now begun to resemble a sizeable areola in exactly the same location as my own native areola (which, by the way, was decidedly less large. TMI? Probably).

Fan-bloody-tastic. In my desperate bid to come across as a professional and credible pharmaceutical industry professional, I was about to give one of the most important presentations of my career to date, with a very visible and highly suspect stain on my cream-coloured blouse. The top half of my reflection in the mirrored panel of the lift door looked not too dissimilar to how I imagined a blow-up sex doll might look: startled expression, pink cheeks, red mouth open in a disappointed little 'O'. And an overly prominent and overly large nipple-like feature, which very much drew the eye.

"Oh my god! Why did no one tell me?"

"I'm telling you now, but possibly a bit late to do anything. Sorry about that," Dominic replied smoothly, just as Richard swung the door open in front of us, and dragged me inside the dimly lit auditorium.

Chapter Three

"You're up, come on," Richard muttered darkly and, not so gently, I was thrust onto the brightly lit stage.

The title slide of my presentation was already up on the screen behind me, my name and position in Times New Roman, font size forty-four thousand, leaving no room for confusion who this late and slightly flustered interloper was. Turning my body a little to the right, I hoped that the chocolate nipple was not so evident, and I took a deep breath and began my carefully structured and rehearsed presentation.

Only, when I clicked through the slides, I realised that Richard had done a hatchet job on my talk, and there was very little of the original content left. The only thing that kept me going and stopped me from looking like a right tit, was a semblance of professional pride, and the crushing fear of humiliation, both of which prevented me giving in to the unmistakable urge to burst into tears in front of everyone.

But I had this. I could do this. Bloody hell I had worked really hard to get to this point. Pushed by the one science teacher who believed in me at my under-achieving state school, I was accepted to Oxford, who welcomed me with open arms, while my presence pretty much doubled their quota of poor kids in my college. Desperate to prove my worth, I'd exceeded my own expectations when I'd successfully completed my doctorate, which was a feat really considering the extra-ordinarily high standards I held myself accountable to.

I squared my shoulders and blindly stared out at the dark, unrecognizable faces of the audience, deciding that there was absolutely no way on earth I was going to let a real-life pantomime villain get one up on me.

Fifteen minutes and several narrowly avoided panic attacks later, (while wondering more than once where a person could find bulk suppliers of voodoo dolls on the internet), I finally sat down in the front row, next to my boss, and watched the following statistics presentation in numb silence.

"We need to have a word about this, Clara. My office at 3pm," Richard said in a very loud stage whisper, and I heard a faint snigger from the row behind us.

"Right," I replied. I'd definitely be updating my CV when I got back to my desk then.

When the tortuous meeting was finally over and all questions had been asked (luckily, and unsurprisingly, none directed at me), the collaborators and investors were offered a tour of the offices, followed by refreshments before being bussed out to the drug manufacturing and packing plant a few miles away. I used this distraction to extricate myself from the conference room, before anyone could make eye contact and start talking to me about any of the random bits of largely irrelevant information which Richard had seen fit to put on my slides. Quickly bounding up the emergency stairwell with all the energy and coordination of a hyperactive rabbit, I ensconced myself safely in the loo.

Dabbing a wet paper towel at the stubborn and persistent chocolate nipple, my attempts merely ended up making it larger, and the material wetter, so that my previously very respectable top became entirely see-through, revealing much more than just a hint of the cotton and white lace bra underneath. Damn it. I now looked like a bad advert for a wet T-shirt contest where muddy pond water had been thrown at the contestants.

"Crap," I said aloud, staring at myself forlornly in the mirror, the stained and dishevelled woman staring back, a million miles away from the poised scientist I had endeavoured to be first thing this morning. Someone who you'd definitely trust with your multi-million pound account? Someone who you'd be happy representing your company at an international medical convention? Nope, neither of those things sprung to mind. The bloody bastarding chocolate nipple of doom, that's what they'd remember, and the bumbling bubble head attached to it. Fuck my actual life.

Coming out of the bathroom, head down, intent on returning to the safety of my office as quickly as possible, I ran headlong into a firm, broad chest, causing a huff of air to be expelled above my head as I gripped an unknown arm and tried not to ricochet off into the wall like a pinball.

"Clara?" Dominic's voice was a little hoarse as he tried to recover from being winded by a Clara-shaped missile to the sternum.

"Shit, sorry, didn't see you there." Fuck sake, Clara, why him, of all people?

"It's ok." He gave a pointed look to where I was still clutching his forearm tightly, and I dropped it quickly, taking a step backwards in an effort to compose myself from this latest blunder.

Chancing another look at his face, I was simultaneously repulsed and shocked to catch him staring at my entirely unrespectable blouse situation and licking his lips in a way that my brain interpreted as suggestive, and I was subjected to a whole-body shudder. An innate human pathogen avoidance response: the sort of shiver usually reserved for confronting something disgusting like a mutilated corpse, or the soul-sucking and ruthless expression of a serial killer. But the glint in his eyes showed he'd seen it, and probably misinterpreted it as something other than revulsion, because he licked them again, flicking his tongue out like a snake, and I swear I was a little bit sick in my mouth, and fled, in an ungainly trot, as fast as my pencil skirt and heels would allow.

As I slumped back down at my desk, ferreting about for a notebook and pen, Simmy looked up from her teleconference, no doubt in response to the huge and desolate sigh I emitted.

"Are you ok?" she mouthed silently. Then began frantically pointing at my chest and dramatically dabbing at her own ample cleavage, in an attempt to convey to me the need to look down at the brown, transparent disaster that my top had become.

"I know," I mouthed back at her and quickly slipped on the emergency granny cardigan that I kept on the back of my chair, for when the air con was turned down to sub-zero. It was grey, and bobbled, there were numerous cat hairs now interwoven into the fabric of the garment that no amount of rolled up Sellotape had been able to remove. It was saggy and worn, and not strictly office attire, but at least I could pull it around myself so as not to be constantly reminded of the glaringly obvious stain.

"Excellent news. Thanks, cheers. Yep, you too. Thanks, cheers, yep, bye. Bye. Byeeeeee." Simmy finished her call and took off her headset. "You look like a complete mess, what on earth happened to you?"

"Chocolate-related nipple faux pas, slightly creepy run-in with Dominic in the corridor, and Dick Dastardly changed all my slides and didn't tell me. This morning has been an unmitigated bloody disaster," I groaned and put my head in my hands.

"What did Dominic do? And how on earth did you get chocolate on your nipple?" Simmy asked loudly in confusion, just as our office door opened to a group of suited men and women, led by none other than Richard himself, their curious and incredulous faces demonstrating that they had clearly heard at least the latter part of our conversation.

"Yes, well, Dr Clara Clancy, who you saw earlier and who is part of the cardiovascular team, and Dr Simran Anand from oncology, who both head up the clinical trials and medical communications side of things here at Pharmavoltis." Richard glared at me, in full cartoon villain mode. He was just missing the hand wringing and evil laughter.

I gave a small wave, which caused my cardigan to fall open once more, and I saw Dominic's face in the crowd as he grinned and waved back. The urge to poke him in the eye was strong, but I valiantly resisted, instead pressing the end of my favourite pen so hard that the plastic casing disintegrated into pieces, just as the throng of suits turned away and began to disperse.

"Shit," I murmured quietly, placing my forehead on the desk with a bump. Now was a time for inward reflection and self-annihilation for being quite so inept. Probably also a good time to update my LinkedIn profile and start the job hunting in earnest. And invest in some new stationery.

"I seem to remember saying that rather a lot when I was in your presence, usually in a lab coat and goggles," a deep voice said from the doorway.

A sense of familiarity flooded my brain, nostalgia creeping up from my toes. I knew this voice, and it didn't fill me with dread. No, in fact quite the opposite was occurring, a blooming warmth on my skin, a tingling rush of butterflies in my stomach, my whole being lighting up with happy hormones.

Swivelling my face so that my cheek was flush with the cool surface of the desk, I gazed up at the rotated view of a tall man in a suit, leaning against the door frame, hands in his trouser pockets.

"Hello, Clara, nice to see you again after all these years."

My head shot up like a meerkat who'd spotted a hawk.

"Henry, what on earth are you doing here?"

Chapter Four

Henry Fraser looked pretty much the same. His hair slightly shorter, now cropped into a corporate and smart style, rather than flopping across his forehead like I remembered. Perhaps he was a little more well-built, definitely broader across the shoulders, but totally recognisable as the charming and affable PhD student I had known. His sudden appearance was a complete jolt to my whole system, my mind struggling to process the fact that he was stood here, in my office doorway, looking drop-dead gorgeous, and perhaps a touch nervous, in a tailored navy-blue suit.

"Well," he said, shuffling uncomfortably and focussing his gaze on the carpet near his feet. "My company has designed a new heart valve system and…"

As his voice trailed off, I realised what he was about to say and finished the sentence for him, "…you are looking to collaborate with us on our heart failure pipeline."

He nodded, briefly meeting my eyes, almost apologetically.

"Urggh," I groaned, "so you were in the presentations just now?"

Another nod. A faint blush coloured his cheekbones, he was clearly as mortified as me about witnessing my car crash of a life on stage this morning.

This was just excellent. No anonymity for me, my disastrous representation of myself, and my department, permanently etched onto the mind of someone who actually knew me outside of work. I laid my head back down on the desk.

"Are you going to introduce us?" Simmy asked, clearly intrigued and not one to sit quietly by.

Simmy was my partner in crime, my work wife. We led our respective therapeutic areas separately but collaborated on all things, and I loved her dearly. But she had a voice like a foghorn and an unshakable confidence in her own opinion on things, and I was quite sure she was going to have an opinion on Henry Fraser.

"Sorry, Dr Simmy Anand, Dr Henry Fraser. Henry and I spent some time in the same lab at Oxford," I said into the safe, dark space of the crook of my arm, my other hand waving ineffectually between the two of them.

"Nice to meet you, Henry," Simmy exhaled. Huskily. I raised my head at the ridiculous porn-esque quality that her voice had taken on. Was she fluttering her extraordinarily long eyelashes at Henry? Looked like it. Her coffee-coloured eyes were round and impossibly dark, and she was resting her chin in her hands, elbows on her desk, red nails tapping her cheeks rhythmically. I cringed inwardly as she blew out a sigh in his direction.

"And you, Simmy. Although, I think Clara has under sold

herself here. She tried very hard to teach this hopeless engineer about stem cell culture, which was an entirely difficult and onerous task," Henry said quietly, the hint of self-deprecation endearing himself further to Simmy, as she almost began to pant like a dog in a heatwave.

"*Tried*, being the operative word," I muttered.

And then there it was. The trademark Henry Fraser smile that could set a heart into atrial fibrillation at twenty paces, the killer blow that could seemingly turn the most cynical or prudish of women into a bone fide sex pest.

You see, the thing about Henry Fraser, his modus operandi if you will, his get out of jail free card, was that easy-going, self-effacing, yet totally sincere smile. It was bonkers how just the curve of his mouth, the hint of a dimple, and the crinkle around his eyes could be both quietly reassuring and hugely disarming. He had, in actual fact, got a whole repertoire, from shy and unsure, just a twitch of the lips, to boyish and mischievous, all lopsided and charming. There was also the trying-not-to-smile smile (my personal favourite), and then the huge megawatt, pulse of radiation, beaming grin, which could obliterate all in its path, reducing the most hardened of hearts to a warm, gooey mush. And here he was in the flesh, like he'd not been AWOL for seven years, flattening me with that small, personal smile, that one he had used to soften an apology, or worm some extra lab time from me. The one he'd used to very great effect so many times before.

"I'm afraid I was a truly useless student, but she never complained," Henry countered, his tone playful but still a touch unsure.

To his credit, Henry didn't seem to notice the excited little squeak that escaped Simmy's mouth or the highly indiscreet clap of her hands as she mouthed something indecipherable at me from across the room. No, his unwavering gaze remained focussed on me, just as it had been all those years ago, like he was waiting for my next words with bated breath, almost as if they would be so truly monumental and ground-breaking that he dared not miss a moment.

"You were pretty dreadful in the lab, and I did complain, a lot," I finally said, in a desperate attempt to gain some rational thought, reminding myself that I was no longer a gangly graduate student, but a qualified and intelligent scientist. I'd proven myself and was on a respectable career trajectory. I was a professional, meeting with another professional. Being, well, professional, together. I could do this, and not make even more of an arse out of myself in front of him than I already had today.

Henry huffed a small laugh and toed the carpet with his shiny dark brown brogue. "Yes, actually now I come to think of it, you really did complain a lot. I guess I'm just better with a ruler than a pipette," he said with a shrug.

"And with inanimate materials rather than living things?" I quipped, matching his teasing tone.

"Ouch." He winced and feigned an arrow to his heart. "You wound me."

From outside the office, I heard Henry's name being called, and he leant backwards out into the corridor, before returning his gaze to mine.

"I should go," he said quietly.

I nodded, now suddenly mute. Why, when I hadn't seen him for so long, was I suddenly desperate for him not to leave, desperate to continue talking to him?

"It's been really nice to see you, Clara." Henry glanced up

at me cautiously before stepping forward and taking a card from his jacket pocket, and placing it on my desk. "Here are my contact details, although I think you should already have them, but just in case you want to grab a coffee and catch up on old times."

I gingerly took the card. "Thanks."

"Nice to meet you too, Simmy," he said again with a small, genuine smile and wave of his hand, before striding out down the corridor, in pursuit of the rest of the group.

"Ooh la la!" Simmy exclaimed, fanning herself with a copy of the British Medical Journal. "He's a particularly mesmerising specimen of man meat, isn't he?"

"Man meat?!" I choked out incredulously.

"Yes, hunky and gorgeous, and a little bit shy? Oof, I would definitely not say no to a piece of Dr Henry Fraser." She grinned, not even embarrassed by her blatant thirsting over him.

"You'll have to get in line Simmy, mother of three and married to Bhavin the accountant," I replied with an exaggerated grumble. "If it's anything like our university days there will be a queue a mile long of fawning admirers following him wherever he goes."

"And you're not one of them?" she queried, eyebrow quirked.

"No, definitely not. I mean, he's a nice enough guy—"

"*Nice enough guy*?" she spluttered, interrupting me, "He looks like a freaking male model!"

"Yes, I know that, I'm not blind. But we're firmly in the friend zone." I was resolutely holding on to that fact, despite the weird fluttering that was still going on in my stomach at his sudden appearance back in my life.

"Well, maybe you were, when you were students. Now he's all like 'It's really nice to see you' and 'Let's grab a coffee and catch up on old times'," she said, throwing her voice as low as it would go, in a fairly poor attempt at mimicking Henry's deep luxurious tones.

"And I'm sure he was just being polite."

"If you say so," she said with a smirk.

"Don't be fooled, he has a special gift for being able to charm even the most cynical and bitter old spinster. I'm sure he's mortified and doesn't want to be associated with me at all, after my disastrous performance today, probably just beholden to some gentlemanly etiquette that made him say 'hello' to an embarrassing old friend." The creep of humiliation began climbing back up my spine.

"Pfft. Talking of cynical and bitter spinsters, are you going to call him?"

"No. Most definitely not."

"Why not, Clara? What have you got to lose?"

"My self-respect? It's bad enough that he saw my epic levels of professional failure today, I really do not want to meet up with him and chat through it, so he can point out all the reasons that he'll be telling his boss not to collaborate with us."

"I think that sporting a chocolate nipple for the entirety of your presentation has put pay to any self-respect you may have had, plus he didn't mention it just now, so why would he if you met for coffee? And what did he mean that you should already have his details? What are you not telling me?"

"I don't know?" That comment was puzzling, I hadn't been in contact with him in over seven years. Turning over the business card in my fingers, I read the embossed gold lettering with growing dismay.

. . .

Dr Arthur Henry Fraser MEng PhD
    FraserTech, Unit 14, Oxford Science Park, UK
    Email: AH.Fraser@frasertech.com

"Oh no," I murmured in horror, faint alarm bells ringing in recognition of that email address. Shit, what an awful and hideous brain fart moment this was.

"What now?" Simmy looked up.

Scrabbling for my mouse, I pulled up the poster that we were currently getting printed for the upcoming World Congress of Cardiology in San Francisco, and sure enough, in the list of twelve authors, there was A.H. Fraser, second from the end.

"Shit, why did I not research this properly?" I'd been so busy of late that I'd not had time to go through the details of all the authors on the list, relying instead on the medical writer to make sure everything was correct, I'd not had the chance to double check it like I normally would.

"What is it?" Simmy came over and took the card from my hand.

"He's one of my authors, he's been on emails about one of my posters for WCC for weeks. I do have his contact details." My head hit the desk again. The thunk loud and vibrating through my skull, so that my teeth clacked together.

"Oh, and you didn't twig?"

"No, because he's actually called Arthur Henry, and only goes by Henry for day-to-day stuff, I had forgotten this. Plus his secretary has replied on his behalf in all correspondence, so he's never actually signed off any emails as Henry or been on any of the kick-off calls as he's not one of the main contributors." I paused and looked up into Simmy's commiserating eyes. "I haven't even been on the FraserTech company website because I've been so busy, his face is probably all over it – he must have thought I was being a right arse." My voice came out muffled as I buried my head deeper into the crook of my elbow again. "And what makes it so much worse is that when he said that his company was looking to collaborate with us, he meant *his* company, as in he owns it!"

"Ooh, rich too!" Simmy said gleefully.

"Gah! Simmy, that's not the point! I thought that maybe he'd come as a representative and wouldn't necessarily have the sway to ensure that his company didn't work with us, but it turns out he can make that decision all on his own," I replied miserably. "Richard is so going to fire me, unless Claus already has, after the shit show this morning has turned into."

"Come on, your presentation was just one amongst many today, and you've already done some good work for this collaboration with an abstract accepted. I'm sure it's not that bad." Her voice was attempting to be soothing, and I wondered if this was the tone she used to placate her tantrumming two-year-old daughter.

But I just humphed gloomily into my arm, and tried to imagine ways in which to give myself food poisoning, or some kind of contagious disease so that I did not have to face Dick Dastardly later.

As 3pm approached I tentatively made my way to Richard's office, determined not to be late. In preparation and hoping to make myself feel a bit better, I'd popped out at lunch and bought a new top from town, no nipples on show (chocolate or otherwise), and navy blue so as to hide any other unfortunate spillages. I'd also made a good stab at updating my CV and sent it to a couple of recruitment agencies already. No harm in being proactive in the face of imminent doom and unemployment, right?

With a deep breath I lifted my hand to knock on the door, just as Richard opened it and beckoned me inside with a large and unnerving grin.

"Clara, Clara! So good to see you, thanks for stopping by." He leant forward as if to give me a hug, which in itself was very strange, but with my hand still held aloft between us, fingers clenched in a knocking position, he ended up awkwardly fist bumping me instead. "Come in, come in."

He was far too jovial, and this felt like a trap, my nerves immediately on edge, waiting for the bollocking that I was sure was going to be levelled at me any minute now.

Bracing myself and trying to figure out how to gracefully accept my P45, I perched on the seat opposite him and clasped my slightly sweaty hands together.

"So, the collaborator meeting went well, didn't it?" he said from behind his desk.

Richard's office was stark and empty, no personal artifacts at all, even his laptop bag and coat were hidden from view. I wondered momentarily if he had a secret villain's lair, one that only he could access through the numerous cupboards that filled the back wall behind his desk. I couldn't think for the life of me what he kept behind all those locked doors otherwise.

"Really, really well." Richard was still talking and actually beaming at me now. Disturbingly happy and positive.

Blinking slowly, I nodded, what the actual chuff was going on here?

"We've secured a number of very interested investors and a particularly exciting confirmation of an ongoing collaboration for our heart failure portfolio, which is great news. Great news!" He was almost peeing his pants with excitement.

"Riiighhttt," I replied, still not totally sure that I was out of the woods just yet.

"Yes, yes. And your name came up, such high praise, Clara, I knew I was right to put my trust in you this morning. Bit of a test, giving you some new slides, but you handled it like a pro. Stellar performance, Clara. Super." He was looking a bit maniacal now, eyes bright and moustache twitching vigorously.

What a total and utter bastard. I stayed quiet, not sure I really wanted to speak in case I said something I later regretted. Was there a suitable place in the transferable skills section of my CV to add: 'Works well with dastardly cartoon bad guys'?

"Why didn't you tell me that you were so well acquainted with Henry Fraser?"

Suddenly the penny dropped. Charismatic, do-anything-for-you, all-round good guy, Henry Fraser, had talked to Richard and saved my bacon. I rubbed my temples and closed my eyes, unsure how I felt about this. It was great that I was seemingly off the hook, but having Superman swoop in and save my career felt like a monumental failure on my part.

"Well, we knew each other a long time ago and we've not really kept in touch. In fact, I was very surprised to see him today," I said, keeping the information sparse, not knowing the ins and outs of what had been discussed already.

"Ah, come on now, he says that you have already implemented a number of great ideas for the publication plan for the clinical trial, he is confident his product is in safe hands and is thrilled to be working with you once again." Richard stood up, and began gesturing to the door, my cue that I was to leave, conversation over. "So, I'd like you to officially head up the collaboration between Pharmavoltis and FraserTech on this project, as he really wants to closely align with us on the publication strategy."

"Oh, right."

"And since you are already getting along, both Claus and I felt it would be really beneficial to the company for you to be our single point of contact," he said, talking as though I wasn't really there.

"I see, well it's just that—"

"And of course, he'll be coming along with all of us to the World Congress of Cardiology in San Francisco, so we can present a united front and show all our partners just how well we can collaborate effectively." Richard paused and glanced over, his expression a little less dastardly than normal. "Keep up the good work and all that."

And before I knew it, I was back out in the corridor, the door to his office slamming shut behind me.

"I hope everything is alright, Clara?" Dominic was casually lurking beside the water cooler, partially concealed by a large pot plant and giving me a definite whiff of Christian Bale in *American Psycho*.

"Yes, really rather unexpectedly alright actually," I replied in a daze.

"Good." Reaching into his pocket, he walked towards me and I had a sudden vision of him producing gaffer tape and cable ties and subconsciously started to back away, my sympathetic nervous system gearing me up for a fight-to-the-death situation, eyes darting for the nearest exit, hands assuming what I hoped was some sort of kung fu, self-defence pose.

"Dominic, I—"

Oblivious to my newly awoken inner ninja who was wielding some serious mental nunchucks, Dominic carried on, "I have a few left over from the investor meeting this morning, and it looked like you might need a new pen after the grief you were giving yours earlier."

And handing me some fancy company-branded fine-liners, he smiled a broad smile, before nonchalantly walking away down the corridor without a care in the world.

Chapter Five

"You have to call Henry now, to say thank you," Simmy said smugly over her cup of coffee the next morning, after I had recounted my meeting with Dick Dastardly the day before.

"I know, and admit that I had no clue I had been working with him on the collaboration until now," I sighed. "What a complete moron I am."

"Just meet him for a coffee and explain everything, I'm sure he'll be fine. Then you can just stare dreamily at his perfectly symmetrical face and fantasize about running your fingers through his hair," she murmured, a faraway look in her eyes.

"You said that last bit out loud, just so you know," I said as the ping of my email alerted me to a new incoming message.

"But his hair is so thick and shiny! And remember that I'm living my life vicariously through you. Don't let me down!" she replied with a wink, stuffing her laptop in its case and grabbing a stack of papers from her desk drawer.

Turning to my computer and opening my emails, a

message from the man himself popped up, spookily, almost as if he knew we were talking about him.

From: AH.Fraser@frasertech.com
To: clara.clancy@pharmavoltis.com
Subject: Catch up
Hi Clara,

It was really great to see you yesterday and I just thought I'd send a follow up email to say 'hi'.

Not sure if Richard Holmes has told you but we're going to be collaborating on some projects ahead of WCC, so I thought it would be a good idea to meet and go over a few things.

I'll be in the Pharmavoltis offices on Friday, please let me know if you're free.

Best regards
Henry

Right, here was my chance, suck up the embarrassment of yesterday, draw a line under it and move on; time to be the professional, successful scientist that I knew I was. And bloody well resurrect my own career, I didn't need Henry to-the-rescue Fraser pouncing in again.

From: clara.clancy@pharmavoltis.com
To: AH.Fraser@frasertech.com
Subject: RE: Catch up
Hi Henry,

What a blast from the past to see you again!!! I was just about to email you when your message popped up, how funny is that?!

What about Friday at 10:30, then we can grab a coffee too, and I can bring you up to speed on our pipeline for this year.

Looking forward to seeing you then!!
Best wishes, Clara

I reread it several times, did it sound a bit desperate? Or clingy? Or unprofessional? Was I just overthinking a simple email in an effort to make my brain actually explode?

"Christ Clara, don't write that – he'll think you're a complete weirdo!" Simmy had sneaked around the back of my desk, proffering a biscuit and was reading judgmentally over my shoulder.

"What's wrong with that?" I said, taking a chocolate digestive and dunking it in my tea.

"Errr, you sound like a bit of an unprofessional, desperate loser? And only a children's television presenter would use that many exclamation marks, Clara. Just take that first sentence out. Then ask what underwear he'll be wearing and what kind of shampoo he uses."

"Really? And how is that even remotely professional, Simmy?" I moaned, swatting her hand off my mouse.

"Call it professional curiosity." She giggled before skipping out to the investigator meeting that she was attending for the rest of the day.

Listening to the girly, flirty noise that had come out of my friend's mouth, I wondered if Henry was still so unaware of the effect he had on people, primarily women. Surely, he couldn't possibly have remained oblivious to the carnage that he'd left in his wake? The 'Hot Henry Effect' as my best friend Jo had termed it, where she hypothesised that an increase in oestrogen levels in the subject was directly correlated to time spent in his company, or just looking at his face. Or actually even just thinking about his face. Or hair, apparently, in

Simmy's case. But I had never been so sure, having managed to successfully dodge that particular affliction.

Henry and I had got on really well (I had forgiven him fairly quickly for the stem cell disaster), teasing each other mercilessly on a regular basis, yet also able to go for a pint and discuss complex scientific theory until late into the night. Spending time with Henry had always been enjoyable, and I'd considered him a good friend at the time. I couldn't recall why we'd lost touch when he returned to the States, I guess we had both just been busy getting on with our lives, thousands of miles apart. I had sent emails in the beginning, just friendly ones asking how he was getting on, or if he wanted any help writing up his final chapter of his thesis. But I had never got a reply, no acknowledgement that he'd even received my messages, so it had been clear to me then that he had moved on. Part of me was happy for him, happy that he'd clearly found his place back in America, gone back to his pre-Oxford status quo. But part of me was also gutted if I was honest with myself, a bit resentful and hurt that he'd walked away from our friendship without a backward glance, leaving me behind.

I studied the email again. Navigating a new work relationship with him may prove tricky, particularly considering the shift in power dynamic between our two respective job positions, and the pressure that Richard was placing on me to get this right and not screw things up for the company. While I wasn't sure if I wanted to stay in my current job for too much longer (and was most definitely manifesting a role with a significantly less villainous manager), my perfectionist nature would never tolerate the notion of being fired. No, I knew I had to strive for professionalism from the off, in order to garner even a shred of respect from Henry, and to ensure Richard let me keep my job.

On reflection, perhaps that email was a bit too informal to send to the CEO of a collaborator company and Simmy was right, apart from the pants and shampoo thing. I deleted the draft and started again.

From: clara.clancy@pharmavoltis.com

To: AH.Fraser@frasertech.com

Subject: RE: Catch up

Hi Henry

How about Friday at 10:30 in the coffee shop by reception, and I can bring you up to speed on our pipeline for this year?

Best wishes, Clara

Feeling pleased at my concise and perfunctory communications, I was filled with a growing self-confidence as I hit send and his reply came back almost instantly.

From: AH.Fraser@frasertech.com

To: clara.clancy@pharmavoltis.com

Subject: RE: Catch up

Perfect, see you then.

H

It's funny how I desperately wanted to give off some serious I've-got-my-shit-together vibes to the guy, who once saw me hugging the ancient nineteen sixties centrifuge in our lab, crying and begging it to 'release my babies' after the Bakelite knob broke in my hand, trapping all my samples inside. Henry had rescued me that day too: he took the whole thing apart to get my tubes of bone marrow out, before mending the handle and putting it all back together again. Pheena, the lab manager, was quite-rightly flummoxed the next day as to why it now ran as smoothly as a well-oiled Bentley, when it had previously tried to shake itself to death on anything other than its slowest setting. But in his usual self-effacing way, Henry kept quiet about his fix-it superpower and no one, other than me, was aware that he was methodically working his way through the machines in the lab and secretly and efficiently repairing them all, like a technological superhero repairman.

Closing my emails, I grabbed a glass of water and mentally prepared myself for three hours of back-to-back teleconferences, firmly putting Henry Fraser out of my mind. His reappearance in my life was disturbing my inner equilibrium, I just couldn't place a finger on why.

Chapter Six

Friday came around pretty quickly, and just before half past ten I skipped down the stairs to the coffee shop in the lobby, surreptitiously checking my appearance in the large mirrors in the stairwell (no food-related decorations to the mammary area, I noted with relief). My knee-length, belted, black shirt dress and favourite heeled boots gave me the smart-casual look I was going for on dress-down Friday. Yet, I was still inexplicably nervous to be seeing Henry again, and my innate brain gremlins were having a field day simultaneously ramping up my social anxiety and annihilating my self-confidence.

He was already sat at a table in the far corner when I arrived, looking more Clark Kent than Superman today, wearing a pair of black-rimmed glasses, his light-blue shirt open at the collar, and he looked up and flashed a grin, before waving in a slightly redundant manner.

I gesticulated what I hoped was the universal sign

language for *'Do you want a cup of coffee?'* which was just me trying to make a cup with my hand that, in hindsight, ended up looking rather indecent. Even from this distance, I could see him frown and blush slightly as he distractedly watched my hand moving up and down on top of my other one, and when he finally brought his eyes up to mine, so I could stop the imaginary hand job that I was performing in the foyer of my company, he shook his head in clear confusion.

Frustrated at his complete lack of comprehension, I mouthed "Do you want one?" and pointed repeatedly at the counter with my thumb, where a bored-looking teenager in a brown and red uniform was staring at me with morbid horror.

Henry cocked his head to the side, and I could almost hear the ginormous, resigned sigh as he rose from his chair and walked towards me.

"Hi, I already got you a latte, is that ok?" he said when he was near enough not to have to rely on lewd hand gestures or lip reading to communicate, and it was then that I noticed two steaming cups of coffee set out on the table he had occupied.

"Right, thanks," I muttered, tucking my hair behind my ear, a well-used reflex that attempted to deflect attention away from my most recent self-inflicted mortification. "You didn't have to."

"I hope a latte is ok? I asked for a hazelnut shot as that's what you always ordered when we had coffees after the weekly lab meetings. You're not vegan now, are you?" he asked, suddenly horror-struck that he might have offended me with a splash of milk when all I could think about was the little X-rated hand puppet show I had performed for him in front of everyone in the coffee shop.

"No, not vegan," I replied, cheeks still maddeningly red as I sat opposite him at the small table and placed my laptop in front of me. It was at that moment that my brain registered the fact that Henry had remembered my drinks order from seven years ago, and a funny feeling tingled up my spine.

"Phew, that's a relief." He smiled, sliding into his seat. "Do you remember Simon, who never drank anything hot? Oh, and Emily who had to have about twelve sugars in her tea? Mad!"

Ah, he just had a beverage-related photographic memory, the tingle fizzled away to a numbness, like I'd received a karate chop to my lumbar region, and I nodded and forced out a small, insincere chuckle.

"Glasses?" I asked, grappling for something to say, not really sure if the neuronal pathways between my main frontal cortex and speech centre were still connected.

"Yes," he replied, and touched the frames self-consciously. "I've worn them for a while, I do have contacts, but I hate wearing them. Myopic in my old age, I'm afraid."

"You look a bit like Clark Kent," I blurted out. Shit where was my brain to mouth filter today?

"That's exactly the look I was going for." He laughed and took a sip of coffee, eying me over the paper cup.

I was instantly transported back to my graduate school days, all of us dressed in ripped jeans and vintage T-shirts, with messy hair and big opinions sitting in a large group having coffee. We would usually be complaining about experiments that had gone wrong, unreasonable demands from our professors, or just planning a night out at some dodgy pub nearby. It was a time when I was completely focussed on getting a doctorate and proving myself worthy. I'd put a lot of pressure on myself back then, determined not to fail, to make something of myself, and it was a bit disconcerting to be reliving some of these moments, moments that I'd long since put away in a sealed box in my mind, forgotten in the fog of time.

"How have you been?" Henry asked softly, interrupting my reminiscing. "I was surprised when your name appeared on an email from someone working here, I thought you'd be a professor heading up your own department at Oxford."

Now was my time to apologise for completely ignoring him on all our recent correspondence. "Ah yes, about that, Henry. I am so sorry I didn't recognise you on the WCC poster we've just worked on, if I had known you were one of the authors I'd have definitely said 'hi' over email. I forgot that your real first name is Arthur."

Henry grimaced. "Think nothing of it, I wasn't totally sure it was you either in the beginning, but then I thought that there can't be that many Clara Clancys working in pharmaceuticals, so I scoured the web for pictures of you to be sure. When I knew I'd be coming here to meet with the team, I thought it would be nicer to say 'hi' in person." He gave me a funny little wave. "Hi, again."

"Hi." He hunted me down on the internet, why did that knowledge make me equal parts alarmed and happy? "Stalking women on the internet is probably not something you should admit to, Henry."

He nodded. "Noted."

We stared at each other for a moment, until he asked again, "So how have you been?" His fingers fiddling with the wooden stirrer on the table, nervously.

"Not too bad," I replied lamely, the stock British response

to this question, feeling reluctant to give too much away when he was clearly so successful. "I couldn't get funding for my postdoc, so ended up moving to the dark side and taking a post in industry. I think it's probably worked out for the best though in the end. You?"

"Not too bad either," he said.

"Ah, come off it, Henry, you own your own company. *Not too bad* seems an understatement!"

He shifted a little uncomfortably in his seat and drank another mouthful of coffee. He'd always been a bit reluctant to blow his own trumpet, uncomfortable with praise and preferring to stay out of the limelight. It seemed that this hadn't changed, and it was still infuriatingly endearing.

"Well, I finished my PhD at MIT and the valve system I had been working on was trialled in humans, so I carried the project on as a postdoc. The surgeons liked it and it has worked in most patients, so yeah, not too bad." He paused and looked at me with an expression I couldn't interpret, before continuing. "I missed being in the UK though, so I moved back last year and set up manufacturing here on the Science Park. Things have taken off a little quicker than I'd anticipated."

"Well, that's great news!"

"Yeah," he murmured. "So, what else other than work? Married? Family?"

I snorted in a most unladylike fashion and his boyish grin returned.

"No and no. You?" I said, blowing on my coffee and taking a small sip. Delicious, why hadn't I kept up with the hazelnut shots in my lattes?

"I was married for a short time, but it didn't work out, and we're definitely not married now. No kids."

"Sorry to hear that," I sympathised, the look on his face clearly showed this was a painful topic and that he'd like to move on. And while a curious part of me was dying to interrogate him on this titbit of information, another part was a little sad that there was a whole load of stuff that had happened to my old friend that I would never be privy to.

"Are you?" he asked in surprise.

"Yes of course. Divorce is shitty."

"Yeah, I suppose it is, but for the best," he replied, repeating my phrase and staring down into his cup in a maudlin way. We sat quietly for a moment, in contemplative silence.

"Christ, this conversation has become boring and depressing pretty quickly. Shall we just go back to talking about work and less about icky grown-up stuff?" I muttered eventually, keen as ever to move away from the kind of feelings-based discussions that I found so hard.

"I'm glad that I can still rely on you to get to the point, Clara." Henry sighed, but he was definitely trying to stop a smile from spreading over his face.

"Don't expect me to sugar-coat the truth, Fraser." I grinned and bent across the table, punching him playfully on the shoulder.

Which, for the record, was just solid muscle that made me want to touch him and, more worryingly, kiss him all over to see if he was this firm everywhere. I quickly leant back into my seat, holding my coffee cup in a death grip to stop me from shamelessly feeling up the rest of his body.

In shocked surprise, holding his bicep and leaning back in his chair, he pouted, hilariously. "Ouch, you've clearly been lifting weights since we last met, Dr Clancy!"

"You know it. Now, no more emotional crap: we are logical, objective scientists. Feelings have no place in research," I quoted my PhD supervisor in a rough imitation of his gruff Geordie brogue.

"Don't tar me with your unsentimental brush, I'm an engineer, we have feelings too."

"Urgh. I forgot that part. I'm not sure we can be friends anymore," I joked, standing up and making to leave the table.

Despite my best intentions, it seemed as though we were falling back into the patterns of informal friendship rather than the professional new relationship I had been striving for. Henry's teasing and subtle humour was still there, hitting me full in the face, strong and kind and familiar as if we had never spent any time apart. Being with him again was filling my chest up with warmth and a thousand glittery butterflies, and I realised just how much I had missed my friend, missed his uncomplicated presence and ability to lift my mood instantly. His gentle and patient aura like a woollen blanket on a cold winter's day, secure and comforting, and I wondered again, with a pang in my heart, why we had lost touch for so many years.

"Ah, come on, even scientists need friends. We'll just talk about work, and I'll try not to make you have any of those icky feelings," he quipped, taking my hand and gently tugging until I returned to my seat with a bump.

Now very hot and bothered, I looked across at Henry's face, the slightly bashful, lopsided smile and twinkle of amusement in his eyes playing havoc with my rational thought, which had seemingly deserted me in my hour of need. In complete sensory overload, my nervous system was acutely aware of his long, warm fingers wrapped around mine, the electrical sensations from this point of contact flooding my whole system and temporarily erasing everything else from my brain.

Yes, damn it, icky feelings were exactly what Hot Henry Fraser was making me have. And it was highly alarming.

Chapter Seven

Pulling my hand away and trying to rein in my unstable physical reaction to his touch, I opened my laptop and brought up the publication and clinical trial plan for our heart failure portfolio, dragging my chair round closer to Henry's so we could both see the screen.

"So, here's everything that we've got organised for the next year, five years and ten years, and I reckon with some more data from your latest valve trial, we could submit at least three more abstracts and get a couple of papers published before the end of this year."

"I'm so glad you're here." The deep timbre of his voice reverberated through me now that I was sat closer. "I am completely out of my depth with trying to organise this stuff in any kind of logical way."

I patted his hand that was idly fiddling with a Montblanc pen, spinning it on the table between us, my subconscious seemingly still unable to resist wanting to touch him. "Don't you worry your pretty little engineer's head about it, let us clever scientists work it out for you."

Henry gave me a sideways smirk just as a dark shadow fell over us.

A sixth sense told me it was Dominic. Since I'd run into him in the corridor, my overactive imagination had gone into overdrive where he was concerned, and I now felt his presence just how I supposed Harry Potter would sense Voldemort, a sort of inevitable sense of my own doom. But when his hand landed on my shoulder and squeezed firmly, I knew without doubt that the psycho that lingered inside him was about to be unleashed. Henry glanced up behind me, and then back down to the icy claw that was gripping my upper body in an oddly possessive manner.

"Hello, Dominic," I said warily, without turning around. "Have you met Dr Henry Fraser from FraserTech?"

Henry stood up, towering over me and puffing himself up so he appeared even bigger. He reached out a hand over my head and I felt Dominic's grip loosen as he went to shake hands. Now free and able to stand up, I ducked under Henry's outstretched arm, ending up stood between the two men.

"Dominic Graham, Director of Marketing, we met briefly after the meeting on Monday," he said coolly to Henry. Who nodded and released his hand, taking a small step towards me.

"How are things going?" I asked apprehensively, and both men turned to me in confusion as I flapped my hands wildly. "You know, marketing things?"

Dominic narrowed his eyes and looked between us, before ignoring my question and concentrating entirely on Henry. "So, I hear that you're collaborating with us now?"

"Yes, with Clara and the medical team," Henry said with a soft, affectionate tone to his voice.

"Yay me," I murmured, and gave a half-hearted little fist pump. Henry moved infinitesimally closer, his hand now resting on the small of my back in solidarity.

"How excellent," Dominic said silkily, his demeanour altering as he zeroed in on the obvious contact between us, eyes turning to slits as Henry shifted and curved his body slightly protectively around me. And when Dominic's spear-like gaze settled on me, his expression so psychotic it made my soul shriek in alarm, he quietly continued, like he was reading an obituary, "We're all very fond of Clara."

"Yes, I can imagine that you are, she is a brilliant scientist and someone that I am delighted to be working with," Henry replied.

"Well, we've got lots of important medical stuff to talk about, that you marketing types shouldn't know about just yet," I babbled with forced joviality, wagging my finger in a mock stern way. Probably looking like a deranged primary school teacher in an attempt to break the Mexican eyeball stand-off that was now occurring over the top of my head, and to extricate myself from this particularly awkward encounter.

"Of course. Nice to meet you Henry, we should get together and discuss how my department might be able to work with your company in the future," Dominic muttered through gritted teeth. And with a final look, which left me feeling dirtier than if I'd just bathed in raw sewage, he turned on his heel and stalked out of the coffee shop.

"He seemed…" Henry trailed off, apparently at a loss for words as he tracked Dominic's exit with undisguised consternation.

"Yes, he's very…" I was unsure how to finish this sentence too, desperately striving for professional, I eventually settled on, "Intense."

Henry stared at me. "That is not what I thought you'd say."

"Really, what did you think I'd say?" I was genuinely interested in his insight on my apparent thoughts and opinions.

"Creepy? Slimy? Peculiarly smarmy? Shall I go on?"

"Well, *you* may think all those things about my colleague, but *I'm* being professional, and couldn't possibly comment."

"Professional, huh?"

The way he was looking at me, I could tell he was recounting in his mind all the ways in which I had been wholly unprofessional since we'd become reacquainted. Oh god, please don't mention the chocolate nipple, or the see-through shirt, or the dreadful presentation, or my lewd hand puppetry, I silently begged him. Aware that I probably looked like some large-eyed and pathetic cartoon puppy.

"He just reminds me of someone, but I can't think who." He pondered thoughtfully, tapping his forefinger on his top lip.

"Patrick Batemen?" I replied, before clapping my hand over my mouth, unable to believe I'd said it out loud.

"Ooh American Psycho – yes!"

"Or maybe Hannibal Lecter?"

Henry grinned. "Ah yes, there she is, I knew the real you was in there somewhere."

"Damn it, I thought I'd be able to remain professional about him, but I think he might be the creepiest, slimiest and most peculiarly smarmy person I've ever met."

"Definitely Hannibal Lecter, and I think he really likes you, Clarice." Henry was trying very hard not to laugh out loud.

"Stop it, I'm pretty sure I've just been selected as his next victim." I groaned in despair, burrowing my face into the palms of my hands.

"The way he was looking at me, I think I'm the one he wants to kill, he wants to do *other things* to you." He nudged me playfully with his shoulder. "Come on, let's finish off this plan, I've got another meeting in twenty minutes."

Gently he prised my fingers from my eyes, and gave me an encouraging smile as we sat back down. "I'll check his desk for cable ties and gaffer tape later, don't worry. I can, and will, absolutely kick his arse if you need me to."

"My hero." I blinked up at him, realising that he had, in actual fact, saved me again, since Dominic had definitely backed down to Henry's macho posturing. Damn it, less than a week since he had shown up and he'd already rescued me, twice. This was not good for my independent woman street cred. What would Beyonce say if she knew?

We had settled companionably into the task of publication planning, and it was good to note that he was as studious and meticulous as ever. We'd achieved a lot, and were just finishing up when an abruptly loud burst of laughter filled the atrium outside the coffee shop, and a small group of medical sales reps wandered in. The bright orange perma-tan, lurid nails, and bleached hair extensions revealing the larger-than-life character of Marina Montgomery leading the party. Her tailored skirt suit and high heels were undoubtedly expensive, and hugged her surgically enhanced frame to perfection. She scanned the coffee shop like a sniper on lookout, her gaze skittered dismissively over me, but froze when she saw Henry, who was furiously making notes on his iPad, completely unaware that he was in her sights. My heart sank when a predatory smile graced her collagen-plumped pink lips and she trotted over towards us.

"Clara, dahling! How are you? Long time no see! Must do coffee soon and catch up! And who is this?" She hadn't once looked at me during this quickfire conversation starter, instead focussing all her energy on staring at Henry and willing him to look up from his notes.

"This is Dr Henry Fraser from FraserTech, he's going to be collaborating with us on the heart failure portfolio," I replied.

At the mention of his name, Henry looked up and took in Marina in all her flamboyant glory, and gave a sizeable gulp. She was most definitely at her most cougarish in this situation, and a hunger like I had never seen before was written all over her face. If I hadn't been there, I am fairly sure she would have just ripped his clothes right off him. This was a far cry from the usual simpering and giggling that most women employed around Henry, and I watched on with interest, feeling a little like David Attenborough observing large cat mating rituals in the Serengeti.

"Dr Fraser, so nice to meet you. I am *Miss* Marina Montgomery," she said, stressing the miss almost to epic proportions. "And I lead the sales team on our cardiovascular franchise here at Pharmavoltis. It would be so great to get to know you and work together, let's do lunch or dinner," she purred at him.

Pulling out a business card she bent over, pushing her sizable assets together until they almost spilled out of her low-cut top, and handed the card to a rather petrified-looking Henry. She stayed bent over for a fraction longer, clearly ensuring that he got an eye full, before straightening up and flashing him another smile.

"Thank you, nice to meet you too," he murmured, not quite making eye contact with her, instead choosing a point just up and to the left of her coiffured hair to focus on.

I smiled smugly at his discomfort as she walked away, hips swaying and heels clacking on the polished floor, and he breathed a sigh of relief.

"She seemed…" I queried, deciding to let him finish the sentence.

"Intense?" he replied, "No, scrap that, she's terrifying." With a desperate and haunted look in his eye, he whispered, "I'll help you to escape the clutches of Hannibal Lecter if you save me from Ivana Trump, deal?"

"Ah, she seems very interested in you, Henry, and I'm sure she's got *other things* on her mind." I sniggered.

He shuddered. "How many poor doctors has she tormented in her career?"

"Oh, they love it, she has the highest sales figures of any of them." I took another sip of coffee.

Henry's iPad began to chime, and he looked at the message that had popped up on the screen.

"I have to go to a meeting with Claus now, can we carry this on another time? I've been given a temporary office here to work from, just down from yours, so I should be around a few days each week. When is good for you?"

"I'll check my calendar and let you know," I said.

Inside my head, a little voice screamed *Yes, yes, yes, I'm free any time you want*, which I valiantly tried to ignore.

"It's been fun to catch up," Henry said, before looking over his glasses and adding meaningfully, and only a little sarcastically, "And obviously also hugely educational and professional." Gathering his belongings, he stood up. "See you next week."

I stood as well, turned to face him, and was just about to speak when he leaned in close to me to grab his pen from the table next to my laptop. The scent of fresh washing powder mixed with a hint of a woodsy scent assaulted my senses, evoking images of naked wild swimming, and romps in the forest together. Yes, damn it, Henry smelled delightful, clean and outdoorsy, utterly masculine, and so absolutely and completely delicious that this one sniff had reignited the urge to kiss him all over.

"Err, yes, see you on Monday," I replied, but my voice sounded weirdly high-pitched.

He hadn't changed, at all. He was still the funny, generous and slightly shy Henry from all those years ago, and that we had easily fallen back into our old habits so quickly was disturbing and reassuring in equal measure. However, it also seemed as though a previously inert part of my brain had suddenly been awakened, battered by a cacophony of sexual attraction, which was screaming like a fog horn in the mist of denial as I watched him walk away.

Holy hell balls and shit sticks, I'd lost my previous immunity to the Hot Henry Effect, and this was not good, not good at all.

Chapter Eight

"Hey, Professor Jo, how's it hanging?"

"Dr Clara, what an unexpected surprise!" Jo Harrison answered on the fifteenth ring and her slightly groggy but melodious voice immediately made my spirits rise.

We'd been best friends since our first day of graduate school, sharing an obnoxious supervisor, commiserating and cheerleading for each other, attending conferences and drinking far too much cheap wine in our rented flat. Weirdly, we had both grown up on the outskirts of Manchester, living only ten miles apart but had not known each other until we met at Oxford. We held a lot of secrets for one another, and I knew she always had my back, but would also absolutely and categorically tell me things straight, not fannying about for fear of hurting my feelings. Considered blunt and abrasive by some, she was the exact opposite of my inherent people-pleaser nature, but she got me, and was exactly the person I needed as a best friend.

"Yeah, sorry about my infrequent calls, but considering you

moved to the other side of the world and neither of us like early mornings, it's kind of hard to schedule time with you."

"Bollocks, I'll always take your call even if you do work for the dark side. How are you?"

Jo had moved to Australia to pursue her postdoc and was now hugely successful in the field of neuronal biology, rapidly making assistant professor and heading a small research group. Jo was one of those annoying people who always seemed to excel in anything she put her mind to. If I didn't love the bones of her, I'd have definitely made her my arch enemy.

"I'm good, you?"

We briefly chatted about life and the things that were going on with us. Her Australian boyfriend, Coen, had been promoted and they were moving to a bigger house. She seemed excited, her life was speeding along just how she wanted, and I was totally and utterly happy for her. It saddened me to think that she would probably never return to live in the UK, but I was proud of her success too, and would always be there on the sidelines, cheerleading her unfettered resolve to be the best she could be.

"So, do you want to hear something funny?" I asked, suddenly nervous to get to the real reason for my call.

"Go on?"

"Do you remember Henry Fraser?"

"Of course, who could forget that bone structure?" I could hear her heart rate increasing at the mere mention of his name.

"Are you drooling over there?"

"Shush, just give me a minute to remember him in all his gorgeousness."

"Just let me know when you're ready," I said with an

almost audible eye roll. There were a few moments of silence, well, not quite silence as I could hear her heavy breathing down the line. "You do know that some men would pay big money to listen to this, Jo. If the professorship doesn't work out, this right here, this is your calling."

A bit more silence. "Where is Coen anyway?"

Jo grumbled in annoyance at my insistent interruption to her obvious fantasising. "He's gone fishing. Fine, what do you want to tell me about Hot Henry?"

I took a deep breath. "He turned up here, at work, last week and now we're collaborating on a load of projects together."

"Get out of here?! You lucky cow!"

"He's still just the same you know, nice and funny and clever, it was great to catch up," I said cautiously.

"I bet it was, you sly dog. Has he aged well? Is he married? Did you lick his face?"

I snorted the mouthful of tea I had just swigged and burst out laughing. "Did I do what to his face?!"

"Sorry, that's my fantasy, moving on…" Jo replied, a smile in her voice.

"I did not lick his face, for the record," I muttered, not revealing that the thought of kissing him all over had gone through my mind at least once. "Not married, divorced. Has aged well, he looks just the same but with shorter hair and now wears glasses."

"Ooh, like Clark Kent?"

"Yes!" I said excitedly, feeling reassured that despite the distance between us and the irregularity of our chats, we were still on the same wavelength. Jo was silent for a while, and I wondered if she'd got caught up in another Henry-related fantasy. "Earth to Jo, if you're imagining dirty Clark Kent shenanigans, please stop."

"I always knew he would come back from America for you," she said wistfully.

"What are you talking about?"

"Oh, come off it, you were the only one he ever looked at twice and you were always sneaking off just the two of you for *chats and drinks*," she joked, placing a weird emphasis on the last three words.

"Are you doing air quotes over 'chats and drinks'? Because I can tell you now, that's all they ever were. I was mentoring him, so of course we went off for chats and we sometimes had them over a drink," I replied, a little defensively.

"Yeah, but he never went for 'chats and drinks' with me when I was assigned to teaching him protein extraction. In fact, he was so shy, he barely talked to me at all," she muttered.

"Okay." I wasn't sure exactly what she was suggesting here.

"I wanted to have 'chats and drinks' with him too, maybe in the lab supplies cupboard or in the stacks of the medical library," Jo went on, her voice now had a slightly sulky undertone.

"Are you using 'chats and drinks' as a euphemism for sex? Because Henry and I were definitely platonic, no funny business went on, definitely not in the lab supplies cupboard or in the library stacks. I'd have definitely told you if they had. Plus, you were too busy snogging what's his face, that postdoc from the biochemistry lab, to have any time for Henry-related shenanigans."

"Oh, but Henry wanted to have shenanigans with *you*," she insisted.

"I don't know what you're going on about, he made it perfectly clear that I was in the friendzone." I was a little alarmed at where this was going, my heart rate galloping along as if I'd just run the London marathon.

"That's only because you put him there first. Everyone else was acting as if they were in a Jane Austen novel in his presence, and you were busy taking the piss out of his Bon Jovi tee shirt and shitness with a pipette. You totally friend-zoned him first."

Had I? It was hard to remember who started the leg pulling, had it been me? He certainly gave as good as he got when we had got to know each other.

"If you knew this, why didn't you ever say anything to me about it?" I asked quietly.

"I assumed you knew he fancied you and didn't care that he wanted you undressed and laid out on a lab bench, Clara. It was bloody obvious to everyone else."

"Was it?" I took a deep breath, how could I have missed this? And why was this revelation from Jo acting like some mind-altering drug on me now?

"Yes, you numpty, how you could have missed it is beyond my comprehension."

"But he never said anything."

"He probably did, you just didn't hear it, oblivious little weirdo that you are."

"Thanks for that assessment of my character, Jo."

"You're welcome."

"Do you think that is why we ended up being friends, because I didn't throw myself at him?" Realisation dawned. Perhaps he only liked hanging around with me because I wasn't some eye fluttering, heavy-breathing sycophant, I told it to him straight instead of just trying to flatter him. The only person, other than Jo and Simmy, that I seemed capable of doing this with.

"Yeah, probably, must get a bit boring being that perfect, mustn't it? Although, I'm not totally sure he always registered the sheer volume of lust directed at him. Maybe when you can have anyone you want, you end up wanting the person who doesn't want you." She paused and let that sink in. "Look, I've got to go, it's six am on a Saturday morning here and I want to go back to sleep."

"Sorry," I answered distractedly, still mulling over the reasons why Henry and I had become friends in the first place.

"Listen, if you just want to be friends with him, carry on as you are and enjoy being in his company again," she said softly. "But I can tell you now, Hot Henry Fraser did not just want to be friends with PhD student Clara, and super scientist and pharmaceutical industry superstar, Dr Clara Clancy, is way sexier, so I expect you'll end up licking each other's faces sooner or later. Byeeee!" And she hung up.

Right. Shit. What to do with this information? We'd definitely just been friends, hadn't we?

I stared at my mobile phone, trying to recall how it was with Henry when we had first met. I remember being inordinately irritated that my supervisor was dragging me off my own experiments to tutor a grad student from MIT, I was so close to finishing and could really do without the distraction. Then he turned up, all shiny hair and shy smiles, with girls following him around like groupies, and I thought there was no way on earth he could be a nice person when he looked like that. I clung onto that fact initially, safe in the knowledge that he might resemble Adonis, but he was surely rotten on the inside, and I could just teach him some cell culture and move on. But it soon turned out that not only was he attractive, but he was also a genuinely lovely person. A flawless mix of genetics.

And totally out of my league.

Looking back with the benefit of hindsight and a raft of life experience, it was easy to see that I had refused to let myself even contemplate anything other than friendship, despite what I now realised to be a very definite spark of attraction from the get-go. I had buried my feelings deeply, holding them close to protect them from being trampled, protecting my fragile heart from rejection, using humour as a façade, while trying to act completely indifferent to his presence.

It was hard to admit that twenty-five-year-old me had not, in actual fact, been immune to the Hot Henry Effect at all, merely better able to pretend that she was. Sadly, my thirty-two-year-old brain, which although vehemently opposed to the societal pressures of a rapidly ticking body clock, was actually intent on ensuring that I too now suffered along with every other female in a fifty-mile radius of Henry Fraser.

I blew out a long sigh and slumped back on the sofa, staring at the ceiling as Spencer, my cat, climbed up alongside me, kneading painfully on my stomach and giving me a half-hearted swipe and a grumpy growl when I went to rub his chin. I needed to tamp down these feelings, crazy cat lady was my destiny, because there was no way on earth that Henry Fraser would ever consider me girlfriend material, whatever it was Jo thought she knew.

Chapter Nine

R ichard had organised welcome-to-the-department drinks for Henry after work, and we all bailed out into the wet and windy evening and walked into town together, huddled in winter coats and various other cold weather accoutrements against the inclement conditions.

The Bay Horse was a cosy pub, popular with academics and one we had frequented when we had been in the lab at Oxford. Its heavy, wood-panelled walls and dark red swirling carpet design were so familiar that a comforting nostalgia settled over me as we ordered our drinks at the lowly lit bar. Henry too seemed happy and relaxed here, shepherding us towards the back of the main room to find our favourite table located in a secluded booth. The rough wooden table was flanked with two high-backed benches that sheltered us from the drafty side entrance to the main pub on one side, a low hanging ceiling light setting a warm glow, providing a cosy and private space where we had often whiled away the hours deep in conversation many years ago.

"Do you remember when we came here for your birthday, and you were determined to have a flaming sambuca?" Henry asked as he slid into the corner opposite me while Richard paid at the bar. "Errol, the landlord, nearly set his eyebrows on fire with that lethal-looking lighter."

"Yes!" I laughed and hid my head in my hands. "I blew out the flame but didn't let it cool down before I drank it."

"And the edge of the glass was still so hot that you burnt yourself." He chuckled, shaking his head.

"I had sambuca lips for a week after that," I added, remembering the strange little red marks at the corners of my mouth rather like fangs, which I had tried to cover up with concealer, without much success.

"Good times," Henry said and raised his pint to clink against my wine glass. "Fancy another flaming sambuca tonight?"

"God, no, that stuff is revolting!"

"Yes, it is."

"What are you two talking about?" Simmy asked, seating herself next to me.

"The good old days," Henry replied with a smile. "When this one could pretty much drink everyone under the table."

"Shush, you, no one needs to know about my drunken youth. I am a consummate professional these days."

"Of course you are," he said, taking a sip of his beer.

"Oh no, Henry, you have to dish the dirt on little Miss Prim and Proper." Simmy lent over towards Henry conspiratorially just as Dick Dastardly crept into view and sat down, twitching his bushy moustache ominously and shutting us all up in an instant.

"So, when did you two actually work together before?"

Richard asked after a slightly tense and awkward silence, that he seemed unaware that he had caused.

"It was about seven years ago when we both were doing research in the Centre for Cellular and Molecular Biology. In fact, our lab was very close to here," I replied thoughtfully, a touch of longing for my years in academia seeping into my consciousness. But then I remembered how stressful and difficult it had been, the definite sense of it being an old boys club, women often treated as a small indulgence that the pompous male professors allowed, patting us on the head when we had an idea, but not really taking us seriously. I hoped it had changed since I'd left but feared that it probably hadn't, not by much, anyway. Jo had worked so hard, been up against so much misogyny and backstabbing on her route to heading up her own research group, even though she was a truly brilliant scientist.

"I thought you did your PhD at MIT, Henry? Although, you're not American, are you?" Richard said the last bit like he had a bad taste in his mouth, as if being American was akin to having a venereal disease.

"My father is from New York, although my grandparents are British, and my mother is French, but I grew up in the Cotswolds," Henry replied, luckily not seeming to take offence at the obvious anti-American jibe. "My professor at MIT wanted me to bring in some cell biology to strengthen one of my ideas, so he asked Clara's supervisor if I could do a placement here in Oxford. And Clara got the dubious pleasure of trying to teach an engineer the hugely complex science of cell culture," he said, before adding with a blush, "I was useless!"

"He was," I agreed.

"Surely not!" Richard said indignantly and shot me a villainous look.

"Honestly, I really was!" Henry laughed. "And I wrecked a load of her experiments."

"Yes, you did that too. It's amazing that we're able to be friends at all."

"If it makes you feel better, I still feel guilty, all these years later," Henry said earnestly.

"It does, a bit."

"I participated in many years of self-flagellation, just so you know."

"That is good to know. Did you use your favourite ruler for this horrific punishment?" I asked with a grin.

"Favourite ruler?" Simmy spluttered.

"Oh yes, didn't you know that all engineers have a favourite ruler?"

"Maybe not *all* engineers, Clara." Henry shifted uncomfortably in his seat. "And no, I seem to recall that *someone* broke my favourite ruler by using it to try and free a frozen Eppendorf tube from its rack in the minus eighty freezer."

"Oh yeah. Sorry about that," I said, trying to hide a smile by taking another sip of wine. He was right, Henry had accidentally left his favourite ruler, that source of great amusement for me, on my desk, and with no other implement available, I had used it rather cack-handedly and snapped the thing in half. I'd bought him a new one, which was nowhere near as good, obviously, but he had accepted it with good grace, nevertheless.

"And just so you know, you feature in a full and public

apology in the acknowledgments section of my thesis, regarding the lost stem cells, amongst other things," he added.

"Published online?"

"Yes, on the MIT library website, as well as in the numerous printed versions that sit on shelves around the world, including the one at my parents' house."

I nodded in satisfaction. "Alright then, email me a copy and I *may* forgive you."

Henry made a dramatic show of wiping his brow. "Phew."

Simmy had been watching our bantering backwards and forwards as if she was at Wimbledon's centre court. Her eyes narrowed at me, berry-red lips pursed, seemingly trying hard to work something out. Or maybe she was attempting to mentally drill a hole in my skull in order to read my mind. Either way, she looked a little constipated.

"Are you ok, Simmy?" Henry asked, clearly having noticed her pinched expression as well.

"I didn't know that you knew each other *so* well," she answered, still looking at me. "Clara said it was only a few months of lab work."

"It was about eight months, and then I had to return to Boston," Henry replied, his tone suddenly a little clipped, his posture stiffening, leaning back and away from me marginally.

Richard had swiftly consumed his pint of bitter and was standing again, oblivious once more to the shift in atmosphere. "Need a top-up, Henry?"

"Yes, I'll get these, Richard," he replied and also stood. "Another Sauvignon Blanc, Clara?"

"Yes, please." I smiled weakly up at him.

"Simmy?"

"I'm ok, thanks, I've got to drive back," she answered coolly, shooting me a frosty expression.

"Right." Henry looked a bit disconcerted at the change in tone, glancing between us, but wisely chose not to delve any deeper and followed Richard across the pub. The squeak of the door behind the tall wooden back of my chair and a blast of cold air around my feet heralded the arrival of another patron, and I shivered, pulling my cardigan tightly around myself.

When the two men were propped up at the bar, Simmy leaned over and hissed at me, "When were you going to tell me that you two had slept together?"

"What?!" I coughed, choking slightly on the mouthful of wine I'd just swallowed.

"Come off it, you can't deny it, it's obvious."

"It is not!" I replied hotly. "We have never had sex."

"Likely story."

"It's the truth. We're just work colleagues, Simmy."

"I don't believe you," she said in a matter-of-fact tone. "You two have *chemistry*, it's practically visible when you're together."

I twitched uneasily. "You're reading way too much into it, this is not one of your romance storylines, you know."

"Do you think he knows you're in love with him?"

"What?!" Panic was definitely starting to consume my brain in a fiery tempest of incredulity and disbelief. This is fine, I am fine, I muttered internally trying in vain to douse the flames.

"Mooning after him in the office, banter in the coffee shop? Ooh maybe you guys could hook up and explore your connection in San Francisco? Mix business and pleasure!"

"Please stop talking, we have to work together, Simmy."

"Office romances are not frowned upon any more, Clara, and you two would look great together. Like the Ken and Barbie of science."

"Oh. My. God. Stop, please just stop."

"You'd only have to sleep with him the once and then share all the details, just a nugget of what he's like under his clothes would satisfy me," she murmured dreamily.

"I cannot help you with this." My cheeks were now glowing uncomfortably, and I downed a large mouthful of wine, coughing as it burned my throat a little.

"Hmmph, if you're not going to tell me, I'll just have to ask him instead, because I want to know *everything*," she said, rubbing her hands together in a supremely villainous gesture and pouring petrol on the already flaming pyre of my anxiety. "I need the loo, be right back."

And with that, Simmy flounced off, leaving me alone at our table and desperately not looking at Henry in case he had miraculously overheard any of that, or had developed mind-reading-from-a-distance skills since the last time we'd met. Staring intently into my glass, it was only the prickly feeling of being watched and a slight sense of my own mortality that caused me to glance up, and straight into Dominic Graham's face as he loitered on the edge of the booth, a curious and indescribable expression on his face.

"Hello, Clara."

"Hello, Dominic." A bit of awkwardness ensued until, of its own volition, my hand gestured to the space Simmy had vacated next to me and in a strange, disembodied voice, I added, "Are you joining us?"

"It's so nice to see each other outside of work, isn't it?" he said as he slid into the seat, running a hand over his slicked-back hair and giving me a slippery smile.

Was it? I couldn't be sure, but a very primitive part of my brain was awakening and strongly suggesting that a quick getaway flanked by an array of well-built bodyguards might be a good idea at this point. Instead, I nodded and smiled, fiddling with the stem of my wine glass, spinning it in my fingers, and ignoring the warning bells going off in my head.

But despite the waves of unease rolling off me, which I felt sure were visible in the air around us, Dominic continued. "I'm glad you agree, I think we've got to know each other pretty well now, right?"

"We have?"

"I'd say so, yes."

An alien sounding, part strangled gasp, part grunt escaped my mouth, unbidden, a sort of horror gurgle snort, and my glass spinning became more frantic as the awkwardness inside me started to reach epic proportions.

"I know you talk with Simmy about *everything*, but I am here for you too, you can tell me anything and *everything*, as well. Anything at all."

Why did he keep saying 'everything' in this weird way, like it had some kind of hidden meaning. "Everything?"

"*Everything*, Clara, any thoughts you might have, no holds barred." Placing his cold hand on my twitching fingers that were now grasping the glass stem with increasing ferocity, he gently squeezed.

This unexpected contact and the sudden dreaded realisation that he may have just overheard mine and Simmy's very recent conversation caused a violent, whole-body twitch, that sent the wine glass spiralling towards Dominic like a missile, coating his neatly pressed, expensive-looking shirt and trousers with the remainder of my Sauvignon Blanc.

"Oh god, I'm so sorry!" Well, wasn't this a right royal pain in my arse? I stared at the wet patch spreading in his lap, his beige trousers changing colour like a chameleon in front of my very eyes. Shit, what to do, what to do? Desperation grabbed me by the brain and shook it, and reaching for a tissue from my bag I proceeded to dab at his wet clothes, head bowed close to him in the low light as he sat still as a statue next to me.

"What's going on?"

Back in meerkat mode, and as if hearing the call of a hawk, my head shot up from inspecting Dominic's wet crotch to be met with the furrowed brow and confused eyes of Henry, laden with drinks and looming over us.

"I should go and get cleaned up," Dominic muttered, moving my hand and the soggy tissues from his thigh and onto the table, his fingers lingering a little too long over mine. Getting up, he sauntered across the pub to the toilets, and even when wearing wet trousers that looked like he'd had an unfortunate genitourinary accident, he still exuded an air of arrogance, turning to me with a slightly self-satisfied smile before opening the door to the bathrooms and almost barrelling into Simmy coming out.

"Urgh, what's Dominic doing here?" Simmy shot a curious and slightly suspicious look over her shoulder at his retreating figure before sitting heavily next to me and grinning up at Henry, who was still standing awkwardly, holding the drinks. "Ah, good he's back, we can ask Henry now, can't we?"

"Ask him what?" I said at the same time that Henry said, "Ask me what?" He put the large glass of wine down in front of me, the contents of which I had the urge to swallow in one gulp.

"Did Clara have any boyfriends when she was a graduate student? She's horribly and universally single now and she never talks about that time, and I have been with my husband for at least a hundred years, so I want to use her life to jazz up my own."

Henry frowned and looked at me. "I don't know, did you?"

"No," I replied in a slightly hoarse voice, while silently screaming for everyone to stop talking.

"Oh, there you go then, Simmy," he said. Did he sound a little bit pleased?

"Ah, but there must have been someone that you fancied?" she persisted. I was going to kill her.

"No." Glaring, I willed her to close her cake hole. Where was Henry's favourite ruler when I needed it? I could really do with it at this moment to beat her over the head.

"No one at all?" She was staring intently at me, grinning manically with a devious glint in her eyes as she drummed long, red fingernails on the table. A sudden vision of Cruella de Vil entered my mind.

"Nope, I was focused on my studies. I was very boring," I answered evenly, trying to subtly draw a line across my throat in a warning that only Simmy could see, but she just shook her head slightly and continued to smirk.

"You've never been boring, Clara," Henry murmured warmly.

Smug. That is the only way to describe the look on Simmy's face and I concentrated on the image of her stealing puppies and being outsmarted by a group of dogs and a small ginger cat, because I so desperately wanted to lean over and strangle her to death with my bare hands. Luckily, she was saved by the return of Dominic to the table, and the sound of my soul leaving my body rushed in my ears, obliterating all other thoughts.

The next day an email popped into my inbox.

From: AH.Fraser@frasertech.com

To: clara.clancy@pharmavoltis.com

Subject: Full and public apology

Hi Clara,

Excerpt from the acknowledgements section of my thesis. I hope that this apology will suffice.

H

Finally, I would like to thank (and also apologise to) my mentor at Oxford, the soon-to-be Dr Clara Clancy, who unwaveringly supported me in my endeavours in cell culture, and without whom my final chapter would not exist. She patiently and expertly guided me where lesser scientists would have given up, valiantly sacrificing her time and stem cells. She is a truly extraordinary researcher and an all-round brilliant human being, despite having dreadful taste in music. I feel honoured to have been shouted at by her on so many occasions.

Chapter Ten

The water glugged painfully slowly out of the cooler as I looked distractedly down the hallway towards the marketing department, longingly daydreaming that I was still asleep at this time on a Thursday morning, the caffeine of my first coffee not yet having had its full effect. A glimmer of movement caught my eye, a familiar shadowy figure lurking around the door to the stairwell up ahead.

Then, as if it were a contraption of the devil himself, the water cooler bubbled furiously, eliciting a quick head turn from Dominic, the glint of a predator spotting vulnerable prey dancing over his face.

"Shit," I mumbled, abandoning my bottle and dashing around the corner to my office corridor.

"Clara, wait!" Dominic's cry sounded ominously near, and I knew I couldn't outrun him to the safety of my own office (where I could pretend to be in an important meeting with Simmy and ignore him).

"Shit, shit, shit." What to do? The door of one of the empty offices stood ajar, and I quietly slipped in and closed it, the solid wood cool against the fevered skin of my forehead as I leant on it for support. I could just stay here a moment and hide. It would all be fine. Continuing to avoid him would be fine and absolutely the best course of action. Definitely don't think about how he stared at me, barely blinking, for most of the night last night in the pub, or offered to walk me home (I have never been so grateful for Simmy stepping in and giving me a lift instead, even if she droned on about my lack of a sex life for the full twenty minutes in the car).

Muttering to myself, "Deep breaths, in and out. He'll go away soon. There we go."

"Good morning, Clara, do come in." Henry's deep voice made me visibly startle, my feet comically levitating off the floor a fraction.

"Oh my god, Henry, you made me jump!"

"I know, I literally saw it with my own eyes. But sorry, Clara, this is *my* office." He looked like he was in mid-type, hands hovering over his keyboard, head turned towards the door in puzzlement.

"Gah, I thought it was empty. Sorry, but I'm hiding," I whispered theatrically.

"Oh, who from..." but his voice trailed off as he heard Dominic still calling my name from the corridor.

"Hannibal Lecter after you again?" he asked, eyebrow cocked.

I nodded. "Can I stay in here, please?"

Just then there was a knock on the door, and Henry strode over, ushering me back behind an enormous prehistoric-looking pot plant, and a long, navy wool overcoat that hung from a rather elaborate coat stand behind me. With quick, efficient movements he draped the thick woollen coat around my body like a curtain, which fell from above my head to just below my ankles, and whispered, "Cover yourself with this, you lunatic, and stay quiet, then if this is him, maybe he won't see you."

I found myself engulfed in a warm, dark cocoon that smelled entirely of Henry and I took a huge lungful, reacquainting myself with his scrumptious aroma. Peeking out between the lapels, I watched as he opened the door a fraction, holding it with one hand and effectively keeping most of the office hidden from the corridor. He was good at this, and I made a mental note to continue to engage Henry's clandestine hiding services.

Nonchalantly, he leaned against the frame and folded his arms. "Hello, Dominic, how can I help you?"

"Ah, Henry, good morning. I'm looking for Clara, have you seen her?" Dominic seemed keen to come in, but Henry held his ground, not allowing him over the threshold. "I thought I saw her come this way, but she's not in her own office, so I wondered if she had come in here instead."

"No, she's not here," he lied smoothly. Disturbingly and impressively impassive.

"Oh, isn't she? I felt sure she must be," Dominic muttered sceptically.

"What do you need her for, perhaps I can pass a message on when I see her, if it's work-related?" Henry responded with a level tone.

"That's very kind, but no, not work-related."

I cringed, urgh he was going to keep going with this, was he? Any futile hope that I had the wrong end of the stick was fading fast.

"Oh?" Henry enquired.

"Actually, I'm glad I caught you, Henry, may I come in?"

My innards clenched in fear.

"I'm just in the middle of something, so I don't really have time for a chat, Dominic, perhaps we can schedule a meeting for another day?"

"Don't worry, I'll be quick." But when Henry didn't move to let him in, he sighed and carried on from his position outside the office. "I'll get straight to it. I know that you and Clara were at university together, and I suspect you have a long history." He said the word 'history' like it was something dirty, like it had contaminated his brain to even think it.

"Yes, that's right, we've known each other quite a while." Henry was playing along, seemingly ignoring the unpleasant intonation.

"I thought as much."

There was an uncomfortable pause.

"Is that all, Dominic? I am pretty busy today." Henry was starting to sound a little impatient.

"Well, since you obviously know her so well, I'm sure you can't fail to notice that there is a special connection between Clara and I, one which I would like to explore further. Perhaps, as her *friend*, you could help facilitate this for me," Dominic stated, fairly assertively.

Please, for the love of god, stop speaking to him, I silently screamed at Henry, willing my thoughts directly into his head, hoping he'd get the telepathic memo, wrap up this shit show of a conversation, and shut the door.

"A special connection?" Henry repeated, slightly incredulous.

"Yes, I would definitely say so," Dominic replied. "She's a

very attractive woman." His voice had developed a viscous quality, seeping across Henry's office towards me like the slick produced by a stricken oil tanker. I shuddered, overcome with the awful feeling of being covered in flesh-eating ants.

"Yes, she is, isn't she?" Henry paused and a hot little kernel of joy bubbled behind my sternum. "Do you think that she is aware of your feelings for her, Dominic?" There was a slight wobble in Henry's voice, and I knew he was trying not to laugh at this ridiculous predicament that we were now embroiled in. The warmth in my chest that had bloomed when he'd agreed I was attractive was quickly replaced by an urge to kick him in the shin.

"I think we both know that she's aware," Dominic said arrogantly.

Yes, I was aware of his intentions, aware that he most likely had his sights set on storing my body parts in his freezer for consumption at dinner. Or perhaps to keep me as a zombie and feed me slices of my own brain. Urgh.

"So, let me get this straight. You want *me*, Clara's *friend*, to help *you* get a date with her?" Henry enunciated, shifting a sly glance in my direction. I shook my head furiously.

"Not help as such, I'd just rather that you didn't stand in the way. Let things take their natural course, as it were."

Dominic was clearly staking a claim and telling Henry to back off. If he wasn't such a creepy arsehole, this show of alpha male may have been a turn-on. But since my entire nervous system was pointing to him being the actual human embodiment of slime, it just made me cringe even more. This was worse than I could ever have imagined. Burning levels of nausea and black despair was all I could feel now.

"I see," Henry replied, coolly. His demeanour had subtly

changed. He was now standing a little straighter, shoulders squared, the hand now gripping the door was white-knuckled and when his bicep flexed it strained the material of his striped shirt. He was definitely more than a little intimidating. Seeing Henry acting all dominant like this was making me feel a little weak at the knees. Phew. I really could have done with something to fan myself with, but since I wasn't one of Jane Austen's heroines, I had to make do with quietly blowing on my own face, bottom lip stuck out, in an effort to cool my heated skin.

"Well, if I see her this morning, I'll be sure to tell her you were here, looking to explore your *connection*," Henry carried on, his tone vaguely sardonic. Then he gave Dominic a wink. A bloody wink. I was going to have to kill him. In an inordinately painful fashion. "Anyway, while I would love to chat more about how delightful Clara is, I really must go, I've got a meeting shortly and I don't want to leave my colleague hanging about any longer than I have to."

And rather impolitely, Henry shut the door in Dominic's face, leaning on it and shaking with laughter.

"You, sir, are an arse." I glowered from inside his coat.

"What? I didn't reveal your whereabouts, did I? Or let him eat your entrails with a nice Chianti," he whispered, and did that weird Anthony Hopkins slurpy lip thing from *The Silence of the Lambs* and grinned.

"You didn't have to egg him on, you could have got rid of him ages ago," I replied sulkily.

"Oh, but you two have a connection," he said, still smirking.

"Oh god, he's so horrible."

I wasn't really sure how I was going to come out of this

intact, how I was going to rebuff Dominic's advances and maintain a civil and professional relationship with him, and not totally derail my career. I had no doubt in my mind that he would take rejection badly, and my inherent people-pleaser nature made me want to implode at the monumental awkwardness that would most likely ensue.

Seeing the obvious despair leaching out of me, Henry's face fell, and he crossed over to where I stood, still cloaked in my navy blue chrysalis. Reaching out and pulling the lapels of his coat, he tugged me along with it towards him, before rubbing his hands soothingly up and down my arms. His touch zinged my skin, even through several layers of clothes.

"I'm sorry," he murmured. "If he's really creeping you out this much, I'll tell him to back off more strongly, if you like? I have no qualms in pissing him off if it gets him to leave you alone, you know that, right?"

I humphed, partly at this whole unbearable situation, and partly because I'd needed rescuing, by Henry, yet again. "No, it's fine, but I'm not coming out of hiding just yet, he might still be lurking outside the door."

"I'll go and check the corridor, then escort you back to your office," he replied, gazing down at me in concern and stepping away.

"Thank you, that would be much more becoming of a gentleman, Mr Darcy," I said, a reluctant smile tugging at my lips as I let the coat go and dropped into a curtsey.

Henry chuckled and bowed in return. "Of course, Miss Bennett, anything for you."

"You better mean that, or I might not be so helpful when Ivana Trump comes calling, and she definitely will." It was my turn to smirk.

Henry blanched slightly. "You wouldn't leave me at the mercy of that woman, would you? I thought you were my friend?"

There was that word again. Friend. My telephone conversation with Jo replayed in my mind, but I knew she had got it all wrong. If he'd wanted more, he would have told me, and stayed in contact when he went back to MIT. No, I knew him best and he'd only ever wanted to be with me in a purely platonic way, confident that he could rely on me not to fall head over heels in love with him. Probably the only woman in the world who had been able to do that. Staring up into his blue-grey eyes, I smiled, making a concerted effort to dampen down any ridiculous inkling that was blooming in my head that he might want more, to ensure I didn't fail him in this one thing that he needed from me.

"Don't worry bestie, I'll protect you," I said with forced gusto. "But first you need to go and sweep the hallway for our resident psychopath so I can get back to my desk."

Chapter Eleven

I t wasn't long before I was leaping to Henry's rescue as per our agreement.

I had just laid out lunch on my desk, consisting of my most favourite panini from the gourmet panini van who came round the business park several times a week. It was packed with roasted vegetables, pesto and lashings of gooey cheese, and it was a little treat that I allowed myself every once in a while. Even Simmy knew not to interrupt this revered and special moment, leaving me well alone to stuff my face in peace.

I'd cut it in half and was admiring it in the way you might gaze at your first true love, when Henry burst in, looking flustered, not even bothering to knock.

"Ivana Trump," he hissed at me, before turning to look at Simmy. "Oh hi, Simmy, how are you?"

She blinked several times before answering, "Good, you?"

"Yes, great, thanks, excellent." He turned his pleading gaze back to me, nerves quite obviously frayed.

"Fine, pull up a seat," I said with a sigh and a lingering look at the panini.

"You're a life saver." He dragged the spare office chair from over by the window and placed it snug up next to mine, eying my panini with interest. "That looks good."

"Ooooh, you're a brave man, Henry! Clara does not share food." Simmy chortled and ducked back down behind her screen as I glared at her.

"Oh yeah, that's true. Except those cupcakes that you baked to celebrate Ben's graduation, I seem to remember that they had no cake mixture left in the middle and were black on top. You were happy to share those," Henry said with a smile.

"In my defence, they were a trial run, my baking did improve. I made you some flapjack once and you really liked that!"

"Well, *like* is a strong word," Henry said evasively, not looking me in the eye.

"Hey! You said they were nice!"

"I didn't want to hurt your feelings, I almost cracked a tooth on the first bite, even the birds in the garden couldn't break them and one was a woodpecker." He gave me a sheepish grin. "As an engineer, I was more impressed with their properties as a building material."

"Humph. Well, my brownies are to die for," I said, looking over at Simmy triumphantly.

"Yes, sweetie, they are," she replied, smiling. "Especially the ones you buy from the panini van man."

"I don't know why I'm friends with either of you," I grumbled, and lobbed a biro at Simmy's head, which missed and bounced off her largely empty and redundant filing cabinet with a thunk.

"Savoury baking is your specialty though, isn't it?" Henry said thoughtfully. "I fondly remember the mystery quiche that you made for the summer picnic, after much contemplation we decided that it was best consumed through a straw."

"You came here, looking for my help, remember that, Fraser," I replied tersely, and forcibly shoved the wheeled chair that he was sat on, so he scooted off across the office, laughing.

It was at that moment that I heard Marina's sing song voice from the doorway. "Ah, Henry dahling, there you are! I thought that *we'd* agreed to do lunch today. Naughty!"

As if caught bunking off by the headmaster, Henry slunk back over to my desk, long legs crabbing his chair along the carpet in a way that made me snort with laughter into my cup of tea.

"Oh, Marina, was that today? I'd totally forgotten, and Clara and I are doing a working lunch that I couldn't miss, isn't that right?" he addressed the last bit to me, silently urging me to agree.

"Yes, sorry, I just had to pinch him for this project, and it couldn't wait," I added brightly.

Marina narrowed her eyes and pursed her lips, looking at my panini chopped in two and back up at us both. "I see. Well, maybe we should reschedule for next week?"

"Well, erm, about that…" Henry trailed off again, looking back to me for support. Adorably unsure, expression beseeching.

"Listen, Marina, I am sorry but with all the project work we've got going on and the WCC congress coming up, Henry and I are a bit busy," I said as diplomatically as I could, before turning back to Henry. "Why don't you just let Marina know when you're free, you've got her number, right?"

"Yes! Yes, that's right. I'm so sorry, but there's a lot going on and I'm not sure I'll be able to make anything in the next few weeks or so, but I'll let you know," he said, and gave her his best megawatt smile.

Watching this seasoned cougar melt into a puddle of goo because of one of Henry's smiles was beyond nauseating, but it seemed to work. "Oh, ok, of course. I should have known you'd be really busy. Well, see you around, soon, I hope. Bye!"

She gave him a lingering perusal and he just continued to beam at her until she turned with an exaggerated sigh and disappeared from the doorway.

"Thanks for that, Clara." Henry sat back in relief when she'd gone.

"You could just tell her that you're not interested."

"I've tried that, she won't listen. I had one coffee with her last week to discuss potential UK doctors to collaborate with, hoping that would be the end of it, but it's made her even more tenacious," he said miserably.

"Going out for coffee with her is not the same as telling her you're not interested, Henry," I retorted, rolling my eyes.

"Well, erm, I made sure we only talked about work, and not any *other things*," he protested.

"You know what you need to do," Simmy piped up helpfully.

Henry glanced over, hope flashing across his face. "What?"

"Get her to think you have a girlfriend," she said simply, giving me a devious look.

"Do you think that would work?" Henry asked.

I replied, "No" at the same time as Simmy said, "Yes."

I snorted. "That won't stop her, she's nothing if not determined."

Henry's shoulders slumped back down again, and he looked like a puppy that had just been kicked.

"A boyfriend then?" Simmy suggested, waggling her eyebrows.

I laughed and Henry looked as if he was considering it for a minute, then he sighed.

"I should just tell her directly that I'm not interested, shouldn't I?" His voice was dejected, like a man sentenced to the gallows.

"I think that would probably be best," I agreed and patted his arm gently.

We sat in silence for a moment, then he looked again at the half panini that I had pushed towards him, in an attempt to provide a convincing display of shared lunch for Marina's benefit.

"You may as well have it." I sighed. "You've practically drooled on it anyway."

"Really? I forgot to get any lunch and don't want to risk going to the coffee shop." He then silently mouthed "In case I see Ivana Trump" before carrying on, his demeanour brightening instantly, "But I'm starving, and I've got a two-hour teleconference this afternoon."

"Yes, anything to cheer you up, misery guts."

I wrapped the half panini in a napkin and handed it to him, along with the remains of my salad bowl, a banana and a chocolate biscuit. "Now go back and hide in your own office and leave me in peace."

Delighted, he scooped up this meagre feast and bent down to give me a brief kiss on the cheek (which did funny things to my insides that I pretended not to notice). "You're the best, Clara."

"I know I am, now push off," I joked and waved him towards the exit.

Grinning from the doorway, he turned towards us. "See you later, Clara. Pleasure as always, Simmy."

And then he was gone, and I was left a little stunned, to be honest. He'd never, not once, kissed me, even just a brief, friendly one like that. A platonic peck, that's what that was. So why was my skin burning in the place that his lips had been?

I felt the weight of Simmy's gaze and looked up. "What?"

Her mouth was hanging open, wide, like a basking shark in search of its next two hundred litres of plankton-filled seawater.

"You're right, it can't possibly have just been sex that you two had. There is no other explanation, it must be love," she whispered, dramatically, fanning her face with her hand.

"I don't know what you're on about," I mumbled and dipped my head below my screen so she wouldn't witness my skin bursting into flames, while I crammed the remains of the now cold panini into my mouth.

———

Two days later, I got a call from Judy on the front desk. A roasted red pepper and goats cheese panini, Greek salad bowl and a large box of organic chocolate brownies had been delivered by the panini van owner, with a handwritten note.

Thanks for saving my skin and for lunch.
I won't tell anyone if you want to say you
made the brownies
Henry x

Chapter Twelve

E very year Claus Baumann, our company CEO, organised a business away day, designed to test team-building skills and provide a jolly old knees-up for all of the Pharmavoltis staff. Attendance was compulsory and I dreaded it each time it came around.

We all piled into the coach that would take us to the fancy country house hotel, the venue for this tortuous occasion, and I sat heavily next to Simmy and grumbled.

"I bloody hate these away days," I muttered as she excitedly bounced up and down by the window.

"I love them! Bhavin has to do all the nursery and school runs and bedtimes for all the kids. ON. HIS. OWN," she said, her voice particularly high-pitched and loud today. "It's like a mini holiday for me!"

I laughed at her eagerness to be away from her children for the night. "I guarantee that when it gets to 10pm and you've had a few Proseccos, that you'll get teary and tell me how much you miss them, while scrolling through the fifty thousand photos you have of them on your phone."

"Yes, that is also absolutely going to happen," she agreed.

"Morning." Henry's distinctively deep and masculine voice reverberated above my head, and he sat down in the empty pair of seats across the aisle.

"Hello, how on earth have you been roped into coming on this dreadful day of team-building torture?" I was horrified that someone who didn't actually work for the company and was therefore not obligated to attend, had appeared on the bus.

"Claus asked me if I wanted to come, and I thought it sounded like fun," he replied with a smile.

"Fun?" I was aghast.

Henry laughed and nodded. "Yes, Clara, fun."

"There are only two explanations for this behaviour, Henry."

"Oh, yes? And they are?" he asked, eyebrow quirked.

"You're either clinically deranged and enjoy team-building exercises, or you're trying to avoid doing any actual work."

"Those are your best guesses?"

"I actually know the answer. Clinically deranged, I should have seen the signs in other areas of your life, such as your obsessive need to perfectly line up all the coffee cups on the shelf in my laboratory office." I poked him in the arm, and he shrugged.

"I'm not denying it, order makes me happy; mess makes me want to kill people."

And as if on cue, an aura of death and destruction engulfed us, as our company-branded psychopath stepped onto the bus.

"Good morning, Clara, Simmy." Dominic nodded in our

direction as he made his way up the aisle, before turning his head to Henry, "Morning."

"Good morning, Dominic. Clara was just talking about how much she *loves* team-building activities, what about you, are they your thing?" Henry asked, extricating a furious glare from me.

"Not really, I'm only here because I'm contractually obliged," he said over his shoulder as he continued towards the back of the bus.

"That proves that then, not all the clinically deranged like team building exercises, just specific cases," I muttered at Henry's ridiculously happy face.

We were assigned rooms in the hotel and unpacked our things, before congregating to listen to the company performance overview from Claus, followed by an inspirational talk from an ex-sportsman (who Henry actually knew from college rugby days). I couldn't remember the last time I had been this bored. Oh yes, actually, it was coming back to me – the last company away day. Obviously.

After lunch, we were split into teams according to the colour of the little sticker on our name badges. Unsurprisingly, Simmy and I had been placed on different teams, but I found myself in a group with Henry, a couple of guys from regulatory affairs and Melissa Harcourt from medical information, as well as Marina Montgomery (whose sticker looked suspiciously like it had been removed and stuck on again). As she stalked towards us, Henry shifted awkwardly so he was now stood behind me, using my five-foot six frame as a human shield.

"Since you are several inches taller than me, you do realise that she can still see you, right?" I whispered out of the corner of my mouth.

"I am going to use you as a blood sacrifice, so I can escape with my life," he whispered back, lowering his head so that his warm breath tickled against my ear, his now familiar and delicious woodsy scent filling my nostrils. With a huge effort, which involved closing my eyes and a quick mental smack down, I reined in my errant thoughts about how close he was, and quite how nice my body thought this predicament to be.

Now was not a time to get all weak-kneed and ridiculous, especially as I opened my eyes to find myself face-to-face with glossy, collagen-plumped lips and the longest fake eyelashes I had ever seen. Marina was stood uncomfortably close to me, so that I was sandwiched snugly between her and Henry, who had hold of my left hand in a death grip so I could not move away, a peculiar electricity spiking through my nerve endings, radiating from this point of contact and thrumming up my forearm.

"Hello, Marina," I said weakly, the strength of her floral perfume so overpowering I felt sure it must be of chemical weapons grade.

"Clara, nice to see you," she said over my head, not breaking eye contact with Henry. "Henry, dahling, it's *so* lovely to see you here."

She took another step forward and I was now leaning so far back that I was firmly pressed up against the wall of muscle that was Henry's torso.

"Hello, Marina." His voice rumbled sexily in his chest, breath ruffling my hair.

I was instantly consumed with an over-riding image of him slipping his hands inside my clothes and kissing my neck. Oh god, this was bad. I desperately needed to focus on something else in order to prevent any further Henry-related images bamboozling my brain. I had always prided myself on my ability for clear, rational thought, even in the most stressful of situations. Remaining deep inside my own head, I frantically tried to recite the biochemical pathways of respiration, but even this couldn't stop me from breaking out in a sheen of cold sweat as his body pressed closer.

"I've missed you, Henry." Marina pouted.

Henry shifted once again. "Clara and I have been very busy with this new clinical trial."

I smiled a small smile, and mouthed "sorry" at her icy expression, but then, like an angel sent from heaven, the voice of the trainer rang clear from the stage, announcing that we all needed to gather round and pay attention to the rules and aims of the team building exercise for the afternoon. With another flash of annoyance at me, Marina finally stepped away and turned towards the stage, while both Henry and I gave a simultaneous and collective sigh of relief.

"You can let go of my hand now, I think you've cut off the blood supply," I murmured over my shoulder.

"Sorry," he mumbled and moved backwards, dropping my hand and finally giving me the space I so desperately needed in order to breathe again properly. I know I should have been grateful, so why was I missing the contact between us like a lost limb as he walked ahead of me to our allotted table?

As is usually the case with these things, we were given

woefully inadequate materials in order to create an irrelevant feat of engineering, whilst pitted against each other to achieve some infantile objective. In this case it was to create a racetrack, made entirely of paper, paper clips and toilet roll tubes for a car that weighed one kilo, which had to remain one metre above the ground at all times. The winning team would have the longest track, with extra points for turns and loops. The prize was a bottle of cheap wine and Pharmavoltis mugs for the whole team. There was not enough wine in the world that could help me enjoy this, cheap or otherwise, and I toyed with a paper clip, wondering on the most efficient way to gouge my brain out with it.

Henry, however, was in his element and instantly appointed team leader. He was entirely focused on this task, even managing to drown out Marina's constant compliments about his 'impressive muscles' and seemingly able to ignore the huge doe eyes that Melissa was directing his way. Even sixty-year-old Fred from regulatory seemed to have developed a crush on him as the racetrack design took shape. I sat apart from the rest of the group, held bits of folded and rolled up paper and handed them to him when he instructed me to do so, but otherwise I let my mind drift away to a happier place, preferably somewhere with a beach and free cocktails.

"Enjoying yourself, Clara?" Dominic's voice slithered down over my shoulder, wrenching me from my daydream.

With a start, I turned around. "Christ, Dominic, you shouldn't sneak up on me!"

He smirked, the sort of smirk that affirmed to me that he was indeed the living embodiment of a serial killer who was obviously delighting in my discomfort. "Apologies."

"I don't think we're meant to discuss tactics with other

teams, Dominic," I said distractedly, watching Henry as he bent over his masterpiece a few feet away, shirt pulling tight across his broad back.

"I don't want to talk to you about this pointless waste of time. I've been trying to get you alone for a while now, since our little chat in the pub, but you've been quite elusive in the office," he said, his tone vaguely accusatory.

I thought back over the latest avoidance strategies that I had implemented. One day I'd ended up crouched under Henry's desk while he sat in his chair, me holding onto his leg like a koala clinging to a eucalyptus tree, to stop myself falling over, while he categorically told Dominic that he must have been mistaken when he'd seen me come into this office. Then another time, I'd called Henry's mobile out of the blue and pretended to be on a teleconference with him, as Dominic popped his head into my office and waited patiently for me to finish for ten minutes. This time Henry had been about to attend a research and development meeting in his own company building, and had left his phone on his desk so I could fake it for as long as I needed to, while he got on with other things. I had made apologetic faces at Dominic, until he finally got the hint and left. I really hope Janice, Henry's rather lovely secretary at FraserTech, hadn't listened in to my inane wittering.

Henry had offered several times to have a word with Dominic and was getting increasingly concerned and frustrated with the whole situation, but I'd told him not to. I should take responsibility for my own life, I was a grown woman and I didn't need him saving me all the time. But in order to do this I actually did need to stop running away and hiding from such awkward encounters, even if I would rather put something pointy in my eyeball than do any such thing. I considered the paper clip I was holding, but quickly put it down on the table, out of poking range. You've got this, Clara, come on.

"Right, what can I do for you?" I said slowly, stealing myself to take some of the advice I had dished out to Henry regarding Marina. I just had to face, and outright reject, Hannibal Lecter, and survive the ordeal. Simple. Big girl pants at the ready.

"We are both highly attractive and intelligent people," he started, rather conceitedly, in my opinion, and I winced in abject horror at his self-congratulatory tone, but he carried on, obliviously, "and I think we share a mutual connection that should be explored. I would like it if we could spend time together outside of work, *alone*."

I suppressed a revolted shiver at how ominously the word 'alone' sounded coming from him.

"Like a date?" I asked feebly, hoping in vain that I was mistaken as to his meaning.

"Yes, just like a date."

"Oh, right. Well, the thing is..." I began, not really sure what 'the thing' was, nor what was going to come out of my mouth next. My brain was still caught up in the horror show of being anywhere alone with Dominic Graham.

"Dominic, you'd better not be grilling my teammate for engineering tips," Henry said in gentle chastisement, his arm going around my shoulders and literally picking me up off my chair and steering me back towards the group. "No fraternising with the enemy, Clara!"

"You're welcome," he whispered into my ear when we

were far enough away from the scowling psychopath, who was crumpling a toilet roll tube to its death in his hands.

"I was going to handle it, Henry, I didn't need rescuing."

"Oh, I thought you needed me?" He seemed a little put out.

"No, Superman, I didn't," I replied testily.

"Right, you never really did," Henry muttered sadly, releasing me from his grip and returning to his throng of admiring teammates.

After the team building exercise finally ended (our team won, thanks to Henry's engineering know how), we had a brief spell of downtime before the posh dinner reception in the evening.

I spotted Dominic from a distance, loitering around the lift in the foyer. Feeling confident this was a public enough place so he couldn't just bash me over the head without anyone witnessing it, I took a fortifying breath and strode over to him.

"Dominic, have you got a minute?"

"Clara, yes of course." He smiled an oily smile.

"Right, yes, good. Excellent," I babbled. This was going well. "You see, the thing is..."

I was talking about that mystical 'thing' again, gah, I took a deep breath and tried once more.

"Well, the actual thing is, that, well, I'm not really sure that anything other than a professional relationship is a good idea. You know, between the two of us?" My hand holding the team-building winner's mug was flailing between our bodies in an exaggerated gesture, which was entirely too big and unnecessary. "I'm not into dating work colleagues, never good to bump into people in a meeting when you've just had red hot monkey sex, am I right?! Ha-ha!"

Then I winked. Actually winked. And did a weird little clicky thing with my mouth, and pointed my finger at him like a gun. What the actual hell was I doing? Stop all hand actions immediately woman.

Dominic's eyebrows shot up into his hairline. Shit, why had I mentioned sex? And then laughed like a maniac? And winked? And pointed a finger gun at him? He clearly wasn't the deranged one here, I was doing a great job of fulfilling that particular role.

"We could possibly start with a drink or dinner, Clara, we don't have to get straight to the red-hot sex part, unless you want to." He smirked, his eyes flicking down my body, recovering his composure far more quickly than I had.

"Ha-ha! Err, yes. I mean no! No, well, I just don't think that it's a good idea. So, I think I'm going to pass. But thanks for thinking of me." I finished with an awkward mug bump thing to his elbow, before fleeing, like a coward to my room, to lie down in the dark and let the heat of mortification, hotter than a thousand suns, dissipate from my whole body.

Chapter Thirteen

D inner was at 7pm. At ten minutes to, I exited my room, dressed up to the nines in a black fitted dress with long sheer sleeves and a pretty respectable neckline. My hair was left wavy in a slightly unruly blonde halo, only semi-behaving, but I went with it as it seemed to compliment my structured outfit and high sparkly heels. I hated dressing for these work dos. I wanted to look nice, obviously, but not slutty or unprofessional, no one wanted that. I'd brought five outfits with me and tried them all on at least twenty times.

Tugging the hemline of my skirt down over my knees, I wandered towards Simmy, who was waiting for me at the top of the stairs, so we could go down together.

"Whit woo!" she commented, "Who's this sexy lady?"

I laughed and fanned my face. "Stop! You'll make me blush!"

Simmy as usual looked completely and utterly gorgeous, long dark hair falling like a curtain of flawless black silk down her back, pulling off the bright red cocktail dress and matching lipstick better than any Hollywood A-lister.

"I could be persuaded to forfeit my marriage for you, dressed like that," she joked. "But then, I know how you usually look, you know, sporting a chocolate nipple tassel and wearing a granny cardigan knitted from cat hair. Oh, but wait, so does everyone else here…"

I groaned and threaded my arm through hers and we elegantly teetered downstairs together. "Thanks for the pep talk, you're a real help."

"Come on, once more into the fray, my friend," she said encouragingly at the look of indecision on my face, and pushed open the doors to reveal the already full ballroom, everyone glitzed up in black tie, the buzz of chatter accompanying the string quartet playing on the stage.

A young waiter appeared with a tray of champagne flutes, and we gratefully took one each. When I quickly downed one and picked up another, Simmy asked in surprise, "Woah, are you ok?"

"I told Dominic Graham that I didn't want to have red hot monkey sex with him," I whispered and took another long sip, glancing furtively around me. My mouth felt weird just saying the words again. I was a whole big bag of awkward. All the fucking time.

"You did what?!" She choked on a mouthful of Prosecco, her face twisting with horror and disbelief, and a tiny bit of asphyxiation as she continued to cough.

Thumping her back distractedly, I quietly recounted what had happened during the team building exercise and then my conversation with Dominic by the lift.

"I cannot believe I alluded to having sex with him. In fact, I can't believe I actually said 'sex' in his presence at all." I groaned again.

"No, that's a spectacularly awful way to tell someone like him that you're not interested. Maybe I need to have a little word with him on your behalf..." She trailed off thoughtfully, before adding, "But let's take it back a step, Henry came to your rescue in the team building?"

"Yes," I muttered.

"Interesting," she pondered, thoughtfully.

"Not really, he's been complicit in helping me avoid Dominic for the past couple of weeks."

"Has he?"

"Yes, he has, Dominic has been a fairly persistent and shadowy presence recently," I told her, glossing over the many times that Henry had hidden me or deflected Dominic's attention recently, I was not proud of my cowardice at all, and knew I'd get a right telling off from Simmy if she found out. No, if my latest bumbling shit show of a conversation didn't put him off, I'd just have to come up with another brilliant plan to extricate myself from Dominic's attentions, without the help of anyone else.

"I knew it, he's definitely still got a thing for you," she said slyly, with a whole lot of squinty suspicious side-eye.

"Yes, isn't this what we're discussing? He overheard us in the pub the other night and I think he assumed that we were talking about him. I'd hoped that I could be professional and give him a gentle brush off but then I mentioned having sex, winked at him and ran away, so I've no idea what he's thinking now," I moaned despondently.

"Not Dominic, you idiot, *Henry*," she whispered, as subtle as a town crier on market day.

"What have I done now?" Henry said, appearing out of nowhere at Simmy's side.

He looked so good in a tux that I nearly swallowed my own larynx.

"Nothing," Simmy replied smoothly, looking over at me, calculating, back in character as Cruella, I thought ominously. "Clara was telling me how you saved her this afternoon."

"She was?" He raised his eyebrows as he took a sip of his drink.

"Yes, then she rather bravely told Dominic to back off and leave her alone, that she wasn't interested, in *him*," she emphasised with a sideways look at Henry. Then she did a double-take and a little 'oooooh' noise, mouthing 'damn' and letting her eyes trail up and down his body.

"Did you?" Henry murmured in surprise, ignoring Simmy's blatant perusal and meeting my gaze.

"In a fashion," I replied, looking away and scanning the crowd, hoping for a distraction, any distraction. Meteor to the planet, alien invasion, global viral pandemic, anything really that would take the focus off me, and my distinct inability to act even remotely normally around other people.

And, as if the angels in charge of socially awkward situations were finally on my side, a large dinner gong was rung, and we were ushered to the dining hall and to a detailed seating plan. I saw with dismay that I was on a table with Dick Dastardly, who I'd managed to avoid for much of the day. Henry was sat on a table with Claus and various other big-wigs and investors. Luckily Simmy was sat next to me, and Dominic was with the marketing team on the other side of the room. Hope bloomed in my chest: I should be able to get through this unscathed.

As the evening wore on, the atmosphere became rowdier, inhibitions forgotten as the alcohol flowed and the disco started and got cheesier. Determined not to make a total tit of myself, I had switched to lemonade and watched in amusement as Simmy got to the teary, child-missing stage and excused herself to go and ring Bhavin to make sure that their offspring were ok, and maybe partake in a video call or three of her children fast asleep.

Enjoying a quiet moment to myself, I felt the tell-tale rumble of my phone in my handbag and checked it to find a text from Henry.

Henry: This is dull, when can we get back to the bridge building bit?
Clara: You are a weirdo. Drink more alcohol.
Henry: We could sneak off and get some flaming sambucas?
Clara: My face has only just recovered from the plastic surgery after the last one.
Tell me a joke.
Henry: What is a nuclear engineer's favourite food?
Clara: What?
Henry: Fission chips.

I giggle-snorted into my drink and was about to type my reply when Simmy's vacated seat was filled by Richard, who clapped me on the back with some considerable force, so some lemonade spilled from my glass into my lap.

"Well done, Clara, Henry has been singing your praises to Claus, puts our department in a good light. It'll be good to get you both seen out together at the conference in San Francisco, really highlight the work we're doing together. Excellent,

excellent. He's an excellent chap," he said wistfully, staring up to the top table where Henry was looking a little bored and had made a swan out of his napkin.

"That's great, it's been really good to see him again, he's actually a very brilliant engineer," I replied, feeling it was about time I repaid some of his compliments, as I dabbed at my wet dress.

"He is, fantastic invention of his. He's got another one in the pipeline, a valve based on a mesh scaffold seeded with stem cells from the patient's own body," Richard said reverently.

I sniggered at the thought of Henry struggling with stem cells again and caught the weird look Richard gave.

"Yes, totally brilliant idea," I said, covering my mouth to hide my smile.

Richard resumed staring at Henry, and I felt it was time to make a hasty exit. "Excuse me, I'm just going to nip to the loo."

"Yep, yep. Enjoy," he said distractedly.

When I came out of the bathroom having dried my dress under the drier, I was quickly grabbed by the hand and whisked off down the corridor in a whirlwind, with no chance to object.

"Henry, where are we going?"

"It's a Marina Montgomery emergency, I need to disappear," he muttered with a grimace, his head whipping from side to side, clearly in search of a spaceship or something to fly us back to his home planet where all the perfect people lived. Or maybe a telephone box to change in?

"And remind me again why I need to be involved in this?" I grumbled, stumbling along behind him like an uncoordinated giraffe on stilts in my ridiculously high heels.

"Because we are hiding partners, and it's your turn to help me. In here, quick," he urged, pushing open a door and tugging me inside.

We stood quietly in the pitch dark and listened. It was silent and oppressive, and for a moment I wondered if Superman had actually transported us into another dimension.

"Can we at least put the light on?" I whispered after a beat.

Henry sighed. "What if she followed me and opens the door? She'll see us!"

"If she has seen you come in here, she'll just turn the light on when she opens the door and see us anyway. And it will be even more weird that we're in here, wherever we are, stood silently in the dark."

More silence.

"Good point, Clara," he conceded.

There was the sound of fumbling and a little grunt of pain as Henry moved around. Then a flash of blinding light lit up the space, revealing the cleaning cupboard that he had dragged me into. It was very small, made smaller by the sheer size of Henry filling most of the available floor area.

"Wow, what a lovely venue, thanks for bringing me here," I muttered sarcastically.

He gave an annoyed snort, then pressed his ear against the door.

"Are we going to be in here long?" I asked, finding a large cardboard box full of paper towels to sit on, crossing my legs as elegantly as I could in my rather constrictive dress.

Henry turned and leaned on the door, looking at me properly for the first time since kidnapping me from outside the ladies' loo. His expression softened and he smiled, a gentle, sincere smile.

"You look incredibly beautiful tonight, Clara," he murmured, then blushed almost as if he was thinking it and hadn't actually meant to say it aloud.

"Nice try, Henry," I replied sceptically, even though my heart did a little happy tattoo in my chest, and I pushed my hair behind my ear distractedly. "You don't get to flatter me and hope I'll be ok with sitting in a broom cupboard for the evening."

He sighed and ran his hand over his chin, a light scratching sound hinting at the beginnings of stubble. "I actually meant it; I wasn't just trying to flatter you."

"Oh. Well, thanks. You don't look too bad in a tux either really, you know, except for your face, which is hideous, obviously." I grinned up at him.

Henry laughed and came and joined me on a box full of bleach bottles, taking off his jacket and cautiously lowering his large frame onto the fragile cardboard. It crumpled slightly but held his weight. "Thanks, I think."

We sat shoulder to shoulder for a few moments, the quiet between us comfortable and, I pondered, not too bad a situation to be in, considering the relative hideousness of the rest of the day thus far. I shivered as the chilly, unheated air of the broom cupboard leached into my skin through the thin material of my dress.

Henry took his folded jacket and placed it around my shoulders gently. "Better?"

"Yes, thank you," I said, as I pulled the oversized garment around myself snugly. "I expected to see you in your Superman outfit, you know, after rescuing this damsel in distress earlier," I joked, hand against my forehead, pretending to faint dramatically.

"It's on underneath here, just in case, not that you need anyone to save you," Henry answered, amused, tugging at his bowtie until it unravelled, and he undid the top two buttons of his dress shirt. This action did funny things to my eyes, and I had to blink a few times to clear my vision. This, this right here, was the cover shot for GQ and I swallowed thickly, as the Hot Henry Effect hit me full force in the heart. And while the view in front of me was a visual treat, undoubtedly, it was the wonderful everythingness of Henry that was pulling me towards him like a magnet, and I closed my eyes for a moment to try and clear my head. But this was nigh on impossible, actually, and I let out an involuntary little sigh at the Henry-being-really-rather-lovely video that my brain had so thoughtfully created for my enjoyment.

We sat unspeaking for a few more minutes, and I contemplated what on earth was going on in my own head, while simultaneously wondering what he was thinking about in the silent and serious way that he sometimes fell into.

"You did a good thing telling Dominic that you weren't interested," Henry said eventually, and nudged me with his shoulder. "I'm proud of you."

"You'd be less proud if you heard what I actually said."

"What did you say?"

"I'm not telling you, but it's very likely that I will have to avail you of your hiding services in the future."

"You're welcome in my office any time. I think I might have to get some more furniture to accommodate you, in order to make it more interesting," he said with a smile. "Maybe a magician's box?"

"Ooh, yes please, somewhere comfy so I can have a nap at the same time."

"Deal. Although, having you hang onto my leg when crouched under my desk was a particular highlight for me." He grinned mischievously.

"Don't get any ungentlemanly ideas, Mr Darcy," I replied tartly, and smacked his knee gently in retribution. Then regretted it instantly as I made contact with the taut fabric pulled tight over his even more taut musculature. Simmy was right. Hot damn.

"And you'll definitely check Dominic's desk for cable ties and gaffer tape?" I added, a touch huskily.

"Goes without saying."

"Thanks, I really don't want to be kidnapped and made into his zombie bride."

"Can I ask you something, Clara?" Henry asked after a moment.

"Depends on what it is."

"Why have you never been married?"

Oh, we were going to go there, were we? Right. Other than first-date-proposal Guy, I'd never actually been asked, and I don't think he really counted. Because he was unhinged, clearly.

Turning away, I allowed myself a little moment of self-reflection, peeking inside the closed-off part of my being, the place deep inside that held my heart. Somewhere that I rarely went, because it was vulnerable and painful to access, a place I kept guarded and out of reach.

"I think I am incapable of forming a meaningful romantic relationship with a man because I am actually cold and dead on the inside," I answered, only half joking.

"That's not a dramatic or preposterous answer at all, Clara," Henry said with a quiet tut.

"I don't know the answer, then. Never found the right bloke, seems a bit, well, bleurgh, doesn't it?"

But it was close to the truth. In fact, it had never felt comfortable or achievable to imagine myself long-term with any of the guys I'd dated (pant stealer Paul had seemed like a safe bet and look what he did. Or Hugh, with his 'wifely wants' checklist, on which I received an abysmally low score, apparently). So why waste everyone's time? I had always had the niggly feeling that each of them would eventually grow tired of me, look for someone else, somebody younger, prettier, or more intelligent (or more wifely). Realise that I was too needy, or self-absorbed, and not actually worth the effort. Surely, it was better to leave than be left, right?

"Hmmpphhh," Henry grumbled, clearly not buying that answer.

"I have had a few boyfriends, it's not like I am some man-hating shrew, Henry. But nothing ever really felt like it would last, so why bother?"

Because if we were being really honest, doing it half arsed would never be good enough for me. I was greedy for other people's love and approval, but not generous to dish out mine. I would demand that they give me all of themself, while never being able to fully open up to, or trust, anyone else. I knew that the fragile cracks that criss-crossed the entirety of my heart rendered it too unstable to examine closely, and certainly not safe enough to allow anyone else in. So, I ignored the quiet voice in my head that longed for intimacy on some level, and kept myself completely closed off to potential further heartbreak.

"Have you ever even given anyone a chance, or really got

to know them before pushing them away?" He sounded a little bitter.

"I think so. I don't know. I just thought that they'd probably get tired of me eventually, so I cut my losses before I got dumped first."

"What made you think anyone would get tired of you? What did they say?" Henry asked, clearly puzzled.

I sighed. "Nothing really. Maybe that's the problem, I'm clearly looking for something specific in a boyfriend, but I have absolutely no idea what it is. And even if I find this elusive '*thing*' in someone, what is the chance that they'll even like me back? Or stick around?"

"Why wouldn't they like you back?" He seemed genuinely confused.

With a long sigh, I continued, "I don't know, I'll be honest, I think the line 'it's not you it's me' should be my mantra in life."

"Why?"

This question lit a fuse somehow, made me want to lash out. "Because I am damaged inside, Henry, and have been for a very long time."

He recoiled a little at my sour tone, and I made a conscious effort to rein in my irritation, knowing it was completely unfair to take this out on him. But Henry waited patiently, allowing a vacuum of silence to sit between us, deafening in its invasiveness, and in a rush to fill the void I found myself speaking again.

"I'm too frightened to open up and trust someone not to trample all over my already broken heart, and crush it completely," I whispered dejectedly, hardly able to believe I had voiced this inner-most failing voluntarily to him. Especially because I wasn't even drunk.

"Who broke it, Clara?" he asked, quietly angry.

"My own father, Henry. Please can we drop this now?" I begged, voice cracking and tears starting to burn behind my eyes. The overwhelming reality that I was still that unloved little girl weighing heavily on my chest.

The cardboard creaked as Henry moved towards me, the warmth of his hand covering mine, where it militantly gripped the box edge, intertwining our fingers and giving them a gentle squeeze. This simple gesture of friendship and solidarity warmed me right through, a light tingling in my skin, a zip of electricity up my arm, which was as disarming as it was reassuring.

"Of course, Clara, I'm sorry."

We sat quietly together, a strange intense energy seeming to ping around the small space as I desperately tried to compose myself again. I wracked my brain for a change of subject, anything to get the spiral of depressing thoughts out of my head, turn the conversation away from my own insecurities. I could do with some sort of mind-erasing superpower to zap Henry with right about now.

"So, while sitting in this cupboard with you has undoubtedly been the highlight of my evening, I think that you really need to tell Marina that you're not interested, Henry," I said eventually, pausing to take a tentative peek at him. "Just be honest with her."

"I know, you're right. I did try again today, but I think she just uses it as a challenge and has become more determined," he replied, seemingly alright with my abrupt change of tack. "Perhaps the girlfriend idea is a good one?"

He raised an eyebrow and nudged me again with this shoulder when I didn't reply. "How about it?"

"Henry, I am not being your fake girlfriend, it's a ridiculous idea that only ever works in romance novels. Why don't you just get a real girlfriend?" I asked, despite the thought of him with someone else making me feel as though my heart was being squeezed by a giant octopus.

"Do you know anyone who would be interested in such a position?" he said quietly, now staring intently at me.

"Err, let me think," I pretended to be deep in thought, tapping my finger on my lips, which he watched with fascination. "I mean we clearly need to find someone who can look past your obvious physical flaws, which could be tricky, but I'm sure there must be a woman out there for you, somewhere."

His shoulders sagged a little and he leaned his elbows down on his thighs, gazing at the carpet tiles by his feet. "You really need to work on your motivational speeches, Clara."

"How about Suzy in regulatory, she broke up with her boyfriend ages ago and I'm sure she'd like you. Flaws and all."

"I don't even know who you're talking about."

"I could organise a blind date?" I suggested.

"No, I don't think so," he replied without looking up.

Oh, that was pretty dismissive.

"How about Melissa from med info, you know, who was on our team today? With the looks she was giving you over the cardboard bridge, I'm fairly positive that she's into you," I said desperately. Surely, he couldn't possibly feel as though he didn't have a multitude of options in this? How oblivious was he?

He glanced at me and frowned. "She's got brown hair."

"What's wrong with brown hair? You have brown hair. Melissa is really nice and very attractive," I replied, flummoxed at his response.

"Yes, I suppose she is," he started, "but—"

"Well, there you go." I smiled triumphantly, although I felt a little bit of me die inside at his admission.

"Yes, but, Clara, she's just not—"

But before he could finish, the door burst open and a small black-haired woman came into view and screamed when she saw us, leaping forward brandishing a tea towel. She whacked Henry round the head, continuing to scream in Spanish like a banshee. Jumping to my feet with a yelp, I grabbed Henry's hand and pulled him up with me, whilst he used his other arm to defend us from her onslaught, and we ran out into the corridor and towards the foyer in fits of laughter, with garbled, angry Spanish ringing in our ears.

"Come here," I said, stopping and turning to face him, as we came to the foot of the very grand staircase.

Henry's hair was completely dishevelled where it had been assaulted by the cleaning lady, and with one hand on his chest for balance (yes, that's totally why I put it there), I leant up and ran my fingers through its unsurprisingly silky ends, flattening the waves back down so he looked a little less ravaged and a lot more presentable.

"Thanks," he said tenderly, looking down into my eyes in a way that made me gulp.

"My goodness, what have you two been up to?" Simmy commented suspiciously as she walked down the stairs towards us, and we jumped apart, looking very much like guilty lovers caught in a tryst.

"Absolutely not what it looks like," I denied vehemently.

"Methinks the lady doth protest too much," she replied with a wink at me and a curious look at Henry.

"Tell her, Henry," I hissed.

But he was distractedly looking over the top of my head, and I turned round to see Dominic Graham in full homicidal maniac mode, his expression so dark and deadly it was sucking all the light from the room.

Chapter Fourteen

The week between the company away day and the upcoming trip to the World Congress of Cardiology had been particularly hectic and, due to various meetings, I hadn't been in the office much at all. Giving me a lucky escape from facing any more embarrassingly awkward interactions with Dominic. Even Henry and I had just passed like ships in the night, not really getting much of a chance to talk over anything that was said in the infamous broom cupboard confessional. And I was actually pretty grateful for that, hoping that he'd just forget the whole thing, and we could carry on without the need for an in-depth psychoanalysis of why I was so completely bonkers and unlovable.

But right now, I was sat on my bed feeling like week-old roadkill. My alarm had gone off at four-thirty in the morning and even a brisk hot shower hadn't been enough to imbue life into my bones, and it was only the incessant chime of the doorbell ringing that finally stirred my consciousness into action. Grabbing the first piece of clothing I could find, my pyjamas, I put them on as quickly as I could and headed downstairs, flinging open the front door with a flourish.

"Good morning, ma'am, I am your chauffeur for the day." Henry grinned from the step.

How he could be so cheerful at five-thirty on a wet and cold winter morning was beyond me.

"Good morning, Fraser, I'm disappointed that you've forgotten your cap and driving gloves, we follow a strict dress code in this establishment," I joked haughtily.

"Duly noted, ma'am." He nodded, tipping his head deferentially, the wind flapping his long overcoat around his legs. "But I did bring your favourite piece of outerwear, just in case any covert hiding scenarios are required."

"Of that I am eternally grateful," I said, laughing and backing up so he could enter the small hallway. "Come in, I'm not quite ready."

Now that he was standing in front of me, I was suddenly hit with how much I had missed him these last few days, and how accustomed I had become to seeing him regularly again. Before I could stop it, a goofy grin was stretching my mouth almost painfully wide.

"What is it, Clara? Have I got something on my face?" Henry asked with a frown. Obviously my unusually happy appearance was making him uncomfortable, and he turned to look in the hall mirror on the wall by the coat rack.

"Nope, nothing out of the ordinary. I've just missed these revolting features," I replied jokingly, gently pinching his cheek. "Right, let me finish getting dressed and then we can go."

"Probably a good idea, I'm not sure that a polar bear onesie is considered appropriate attire for a work trip."

"What are you talking about, I could totally pull this off!" I said, doing a little twirl at the bottom of the stairs.

"You would wear it with confidence, of that, I have no doubt."

"Help yourself to a tea or coffee while you wait," I added, skipping up onto the first step on the way to my bedroom, then turned back to him, "but don't judge my disorganised mug cupboard, you maniac."

"I can't promise that it won't be completely rearranged by the time you are finished getting ready," he said with a shrug and a smile.

Keeping an umbrella over me and opening the door like a gentleman (did I expect anything else?), Henry ushered me into his car. "Your carriage awaits."

"You have a very silly car," I grumbled, lowering myself into the ridiculously low-slung Jaguar, a difficult manoeuvre in any outfit, but I was particularly glad I'd worn a trouser suit today so he didn't get an eyeful of my knickers while I inelegantly swivelled my legs inside. Small mercies and all that.

Henry came around the front of the car and folded himself into the driver's seat. "It's not silly, Clara, it's sophisticated."

"I don't think I'd feel very sophisticated getting in it in a dress and flashing my pants at passers-by," I retorted.

"This is the reason why a lot of guys buy these types of cars, Clara." He gave me his best boyish grin, a hint of colour high on his cheek bones.

"Pervert."

"But obviously that is not the reason why I bought it," he replied, his tone hinting at mock offense. "I am a gentleman of the highest order, Miss Bennett!"

"Obviously, Mr Darcy," I said drily, but couldn't help smiling back at him. "Let's get to the airport, I am in desperate need of a coffee, and it's so cold I don't even know if I have feet anymore."

"Your wish is my command," he said with a salute and started the engine, turning the heater up high and directing it into the footwell so that my limbs started to thaw almost instantly.

On the way to the airport, we chatted amiably about what we'd been up to since we last saw each other. He spoke of the new project he was working on, and the networking he'd been doing in order to secure more investigators for the joint clinical trial we were running. I told him tales of the office, including the shock news that Dick Dastardly and Dorothy from accounts had been found snogging behind a rhododendron bush at the company away day. He listened intently and laughed in all the right places.

"Do you give everyone a nickname, Clara?" he asked after a pause.

"Most people, I find it helps me to understand how I view my relationship with them," I replied, watching the slow creep of dawn through the car window as we swept up the M25 slip road.

"Do you have one for me?" he asked, trying to sound nonchalant.

"Several."

"Oh? Such as?" he prompted when I didn't elaborate.

"Well, as you have probably guessed, most recently it's

been Superman. It seems especially apt when you're wearing your Clark Kent glasses as well." I gestured at his current eyewear.

"You really see me as Superman?" he queried, obviously pleased.

I sighed. "This is me, over here, rolling my eyes at your obvious attempt at fishing for compliments, Henry."

"I'm not fishing," he denied, shifting a little in his seat. "I'm just curious what you think of me."

"You're Superman, because you always seem to be in the right place at the right time, rescuing poor unfortunate women from villainous baddies and fixing broken laboratory appliances," I said in my best Hollywood blockbuster voiceover voice.

"Oh, I see. That's what you really think?"

I stared at his profile for a minute, was he feeling insecure?

"Well, since I'm very choosy with my friends, and you made the cut, even after a seven-year hiatus, which we should probably talk about at some point by the way, I think that tells you all you need to know about my feelings for you," I carried on, trying to assuage his worries. But the look he gave me was far from pleased. If I had to describe it in one word, I'd say maligned. Shit, *now* what have I said?

Desperately grappling for further words of reassurance, I added, "If you're concerned about your far-from-ideal appearance, I'm sure someone, somewhere, will eventually fall for your charms. Jo used to call you Hot Henry at university, so don't beat yourself up too much when you next look in the mirror."

Henry glanced sadly over at me as we entered the airport long-stay car park. "I know she did."

Interesting, of all the nicknames that I thought he'd like, he didn't seem too thrilled with that one.

We sailed through check-in, thanks to Henry's British Airways gold card and our business class seats, and were soon entrenched in the lounge with coffee and breakfast. Henry seemed a little subdued as he blew gently on his hot drink and read the headlines in the morning papers.

"Are you ok?" I asked. I gave my top a thorough inspection for any stray bits of pastry that were hoping to secretly decorate my clothing and draw unwelcome attention to my chest.

"Yes, why do you ask?"

"You seem a bit down. Is it about what I said in the car? Because, all joking aside, you do know you could pretty much have anyone you want, right?" I mumbled uncomfortably, then gestured around the seating area. "There's a beautiful blonde over there who was giving you 'come hither' eyes when you were getting coffees."

I looked around me again. "Or that petite redhead is really pretty."

Henry looked at me steadily for a moment, and then shook his head. "I'm not going to go looking for a girlfriend in the BA lounge at Heathrow, Clara."

"Oh, right. Well, there's always online dating?" I added, trying to be helpful.

"Are you on any online dating websites?" Henry asked over his cup.

"No. God no! Don't be ridiculous!" I had tried it admittedly, and the direct messages and pictures I'd been sent by some of my matches had made me want to set fire to my phone.

"Exactly."

"Alright, well maybe not that then." I huffed a little, exasperated at his evasiveness on this topic. "There must be someone you fancy?"

Turning back to look at him, Henry's expression was raw and penetrating, conveying an emotion that I was struggling to place. But then, as if it had never been there at all, it flickered away behind a mask of indifference, and we fell into a weirdly comfortable staring contest. Like ridiculous children. But I was nothing if not competitive, and I locked myself in for the long haul, taking the opportunity to unabashedly gaze at him and inadvertently becoming almost hypnotised by the depth of his eyes.

Henry's expression quirked, amused, as I started to pull faces to try and put him off, but he barely flinched, only the tip of his tongue poking out in concentration, until he intentionally touched his finger to his chin and raised his eyebrows. Did he think I was an amateur? Distraction would not work on me. Ha! Until, suddenly horribly self-conscious, my frontal lobe finally kicked in and lit up my highly evolved mortification response.

"Oh god, Henry, is there something on my face?" I frantically delved to the bottom of my handbag and pulled out a compact mirror, checking for a cappuccino froth beard, or breakfast-to-face disaster, but all was clear.

"Ha! I knew I'd out-stare you in the end," he said triumphantly, before gathering his things together and getting to his feet, holding out his hand to help me up. "Right, you funny little weirdo, we should head to the gate."

"Oh, come now, favourite-ruler-guy, we both know that I am definitely not the weird one in this friendship. Scientists are distinctly cooler and significantly less nerdy than engineers. *Everyone* knows that," I replied, grasping his hand and getting up.

"*Significantly* less nerdy? Do you have statistics to back up that bold statement?"

"I am legitimately doing a literature search for the stats when I'm back in the office, there's bound to be irrefutable evidence, Dr Fraser."

Henry gave me a put upon and patient look, before patting me on the head like an indulgent uncle. "Whatever you say, Dr Clancy."

Chapter Fifteen

Henry took the aisle seat, he said it was because he preferred to face forwards and the window seats faced backwards in business class on this plane. But I knew he thought I'd just like the window better, probably because I was a bit over-excited now that the caffeine had finally kicked in. And (more likely) because I was also effusively explaining all the things that I could see outside. It was confirmed when my little squeal of excitement at the free socks in my flight pack, garnered an indulgent smile from him. It should be noted that I too am a frequent flyer, but free socks are free socks, and I am yet to be unamazed at the sheer brilliance and ridiculousness of flying.

The immaculate cabin crew were very attentive, particularly the young slim blonde who spoke very huskily whenever she came close to our row. She must have asked Henry fifteen times if he needed a drink top-up. When she headed off after her sixteenth appearance, I gestured to him over the divider and mouthed, "What about her?"

He rolled his eyes and leaned over to my side, grabbing the book off my lap and turning it over in his hands.

"'*Held by the Highland Barbarian*'," he spluttered, reading the front cover aloud. "What the hell kind of drivel is this?"

"Hey! Give it back!" I launched myself over the partition in an attempt to snatch it back, but he held it out of reach and opened it up to the bookmarked page. One, as luck would have it, that contained a particularly intimate scene and that I had reread several times already. Damn it.

"No, no, let me have a read," he said laughing, holding me back with one hand on my shoulder as I swiped away uselessly towards the book.

And to my complete horror he began to read aloud.

"'She was backlit by the fire roaring in the grate, her luscious curves highlighted to him through her thin, white shift. Angus took a step towards her, a surge of lust coursing through his veins, knowing that this would be quick, and probably rough, and that he wouldn't be able to help himself when he finally touched her alabaster skin. Angus pulled off his shirt in one swift movement, his muscles flexing as he bunched the material in his hands and threw the garment onto the floor. Lily was nervous, he could see it in her eyes, and how her throat worked visibly as she swallowed, her body beginning to tremble as his hands went to his kilt and began unfastening the heavy cloth from around his waist. The course wool was harsh as it brushed over his skin, the sensations raw and almost painful against his straining manhood.'." Henry looked over at me, he was definitely blushing, as was I, furiously. "Shit, Clara, I never expected you to be into this sort of thing?"

Was it wrong that I found the sound of his voice reading

this stuff incredibly erotic? Yes, wrong, wrong, wrongity wrong. Scrub your mind, Clara.

"Judy on reception gives them to me, she says I need some spice in my spinster life," I replied grumpily, slumping back to my own seat. Embarrassment sweeping me from head to toe as I admitted my sad and lonely existence to Henry. Someone whose life was clearly on a totally different trajectory to mine.

"Judy gave you this? Because she thinks you are a spinster?" he asked incredulously.

"Yes, bone fide perpetually single, crazy cat lady, that's me. Now give it back."

"I am not sure I am able to read any more of it without my eyes bleeding," Henry sniggered and handed the offending item back to me, which I gripped tightly in my lap.

"Maybe you should get yourself on Tinder," he added thoughtfully. "Reading racy novels should definitely be in your profile, you'll have flocks of willing romantic heroes contacting you, willing to fulfil your fantasies."

I glared at him. "No thanks. This way, if the guy in the story is an arrogant arse, I can drop him off at the charity shop and I never have to see him again. And I don't have to worry about being stalked by a weirdo. Or teased about my literature choices."

"Calling that book 'literature' is definitely stretching the limits of the definition, Clara." Henry's eyes twinkled with amusement, I could see he wasn't going to let this one go, and the flight to San Francisco was eleven hours. I sharply pulled the divider up between us.

"Don't be like that," he said gently as he pushed the dividing screen back down again. "I'm seeing you in a whole new light!"

"Grrr," I growled and pulled the divider up again rather forcefully, just as the willowy member of the cabin crew breezed past again and I waved to her. "Excuse me."

"Yes, madam?" she responded pleasantly.

"My friend here..." I pointed over the divider, which Henry slowly brought down so I could see him glowering at me. "Thinks that women's romantic literature is drivel and that they need an actual, real-life man in order for them to be happy. I think it's a hugely sexist and derogatory opinion, particularly because he is very grumpy and obnoxious when he's single. You strike me as an enlightened and intelligent woman, what do you think?"

"Well..." She shot an agitated look at Henry and glanced down at the book in my lap. "Ooh – I really loved that one! How far have you got?"

Her expression had become very animated, lighting up her delicate features. "The next one is even better; you should definitely get it. *Really* steamy!"

I nodded enthusiastically and gave Henry a sideways look, and he seemed wholly dumbstruck.

"And you," —she wafted a small, beautifully manicured hand at Henry, drawing his eye to her— "should know that women do not *need* men. In fact, most men couldn't live up to even the most mundane of women's fantasies anyway."

"Wow. That's me told," he said, as she carried on down the aisle.

"Don't be like that," I repeated back to him. "Maybe you should join Tinder and announce your new feminist views, you'll have no shortage of women's lib types falling head over heels and swiping right."

Henry chuckled and stared at me again, a small smile playing over his lips.

"I'm not falling for that you've-got-something-on-your-face stare again, you know."

"You haven't got anything on your face," he murmured.

"Ok, well good then." I twitched in my seat and went to open the pages of the book, the memory of the rich, deep tone of his voice reading the words in front of me, sending a shiver down my spine.

"So, it's men in kilts that does it for you?" Henry was going for innocent, his head cocked to the side slightly.

But I knew him better than that and slid my middle finger up the side of my face, subtly giving him the birdie over the dividing partition.

He smothered a laugh behind his hand. "You do know that Fraser is a Scottish name, right? You only have to ask, and I'll don the clan tartan for you, anytime you want."

"I'm thinking that I might have to come up with a different nickname for you, Superman doesn't seem to fit anymore."

"Henry the Hopeful Highlander?" he suggested and waggled his eyebrows, making me snort with laughter.

It wasn't that long into the flight before I fell asleep (long-haul flying always makes me drowsy), and when I woke up, I found that the airline blanket had been tucked around me and my book was missing. Sitting up with a yawn, Henry gave me a wave, but seemed engrossed in something, craning my neck over to his side I could see he was about halfway through *Held by the Highland Barbarian*.

"Enjoying the drivel there, Henry?" I asked.

"This is filth," he replied with wide eyes. "Is this what women really want?"

"What, to be captured by a barely coherent Scotsman and held captive? No, Henry, they do not. Not in real life anyway. This is just escapism," I answered, a bit uncomfortable to be discussing female sexual fantasies with a male friend and supposed work colleague.

"No, but I mean the sex and dirty talk?"

"Well, dirty talk isn't for everyone. But some people really get off on it, I guess." God, this was like talking to a thirty-year-old virgin about the birds and the bees. "Have you not discussed this sort of thing with any of your past girlfriends?"

"I've never had any complaints in the bedroom," he said, his nose back into the book, and the way he spoke did not come across as conceited, just a statement of fact. That thought did funny things to me. Best not to dwell on that nugget of information too much.

"Right, well, I think most women just want men to take control in bed, at least sometimes anyway. I think this is why the heroes in these types of books tend to be such overt alpha males," I pondered, and he looked up at me questioningly and I carried on, awkwardness bringing out my dark humour again. "But don't go bashing any Tinder dates over the head so you can drag them back to your cave, just because you've read it somewhere, the police take a dim view of that sort of behaviour."

"Got it. You want a perfect gentleman at all times," he replied, then in a low, growly voice he added, "Except in the bedroom, where you want to be roughly manhandled by an overtly alpha, potty-mouthed, caveman with a Scottish accent, is that right?"

My eyeballs popped out of their sockets in shock at the gratuitous image he had just conjured in my mind. My respiratory system going into arrest as I inhaled copious quantities of my own spit, culminating in a coughing fit worthy of a thirty-a-day chain smoker, and drawing so much attention from the other passengers that I was beginning to wish that I had never woken up at all.

When my trachea had eventually stopped spasming, and Henry had finally stopped laughing, I managed to hoarsely respond, "Um, yes, I suppose so, something like that."

Chapter Sixteen

S an Francisco was cool and cloudy as we left the hotel. We tried to stave off the jet lag and make it through until at least early evening, before finally giving in to sleep. It felt good to be out in the fresh air after so long on a plane.

We were fairly close to the conference centre and a short streetcar ride to Fisherman's Wharf, so Henry suggested that we head there and walk along the waterfront to find somewhere for dinner. I blew out a happy and contented breath, inhaling the salty tang on the breeze, the faint smell of fish and sea, the chatter of tourists and the call of gulls, the malaise from travel being replaced by a sort of contentment, settling deep inside. I loved this city, its eclectic and relaxed vibe was unique, a good mix of arts and sciences, and it was really nice to be here with Henry for company.

"That was a big sigh," Henry commented, "everything ok?"

"Yeah, I love San Francisco," I murmured dreamily.

"It's pretty cool, isn't it?" He smiled down at me. For once,

I was wearing flats and I had to really crane my neck up to look at him.

Strolling a little way further in companionable silence, I was relishing the new scenery and the busy hustle and bustle of the city. Occasionally our fingers would accidentally brush each other's as we walked, or Henry's hand would gently touch my back or shoulder as he helped to guide me through the crowds, and I absentmindedly enjoyed this brief and unintentional contact, and the little zips of electricity that accompanied them.

When we eventually arrived at Pier Thirty-Nine, I, like all the other tourists gawking at the sea lions, leant out over the railings to catch a glimpse of the ones right below us. Henry's fingers gently intertwined with mine over the rough wooden bar, his body now close behind me as he too leaned out for a better look.

"I know how clumsy you are, I am not diving in to save you from a sea lion mauling," he explained when I looked at our joined hands quizzically. "That water looks freezing."

"Yeah, yeah. If the big strong engineer is so frightened of the cute sea lions that he needs to hold my hand, he only has to say so."

He shrugged, sliding his hand from mine, before gripping me firmly round the waist, hoisting me off my feet and propelling me towards the barrier and the water beyond. My stomach lurched, but he didn't let go, just tightened his grip as I looked down into the faintly brown and swirling sea below.

"What was that you were saying?" His lips almost brushing against the skin of my neck, amusement lighting up his voice.

"I'm sorry, I'm sorry," I shrieked with laughter. "Put me down, I'll let you hold my hand!"

"That's better," he growled in my ear and placed me back on my feet, resuming the hand holding as if nothing had happened. A happy and relaxed expression on his face.

Only, something had most definitely happened, in fact, the whole world seemed to have shifted off its axis and I desperately gulped the briny air into my oxygen-deprived lungs. The usual zings of electricity that I had felt whenever Henry inadvertently touched me were nothing compared to the feeling of his large hands wrapped around my waist, or his long fingers tenderly and intentionally holding mine. My whole body was suddenly alight, and I had absolutely no bloody idea what to do about it.

Friends, just friends, I repeated over and over in my head, hoping this chant would be able to get me back onto firmer ground, away from the crumbling mental cliff edge where I would most definitely crash down to my doom by falling in love with Henry Fraser. There was a real and sudden danger that this could happen. And I couldn't let it, for his sake or mine.

It seemed as though we were now also one of the attractions being watched by the other tourists, especially Henry, and a little self-consciously, I tried to ignore the glares from several jealous-looking women who had noticed our little show.

"The Ghirardelli chocolate place is near here, isn't it? Can we go?" I asked quietly, shrinking away from the curiosity directed our way.

"Yeah, of course," he answered, that same indulgent smile from the plane on his lips.

As we walked away from the wharf, he still kept hold of my hand. "You can let go now, I'm not about to fall into the sea, and I'm quite good at crossing the road on my own, you know."

"Oh." He looked down in surprise and slowly released me, sticking his hands firmly in the pockets of his trousers. "Sorry."

"That's alright, I just wouldn't want to ruin your macho bachelor image, Henry." I was relieved and disappointed in equal measure that he had dropped my hand so readily.

"Too right," he replied but it was a little half-hearted.

We spent a while perusing the chocolates, and we both bought some boxes (Henry's were presents for his mum and his sister-in-law, mine were for my own consumption, but I kept that to myself), and by the time we had paid it was dark and getting on into the evening.

"There's a really nice fish restaurant on this pier, if you fancy it?" Henry said while we walked back along the seafront.

"I'm starving, that sounds great."

A chirpy hostess showed us to a table overlooking the bay and handed us some menus, reeling off the specials and pouring us each some water as we sat down.

"How do you know about this place?" I asked.

"When I was at Stanford a few years back, one of the PhD students brought a group of us here. She was born and raised in San Francisco and she said, as tourist restaurants go, this one is the best."

"Oh, are you still in touch? Maybe you should meet up with her while you're here?"

Henry gave me a strange look. "I'm not sure that's a good idea."

"Why not?"

"Because, Clara, she is my ex-wife, and we didn't part on such good terms." His tone was clipped, terse. Hurt?

"Oh." His response hit me in the guts, and I was unable to find something to say that I felt comfortable adding to the conversation, so we ended up sat in awkward silence, neither looking at the other.

Eventually I plucked up the courage to ask the question that was burning a hole in my head. "What happened, why did you break up?"

Henry watched me steadily and the waiter came by and took our order, dropping a breadbasket between us, before beating a hasty retreat, clearly sensing the tension now radiating from our table.

Finally, when he spoke, Henry's voice was quiet and he sounded tired. "We met at one of the university's bioengineering social events and then she joined the same lab as me, we hit it off and went out for a while. Getting married was a bad idea and it only lasted six months." He paused and sipped his wine, before continuing. "It was all my fault – I should have never gone through with it, I'm not proud of how things went between us."

A chink in perfect Henry's armour. Sensing his reluctance to continue, I selected some bread, allowing him the space to speak if he wanted to, not pushing him, even though the nosy little she-devil who lived in my brain was yammering to find out every minute detail.

"Can I ask you a question, Clara?"

"Ok, but it better not be a marriage proposal because I'm only looking for a kilted, barbarian husband right now."

Henry stared at me, mouth slightly open. Shit, that was a hugely inappropriate and poorly judged joke. Well done for some more splendid fuckwittery, Clara.

Then, luckily, he chuckled and shook his head. "No, you

don't have to worry, I'm not about to propose. Based on my very recent revelation, you can see that I have fairly poor form in that regard."

Again, I was niggled by the urge to ask more questions, to prod at this obvious blister and ignore the mental warning that pressing too hard could make it pop and unearth something that I might not want to know.

"It's about what you told me in the cupboard last week," Henry added.

Damn it, my telepathic attempts to erase his mind had not worked after all. Looking up, I was met with an intense and stormy gaze from his blue-grey eyes.

"You don't have to answer this if you don't want to, but what did your father do to hurt you so badly?" he asked. It was clear that affable Henry, the one who liked to smile and joke, and put me at ease, was gone. Spanish inquisition Henry had joined me for dinner, it seemed.

Buttering a piece of bread, I thought about the best way to answer this question without sounding like a complete disaster. Or giving away how broken I really was inside. Trying to keep my tone light, I said, "The usual parental abandonment shenanigans." Hoping that would suffice.

"Where is he now?"

"I don't know, I never saw him again."

"Never?"

"Nope, he disappeared and didn't leave a forwarding address."

"Do you want to find him?"

"Jesus, Henry! No! No, I've tried, and he's not interested in having any kind of relationship with me." I paused in an attempt to compose myself after that outburst. Unbeknownst to him, Henry had accidentally lit the touch paper of fiery pain that lived inside me.

"Oh." He seemed at a loss for words, his face sympathetic and confused all at once. "Why not?"

This was the million-dollar question, wasn't it? Why did my own father not want to know me? Why had he chosen to leave and cut all contact? Hurt the one person he was meant to love unconditionally?

"I don't know."

"What happened?" Henry was persistent, but as I gazed at him across the table, there was nothing but compassion in his eyes, an effort to understand what was going on. I could trust him with this piece of me, allow him to see a little bit of the brokenness. That would be ok, wouldn't it?

I took a mouthful of wine followed by a deep breath. Here goes. Kill or cure.

"I was eight years old when he walked out, packed a bag, left the house and didn't look back. His parting words were that my mother and I were suffocating him, that he had to have some space away from us, he needed time to be himself and not be a husband or a father for a while. As a child I tried to contact him, I wrote letters, hundreds of letters but I didn't know where to send them, so I kept them in a little box under my bed. I just wanted to know how I could be better, so that he would come back and love me like he used to. But we never saw or heard from him again." I gulped more of my drink, while Henry's face flitted between sadness and anger. "My mother couldn't cope, she drank away her life, relying on handouts, and left me to grow up pretty much by myself in a grotty flat, a product of the British social welfare system."

"I'm so sorry he did that to you, Clara," Henry whispered.

"I feel like I have a wound that won't heal, and every now and then I knock the scab off, and it starts bleeding all over again. I don't know what to do to make it better, or how to stop it hurting. So, instead, I don't think about it, I lock it away, keep it in the dark, and don't let anyone see." I paused, studying his face, looking for pity or incredulity. "It's a pathetic little story of woe, isn't it?"

Henry shook his head. "What you're feeling is not pathetic, Clara. Have you talked with anyone else about this?"

"Only Jo knows, and you, now. Aren't you glad you're back being my friend again? You get to share all the fun stuff with me," I joked, desperate to disperse the tension and move the conversation on. I was annoyed at my apparent inability to engage my usual steadfast avoidance techniques when Henry was around. Somehow, without even really trying, he had, yet again, been able to coax out my deepest, darkest secrets.

Henry observed me quietly for a moment as I glugged at the wine, trying to ease the dull ache that formed in my chest whenever I thought about this part of my life. My father had never even looked back as my mother wailed and begged for him not to leave us, and my delicate, still-growing heart had broken irreparably. It was a cliché, I knew, but to this day I still wondered what I'd done to send him away, wondered why I was so awful that he'd cut all ties with his own flesh and blood. Even if he could no longer love my mother, surely, he could still have loved me? But he didn't love me. I hadn't been worthy of love, even from my own father. This was the crux of the matter. The chink in my fragile heart made of glass. The reason why I was now ruined for ever trusting or loving any other man ever again. They gave up on those they were meant to love. They left.

"Perhaps you need to talk to someone professionally, a counsellor, maybe?" Henry murmured.

"I know full well that I've got daddy issues, which make me believe that all men are going to leave me, so I don't think I need to pay someone to tell me anything that I don't already know." I was growing increasingly aggravated, mostly at myself, it really was monumentally tragic that I had let the actions of my parents impact my life for so long. I could only imagine how this would look to someone like Henry. Someone whose life appeared as near to perfect as it is possible to be.

"What your father did was unforgivable. I cannot imagine how I would deal with it in your situation; your parents are the people you trust above all others, and when they let you down it must impact your whole world," Henry said, his voice quiet and patient, reassuring.

"I'm just not good at talking about this because I want to move on, but no matter how hard I work, or how well I think I'm doing, it's always there, like a black cloud sucking away my confidence. I didn't want you to despise me for not being able to get over it," I whispered desolately.

Our starters arrived, giving me a much-needed distraction. I dug into the fresh seafood salad, keeping my eyes firmly focused on my food, and we ate in silence. Taking another large mouthful of wine, I let my hand rest on the long, elegant stem of the glass and was surprised when I felt Henry's warm fingers brush against mine.

"I'll always listen, always be here if you need me, and, no matter what you tell me, I will never despise you, Clara."

Chapter Seventeen

I shook off the mental funk I was in. Used to brushing over my emotions and pretending to be fine, and we managed to eat the rest of the meal without too much awkwardness, much to my relief.

I had steadily consumed most of the bottle of wine, while Henry had largely stuck to water, so that when we headed out into the cool night air, I was most definitely on the tipsy side of inebriated.

"Ooops!" I squeaked as I struggled to walk in a straight line and bumped into a bench, giggling. "Naughty little street chair, what are you doing here?"

"Come on, Dr Drunkard, let's get you back and into bed." Henry laughed, taking my elbow and guiding me along Fisherman's Wharf and up the hill towards our hotel.

"That's very forward of you, Dr Fraser, but I'm not that type of girl," I admonished, my stern matronly tone belied by my wobbling stance as I ground to a halt.

"You're right. You need to be tucked up, *alone*, to sleep this off, Clara," Henry agreed, trying to tug me along and get me moving forwards.

"Are you taking me for a walk up Everest?" I grumbled, leaning more and more on Henry's reassuringly sizeable frame next to me.

"Nope," he grunted, propping me up and setting me on the right path again as I veered into him with a thump. "You can do it, one foot in front of the other, Dr Clancy, there you go."

We walked (I stumbled) along fairly slowly for a while and I tried to focus on the pavement and where my feet were, but I still managed to bump into him periodically.

"Can I hold your hand, Dr Fraser?" I asked suddenly, stopping abruptly again, although the world seemed to keep moving around me, spinning gently, so that I felt a bit seasick.

Henry looked at me with amusement. "If that will help you to walk better, then be my guest."

After a couple of ineffective swipes, I eventually had hold of his large hand in mine and I gave it a little squeeze, which was gently reciprocated. The feeling of being mildly electrocuted by his touch was still there, just a little dulled by the alcohol in my veins. I took a confident step forward and my knee buckled slightly, but luckily Henry heaved me back upwards with a resigned sigh.

"Holding hands is nice, isn't it?" I said dreamily, once we'd established a steady march.

"Yes, it is," he replied. I was rewarded with a happy feeling settling in my ribcage, while I gently swung our joined hands backwards and forwards.

"You should definitely do this when you get a girlfriend," I said, giving his hand a tug so that he turned to face me.

"I will, don't worry," Henry murmured, his eyes downcast. "About that, actually—"

"You look sad. Are you sad? Do you need a cuddle?" I interrupted, reaching up and pushing at his cheeks with my free hand, trying to make his lips turn up at the corner. "Want to cuddle away the sadness, Dr Henry?"

I swayed unsteadily for a minute.

"You know you want to." I grinned and took a wobbly step towards him.

"Err, well…" He looked a bit baffled, and adorably unsure.

Without waiting for permission, I went in for the hug, weaving my hands inside his open coat and wrapping my arms tightly around his waist, my cheek snugly placed against his chest. I was enveloped by warmth radiating through his soft cashmere jumper, and the unmistakably delicious scent that was entirely Henry.

"This is nice," I mumbled into his clothing.

Slowly, hesitantly, I felt his arms wrap around me, bringing me further into the depths of his coat, his chin on top of my head.

"You smell lovely," I continued, a bit breathlessly.

"Thanks, so do you." I could feel his voice reverberating through his chest against my ear, as well as hearing the deep rich timbre that was reminding me of hot melted chocolate.

"Oh, but of course Superman would never have *stinky* friends, would he?" I said with a pout.

He chuckled. "Just take the compliment, will you?"

"Humph." I nuzzled in further, like some kind of burrowing animal.

"You're very firm under these clothes, aren't you?" I said distractedly, not sure if it was just in my mind or if I had uttered it out loud. The small coughing laugh that came from above my head confirmed that I had, in actual fact, said it out loud. Damn it.

I held tightly onto Henry for several minutes, and he didn't seem in any hurry to let go. His hands were moving rhythmically up and down my back. I couldn't be sure, but I thought I felt him press a soft kiss into my hair.

"Have you fallen asleep, Clara?" he asked eventually.

"No, but I could. I like hanging out inside your coat, it's become my safe place," I whispered, eyes closed and breathing evenly.

"Good to know," Henry replied, "should we perhaps adjourn this hugging marathon and carry on walking so we can get back to the hotel before midnight?"

I made an incoherent sound, which Henry took as an affirmative and disentangled himself from my monkey-like grip on his torso.

"Have I hugged away your sadness?" I asked earnestly, looking up into his eyes, which crinkled at the corners behind his glasses. Reaching up he swept back a lock of hair that had escaped from my hair tie, pushing it gently behind my ear.

"Yes, you have."

This, I thought through the blurry fug of my intoxicated mind, would be the perfect screen kiss moment, and I looked at his lips briefly, before realising my mistake. Pull yourself together, Clancy, French kissing friends was taboo; if this was me and Jo, she wouldn't be happy about me snogging her face off after a drunken hug. And I one hundred per cent knew that Henry wouldn't welcome it either.

I stepped back, tripping slightly and took his hand again. "Onwards, Hillary, we should make the summit by daybreak."

Henry laughed, perhaps a little sadly, and squeezed my hand again, which I swung along as we walked.

"You know, if you really were Superman, you could just pick me up and fly us both home. But you've come as Clark Kent again this evening, haven't you?" I said, gesturing at his glasses.

"Unfortunately, yes, I've left my superhero suit back at the hotel, I didn't think there would be any damsels in distress this evening, but it seems I was wrong," he quipped, going along with my hand swinging good-naturedly.

"Do you ever just get tired of women constantly throwing themselves at you, Henry?" I asked out of the blue, surprising myself with the directness of my question. Alcohol had a sneaky way of bypassing any thought processes and short-circuiting my mouth filter.

He glanced down at me briefly. "No, because women don't throw themselves at me, Clara."

"Pfft. You can't say that you haven't noticed all the fainting and breathy sighs that greet you wherever you go?"

"What are you talking about?" he replied in confusion. "That sort of behaviour doesn't go on in real life, perhaps in one of your racy novels, though?"

"Let me tell you as an impartial observer, it happens *all* the time, I can't believe you're so unaware!"

But Henry just shook his head in disbelief. "If you say so, I've never noticed."

"Well, maybe you should, because *maybe* if you had, you would have got yourself a girlfriend by now and I wouldn't be having to rescue you from Marina Montgomery all the time." Like a bossy teacher, I wagged a finger at him, or was it two? Things were definitely more than a little blurry.

"Well, if any women who I actually fancied, showed me even an inkling that they fancied me back, then *maybe* I would have a girlfriend to tell Marina Montgomery about by now," he said tersely, holding the door open into the hotel lobby and ushering me through.

Chapter Eighteen

I woke up to loud knocking, pain in my skull a blinding light, completely disorientated and groggy. Urgh, was I in a hospital? Or worse?

The banging finally stopped, and I closed my eyes tightly and squirmed back under the covers into my warm, oblivious cocoon, rapidly drifting off again, jet lag and the residual alcohol lulling me back to semi-consciousness.

"Clara, wake up!" The persistence of the muffled voice coming from the hotel corridor was penetrating my sleepy brain and the banging resumed like a jackhammer to the cranium.

My eyes felt as if they were made of burning sand, and with a groan I lifted the duvet a fraction, squinting at the clock on the bedside table, which read 8.30am. The furious knocking continued, and I reluctantly dragged my corpse-like body from the bed and stumbled over to the door, opening it wide and staring at a fresh-faced Henry, and behind him a member of the hotel staff leaning on a trolley with silver cloches on it.

"I'm awake. What do you want?" Sleepy had most definitely turned to grumpy. I wondered briefly how many of the other seven dwarf personalities I would replicate today, because happy seemed like an unachievable goal right about now.

"Um, can you give us a minute?" Henry turned his very large, very round eyes back to the young man behind him, whose mouth hung open as he stared into my doorway.

What was his problem? I glared my most ferocious glare, the smooth wood of the door frame a steady and grounding comfort as the world still spun slightly around me.

"She has to sign for the room service, sir," he whispered in reply, his voice was unusually high-pitched and slightly raspy.

"Fine, two seconds. Wait there," Henry ordered and shepherded me back into my room, cautious not to touch me as he closed the door behind him and disappeared into the bathroom.

He returned with the large fluffy bathrobe, and keeping his gaze carefully trained on my face he handed it to me.

"Put this on," he said hoarsely, a muscle twitching in his jawline.

It was at this moment that I looked down, a cold realisation sliding over my skin. I had been too drunk to get undressed properly last night and I was just in my underwear, luckily one of my best matching sets, a little indulgence that I allowed myself, but the pale blue lacy bra and knickers that I had on left very little to anyone's imagination. Just when I could have done with a healthy dose of bashful, that little git had deserted me. Great.

"Shit. Sorry to flash you at this time in the morning, Henry," I mumbled, wrapping the towelling material around myself, too hungover to even have the ability to blush at this point.

"Don't worry about me, but that poor lad outside looked like he was about to expire on the spot," Henry joked, seemingly regaining his composure, although a faint hint of colour still edged his cheekbones. "Now go and sign his little bit of paper, maybe without the striptease, so you can have some breakfast."

I opened the door and the waiter looked curiously back in at me, a little disappointed perhaps that I wasn't going to carry on with the peep show. Pushing the cart into my room, he unloaded its contents onto the desk, while I grabbed a pen and signed the bill. Henry dropped a few dollars into his hand and firmly escorted him back out into the corridor.

"Thank you," I mumbled as the door was shut behind the curious waiter, his neck craning back in, probably hoping to get another glimpse of this very poor man's version of a Victoria's Secret model.

"That image of you opening the door in your bra and pants will keep him going for a while, I should think."

"Shush. Where is the coffee? My mouth feels like I've licked a badger's backside."

"I wondered if you might be a bit hungover." Henry was smirking when he handed me a glass of orange juice and some paracetamol, which I greedily glugged down. "So, I thought room service might be a better option this morning. I just hadn't expected quite such an *uninhibited* welcome from you."

Ignoring his last comment, I started rifling through the contents of the tray, noticing pastries and fruit, as well as toast and different types of jam under the metal domes. A large plate of warm pancakes sat steaming gently. Lots of my favourite types of carbohydrates to soak up the alcohol. Henry had done well in his selection.

"Have you had breakfast?" I asked, locating the coffee pot and pouring a large one, heaping in cream and sugar, and stirring vigorously.

"Yes, earlier. I tried to wake you then, but you were dead to the world, so I left you to sleep a little longer. I'll have a coffee though and keep you company if you want?" Henry said, always so thoughtful.

"Help yourself," I replied, waving at the breakfast things on the desk and slumping down into a chair, nursing my cup between my hands.

"We've got a bit of time before the investigator meeting at Stanford today, but we should probably go over some things first." Henry took a seat on the edge of my unmade bed and sipped his coffee.

I drank the heavily caffeinated elixir as quickly as I could, hoping it would infuse some feeling into my shaky limbs, and was relieved when it finally started to take effect.

"Why don't you go through my notes while you drink your coffee, and I'll take a shower to try and feel like a human being again," I suggested.

"Alright, if you're ok with me being here while you shower? I can go back to my room and meet up later if you prefer?" He seemed strangely uncomfortable, swallowing nervously, his gaze darting away.

"I think I can trust you not to peek at me in the shower, Henry. Plus, you already know what I look like in my underwear, so any modesty on my part is largely redundant at this point," I muttered.

"No peeping, Scout's honour," he assured me solemnly, performing a funny little salute.

"Why does it not surprise me that you were a scout?" I said, rolling my eyes.

"I reckon Superman would have been a Scout too, if they'd had the Scout Association on Krypton," he said, before adding, "don't diss the Scout Movement, Clara. Dib, dib."

"Dob, dob," I responded and stepped into the bathroom to the sound of his chuckle.

After an exceptionally long, hot shower and feeling like a new woman, fluffy towels firmly tucked around my hair and body, I went in search of today's clothes, catching Henry lying on my bed, studiously reading my notes. He was on his back, legs hanging off the edge, one arm placed under his head, the other holding the papers aloft. His shirt had become untucked from his trousers, revealing a portion of his toned abdomen and a trail of dark hair that disappeared below his waistband. I gulped, a distinct wave of heat decorating my skin. He really was stunningly attractive, masculine with a hint of rugged, but I was surprised that it was his vulnerability in this moment that had left me feeling truly breathless. While I knew there was really nowhere that this could go, other than a one-way trip to my advanced broken heartedness, I was finding it really hard to stop ogling him.

"I know that you've not had a man in your bed for a while, Clara, but stop staring at me, it's creepy," Henry said with a smile, finally meeting my gaze.

With a huff and trying to cover my embarrassment at being caught staring, I threw one of the breakfast napkins at him, which, much to my annoyance, he caught easily and threw straight back with a chuckle as it hit me square between the eyes.

The taxi to Stanford took about an hour and my hangover had largely abated by the time we arrived and found the assigned meeting room in the medical school.

It wasn't long before the room began to fill with people, and despite my smiles and introductions, I spent an inordinate amount of brainpower just trying to remember everyone's names. Why hadn't we insisted on name badges? Meanwhile, Henry, who already seemed to know everyone, was greeted with hugs and warm wishes, clearly well liked and accepted here.

The last person to arrive was an impeccably dressed young woman, large blue eyes glittering nervously behind trendy, oversized glasses, blonde hair swept up into a high ponytail. She took in the scene, her gaze lingering on Henry, before making a beeline for me, clearly viewing me as the least threatening of this throng of predominantly male academics and doctors.

"Hey, I'm Naomi Porter, nice to meet you," she said politely, darting another quick glance at Henry and pushing her glasses up her nose. She was a little taller than me and had the kind of flawless prom queen beauty that was rarely seen outside of Hollywood movies.

"Nice to meet you too, I'm Clara Clancy from Pharmavoltis. Welcome to this meeting," I replied kindly, shaking her hand and giving her the printed clinical trial information pack.

Naomi's cheeks coloured and she seemed to thoroughly

assess me for a moment, before asking, "You're Clara Clancy? As in Clara Clancy the PhD student from Oxford?"

"Yes, I guess I am. Well, I was, I've graduated now. Hurrah for me!" I answered, smiling and giving a gawky little fist pump that I immediately hoped she didn't see. "Sorry, do I know you?"

"No, probably not, although I feel as though I know you," she said, before laughing slightly and shaking her head at my obviously confused expression. "Sorry, that must sound kind of weird, but Henry talked a lot about his time at Oxford with you."

"He did? Ok, well, it's nice to meet you," I said again, unsure how to continue.

"He's not told you about me?" she asked, a melancholic lilt to her voice.

Well, this was a bit awkward. "No, sorry, since our companies have collaborated we mainly just talk about work stuff."

"Really?" Naomi's eyebrows shot upwards in surprise.

"Yep. I mean, we're friends too, but we're both dedicated to making this clinical trial a success." I needed to keep repeating this mantra in my head just to remind myself that this was entirely the relationship that Henry wanted from me.

"Oh, I see." She glanced wistfully in his direction, and I realised that she was probably another broken-hearted Hot Henry victim, and I gave her a pitying look. We stood in uncomfortable silence for a moment when the man himself suddenly appeared at my side.

"How are you, Henry? It's been a long time," Naomi said softly. There was an open hopefulness about the way she addressed him, an unspoken but perceptible hint of intimacy in her gaze.

"I hadn't expected to see you here, Naomi," he replied, his voice was pitched quietly, sad, and there was definitely a shift in the atmosphere around our little trio as they stared at each other.

The sudden obscure intensity of this meeting made me feel a bit left out, like a complete gooseberry, and a tad jealous, if I was honest. "I'll, um, leave you two to get reacquainted."

But as I made to walk away, Henry reached over, gripping my elbow and preventing me from leaving, whispering almost desperately, "Don't go."

Stopped in my tracks, I offered Naomi a small smile, which she returned slightly tremulously and the three of us then stood looking intently at each other's feet for a few more moments.

"How have you been?" Henry eventually asked.

"I am ok, thanks. You?"

"Not too bad, thanks."

"Where are you now?"

"Back in Oxford. Are you still here at Stanford?"

"Yeah, I have a postdoctoral position in Derek's laboratory now."

Tension was radiating off Henry in waves and the hold he had on my arm was vice-like, the conversation stilted and painfully clumsy. Naomi's demeanour had subtly shifted so that she was now guarded, her expression carefully neutral, but the nervous twisting of her hands gave her feelings away. What the hell was going on?

"Derek thought it would be good for me to come along today, but I can leave if you want?" she said quietly.

"There's no need for that," I said at the same time that Henry whispered, "I think that would be best."

"Henry," I reprimanded quietly.

He glanced at me and sighed, running his hand up the back of his neck in agitation.

"It's ok, Clara, I'll leave, I knew this was a bad idea." Naomi started to back away.

"No, I'm sorry, Clara is right, please stay." The pained expression on Henry's face showed that this was difficult, and he was desperately trying to overcome whatever emotions were militant inside him.

"If you're sure?" She seemed relieved.

"Yes, of course."

"Thank you." With a last lingering look at Henry, her eyes alight with unshed tears, Naomi smiled graciously and headed towards the back of the room, shaking hands with some of the other delegates as she went.

"What was that about?" I asked when she was out of earshot.

"Naomi was the PhD student I was telling you about last night."

"Your wife?"

"*Ex*-wife," he muttered.

Right, well this was bloody tricky. Why would she want to be here? What had gone on between them? How badly had things ended?

"I can see you have a lot of questions, Clara, but we should get on, I'll tell you about it some other time." Then, like the consummate professional that he was, Henry schooled his features back to geniality and turned to the group of potential study investigators who had now found their seats, and welcomed them warmly to the meeting.

After we had been through the clinical trial details and communication plans, we had a coffee break where the attendees could mingle and ask less formal questions. I was soon approached by a kind-looking man in his mid-to-late fifties, sporting a red bowtie and horn-rimmed glasses.

"Hello, Clara, I'm Professor Derek Smith, it's great to meet you," he said, in a relaxed Californian drawl, his face creasing with deep laughter lines as he smiled.

"Nice to meet you too, Henry has told me a lot about you and your team here; we're both delighted that you've agreed to be part of this trial," I answered warmly, shaking his hand.

"Ah, Henry is a bright and brilliant asset to any programme, I couldn't *not* be involved," he responded, gazing at Henry who was talking animatedly near the front of the room. "In fact, I have tried to keep him here at Stanford many times. However, he often talked about his life in Oxford, so I'm really pleased for him that he's found his way back there again."

"It's hard to believe anyone wouldn't want to stay in California, and work here though," I replied lightly, looking over at Naomi happily chatting with a group of other delegates, who were hanging on her every word.

"Isn't it?" Derek's gaze drifted back to me. "But I do believe that his heart belongs back in England."

Chapter Nineteen

I t was quite late when we finally wrapped up the meeting after ordering in pizzas and thrashing out the particulars of the clinical trial protocols and investigator involvement. Naomi had suggested some great ideas about patient recruitment, and the earlier tensions hadn't resurfaced, thankfully.

But Henry was very quiet in the taxi ride to the hotel, he'd taken the passenger seat next to the driver and I was alone in the back; alone with my thoughts and pondering his ex-wife and what little I'd seen of her today. She'd seemed like she wasn't really over Henry, while he'd been horribly uncomfortable around her. What had happened between them? Was this the manifestation of his guilt? Or perhaps she'd done something to really hurt him? Clearly he didn't want to talk about it now though, his face turned towards the window, absently watching the world go by.

The next day, the whole of the Pharmavoltis cardiovascular team had arrived and were loitering in the hotel lobby, including Richard Holmes. Henry was nowhere to be seen, and I had been assigned an early slot on the medical information section of the company booth that morning so couldn't hang around. With a feeling of despondent resignation and after a brief phone call with Simmy to update her on how things were going, I dragged myself over to the conference centre.

The huge exhibition hall was loud and garish, all the major pharmaceutical companies were present and trying to outdo each other with their larger-than-life stands. Pictures of happy-looking patients doing amazing outdoorsy activities smiled down from enormous posters, whizzy mode of action animations, that showed how new drug targets were revolutionizing treatment outcomes, flitted across brightly lit up plasma screens.

Other pharmaceutical industry professionals grinned over at me as I walked by, willing me into their little slice of evidence-based medical utopia, until they saw the Pharmavoltis logo and my exhibitor badge. Then I was shunned with narrowed eyes, disappointment that I was not the world-leading healthcare professional that they'd hoped for.

Pottering over towards our stand, a little part of me was proud to be on the cutting edge of research in cardiovascular disease, a tiny cog in a gigantic machine, playing an infinitesimal role in a hugely controversial industry, but one that ultimately improved – and oftentimes saved – patients' lives. The move from academia to industry was laced with disapproval, and I still remembered my supervisor's obvious dismay when I chose to leave Oxford for a life on the dark side.

But real people were alive today because of the innovation and hard work of my peers, inventions such as Henry's heart valves.

As I got to our booth, hidden in a corner of the huge hall, facing away from me, deep in conversation with some of the US affiliate sales team, was the unmistakable silhouette of Dominic Graham, his presence an almost uncanny manifestation of the dark side. He was leaning on one of the desks where the marketing materials were kept, his outline emitting an aura of arrogant condescension. Great, I would be sharing this particularly onerous task with Hannibal Lecter. Hurrah. I knew I should have checked the booth roster before I committed myself to taking on this slot.

As if he felt my presence (or maybe he'd just sniffed out the scent of my liver, I would no longer have put it past him), he turned around and beckoned me over. With leaden feet and a plastered-on smile, I walked up onto the lurid green and pink platform, the lights from the backlit panels already boring into my skull and triggering migraine-like sensations behind my eyes.

"Good morning, Clara, how are you?" Dominic's voice washed over me like a cup of warm vomit.

"Fine, still a little jet lagged though. You?"

"Really great actually, I don't suffer with jet lag," he stated smugly while I just stared at him. He was clearly some sort of alien, I decided. A murderous, human-eating alien that existed in a dimension where jet lag wasn't a thing. Perhaps he'd even followed Superman here from Krypton? That would explain everything.

With a slightly disingenuous look at the US team, who had now wandered off, he continued smoothly, "It looks pretty quiet here this morning, so it's good to be sharing this booth slot with someone interesting to talk to, isn't it?"

"Mmmm," I murmured non-committedly, locating the budget coffee machine that was situated at the back of the stand and away from public view, and placing a foil pod into the top.

"Yes, I swapped my slot, so we'd be on at the same time," he added, his unwelcome shadowy presence slithering along behind me.

"You did?" Urgh, his creepiness knew no bounds. He nodded in a hugely self-satisfied and congratulatory way, and my fingers involuntarily curled tightly around the handle of the mug in my grasp. Which was the softest part of the skull again?

"How long have you been in San Francisco?" he asked.

"We arrived a couple of days ago, there was an investigator meeting for the new heart valve study at Stanford yesterday," I replied, trying to get something that even remotely resembled coffee to come out of the nozzle of the coffee machine, without much success.

"We?" he pressed.

"I flew over with Henry Fraser." The brown sludge could be coffee, I sniffed it and wished I hadn't. Pouring it down the sink, I suspiciously examined the other pods, deciding that a Starbucks was probably the best way forwards.

"Of course, you did," he said caustically, "you'll do *anything* with him these days, won't you?"

I'd almost got my mind to block out his presence, almost. But as I glanced over at him, surprised at that remark, he was in full serial killer mode, features darkened with a threatening scowl, fists flexing at his sides. I registered then just how tall and intimidating he was, not as tall or broad across the shoulders as Henry, but still a lot bigger than me, and he was blocking my exit from the small kitchenette area.

"What do you mean?" I replied crossly, ignoring my primitive lizard brain, which had evoked an imminent-threat-to-life response in my body, and was urging me to lob the coffee maker at his head.

"Your little rendezvous with Henry Fraser at the company party did not go unnoticed, Clara, and Simmy took great pains to explain to me how well you know each other. Especially galling when you'd only just told me that you wouldn't date a work colleague." Dominic paused and his eyes raked over me. "Oh, but wait, while you won't date, you would, and let me quote you accurately here, have '*red hot monkey sex*' though, right?" he sneered, using air quotes to emphasise the embarrassing turn of phrase I had used.

Speechless, I stared at him open-mouthed for a moment. What a total bastard, of bastarding bastard town.

When I still didn't speak, he carried on. "Any other conquests at work that I should know about? Are you working your way through the medical team? What about Richard Holmes? He's probably a good candidate if you're planning on sleeping your way to the top. I'm sure even Claus wouldn't say no, Clara."

Was he actually accusing me of sleeping around to further my career? And with Dick bloody Dastardly?! I mentally berated myself for how I had handled this whole situation, clearly giving this total arsehole a gigantic heap of crap to throw at me. Fight kicked in over flight in my brain and I felt my hackles rise.

"Maybe it's just us marketeers that you're *not* planning to have sex with?" Dominic added, pretending to focus on something outside of the stand, before gracing me with a contemptuous look.

"Is that what you really think I'm like?" I asked incredulously.

"I wouldn't like to speculate on your morals, Clara, but Henry Fraser certainly came out of that cupboard looking particularly dishevelled and pleased with himself, lucky bastard," he leered.

The urge to slap him was enormous and my palm twitched violently.

"I think it's probably best that you do not speculate about me, or Henry, at all, Dominic. And, for the record, our relationship is purely platonic and always has been, not that it is any of your business," I hissed, pushing my way past him and back into the bright lights of the main booth area.

Shaking with anger, I reorganised some of the journal article reprints in the shelved area at the front of the stand, shuffling and restacking the papers furiously, just as Henry appeared with two large takeaway cups of coffee.

"Hello, that's some pretty livid paper-moving action right there, is everything ok? Want to hug it out?" he asked, opening his arms wide.

"No, I'm cross and I need a minute so I don't kill anyone," I growled, while Dominic skirted around us, shooting a death ray stare in every direction.

"Alright," Henry said, frowning briefly at Dominic's retreating form, before turning back to me. "How about a sugar-laden caramel shot, full-fat latte to brighten your day and clog your arteries?"

"Did you bring some diabetes-inducing pastries as well?"

"Of course." He grinned, placing the cups down on my desk and whipping a couple of paper bags from his coat pocket, like a conjurer. "Ta da!"

"You're like the breakfast equivalent of David Blaine," I muttered, trying to hide my smile, as I rummaged in one of the bags and found a chocolate croissant, much to my delight.

"Just you wait until you see what I've got lurking up my sleeves," he said with a laugh, selecting a Danish pastry and taking a big bite. "I didn't bring anything for Hannibal, I thought he'd prefer something a bit 'meatier'."

"Do not give him anything, unless it is laced with arsenic."

Henry nodded thoughtfully as he ate. "You know, if you ever need an alibi, I can say you were with me the whole time. No questions asked."

"Thanks for agreeing to be an accomplice, but with your pretty face, I don't think you'd do so well in prison," I said, patting his shoulder gently.

"You think I'm pretty?" he simpered, batting his eyelashes and looking altogether ridiculous and gorgeous at the same time.

"Bruno from Corporate Affairs seems to think so, and who am I to argue?"

"Well, if Bruno thinks it, it must be true." Henry smiled warmly at me. "You know, if you want to talk about it, I'm happy to listen. Or nip back there and change into my trusty Superman outfit and kick someone's arse?" He glanced in Dominic's direction again.

I was flattered and reassured that Henry had my back, I knew that he totally would flay Dominic's hide for what he'd just said to me. But I needed to deal with this on my own, I was a big girl, not some pathetic princess who needed a white knight to ride in on his horse and slay the dragon for her. Or punch the serial killer. After all, I knew some ninja moves myself, and even if I'd been a disaster up until this point, Dominic must surely have got the hint now. I could absolutely do this and be the hero of my own life, right?

"Thanks Clark, but I think I can handle it, turning up with proper coffee is definitely the best rescue I could have wished for this morning."

Henry leaned over and chinked his paper coffee cup against mine. "Any time."

Chapter Twenty

The company-sponsored symposium had the whole team in a whirl, desperately trying to get organised and locate the various faculty members. After his appalling behaviour on the booth earlier, I had been mightily relieved that Dominic had been busy for the rest of the day, so I had not bumped into him at any point, allowing my temper to cool but my insecurities to resurface. Had I really given off slutty vibes at work? Did people really try and sleep their way to the top in real life? Did any of my other colleagues think that I was so utterly useless that the only way I was going to progress was by using sex and not my actual brain?

Overthinking Clara had gone into overdrive, and I had begun to feel panicky and physically sick, but luckily Simmy had talked me down off a cliff when I recounted to her exactly what Dominic had said. She categorically stated that no one in their right mind thought my cat hair cardigan was slutty or that I was sleeping with Dick Dastardly, and that she would most definitely be castrating Dominic without anaesthetic on his return to the UK.

"Don't mess about, Clara, though. From what you've said, he's giving me serious psycho stalker vibes. So be careful, and definitely file a complaint against him with HR, because if you won't, I will." Simmy had been clear in her warning so I'd agreed to keep out of his way from now on, and was definitely (maybe) considering telling Richard what he'd said to me on the booth.

In an attempt to turn my brain off from any more thoughts of Dominic, I closed my eyes and leaned back in my seat, taking some deep, fortifying breaths, forcing my mind away from the horror show of this morning and to a golden sandy beach on the Mediterranean, sangria in hand.

My particular role in the meeting was over with, all the presenter slides had been finalised and signed off last week, and I briefly wondered if I could get away with a short restorative disco nap before everything got started. I'd not stopped all day between putting up posters in the relevant poster sessions and attending slide previews and a whole host of competitor company talks, so by the time our symposium slot came round at 6pm, I was trying to stifle a yawn every few minutes.

"How dull is this symposium that you've drifted off before it's even started?" Henry said with amusement, somewhere far above my head.

"Just preparing myself for an hour of intense mental stimulation," I replied, keeping my eyes closed.

"Of course." I could feel him shifting about in the little fold down chair attached to mine as he took his seat, his arm accidentally brushing against me. "If you actually fall asleep, you know I'll draw a moustache on your face, don't you?"

"As long as it's not the same as Dick Dastardly's, go ahead, I look forward to your best artistic creation."

"Challenge accepted," Henry murmured, before he let out a little groan. "Oh no, what is she doing here?"

I opened my eyes to see Naomi walking towards Derek Smith, who was being mic'd up by one of the headset-clad technical staff that made everything actually work at these things. Her hand was outstretched towards Richard Holmes in an elegant pose, high heels and impossibly long legs making her look graceful and feminine.

"Are we going to talk about what happened with her?" I asked quietly. Henry sighed in response.

"If you want to, Clara, but perhaps not now, and maybe somewhere a little more private," he replied. Naomi glanced over and saw us looking at her. Self-consciously, she gave a little wave, which I returned until I caught Henry watching me, upon which I pretended to be swatting a fly and then sat on my own hand.

"Smooth as always, Clara," he said, stifling a laugh and trying to hide it with a cough.

The auditorium was filling up behind us and all the faculty were assembled, microphones attached and ready to go. Dominic was smarming his way around them all, making my skin crawl, even from this distance, and I shuddered irrepressibly. He wasn't really meant to be anything other than an audience member; this was a medical symposium and active marketing involvement was most definitely not encouraged.

"What did he actually do this morning?" Henry murmured,

leaning over towards me, his thigh pressing against mine, warm and solid and comforting.

"Umm, nothing, the usual, you know?" I was being evasive, not wanting Henry to try and swoop in and fix things for me.

"No, I don't know, which is why I asked," Henry responded, before continuing in a gruff voice, "He didn't touch you did he?"

"No!" I almost shrieked, garnering a few curious looks from the rest of the Pharmavoltis team. I gave an embarrassed smile and mouthed "I'm ok", until they turned away and carried on with their own conversations.

"No, he didn't, he was just trying to get a rise from me," I hissed more quietly, quickly turning my head in towards Henry's so that we almost bumped noses in the process.

"Ok, good," he whispered, and I watched his lips moving as if I was in a trance, my whole being now tuned in to how close we were. "Because I will totally kick his arse if he ever does."

His breath smelled vaguely minty and caressed my cheek, heating my skin and simultaneously freezing my thought processes, the air around me charged at his close proximity. I savoured being so near to him, just for a second, but Henry's gaze, which flashed in the dim light of the auditorium as our eyes met, had me pulling away, flustered.

"If he'd touched me, he'd have lost a limb. He's lucky I didn't slap him as it was," I muttered, directing a revolted stare at the back of Dominic's head. Trying desperately to distract myself from the close-up view of Henry's mouth that was now clearly and indelibly etched into my memory.

The symposium went well, and after it had finished and the audience dispersed, Derek, who was a very engaging speaker and an excellent Chairman, came over to speak with us, followed by Naomi.

"Hello, you two," he said jovially.

"Hello Derek, good presentation, as always," Henry said and shook his hand, briefly meeting the sorrowful gaze of his ex-wife.

"Thanks." Derek ushered Naomi forward. "And of course, you know Naomi Porter. Clara, have you two met?"

Henry awkwardly nodded at her, while I replied with a smile, "Yes, nice to see you again."

"Are you going to the faculty dinner, now?" Derek asked pleasantly.

"Yes," Henry said, the tension from the previous day had returned, evident in his creased brow and stiffened posture.

"Good, good. Let's have a chat," Derek murmured, putting an arm around his shoulders and steering him away towards the exit.

Naomi and I were left alone, and we stared at each other uncomfortably for a second.

"Are you..." we both said at once.

I laughed and was relieved when she chuckled in return.

"...going to the faculty dinner?" I continued.

"Yes, Derek asked me to come. But I'm not sure Henry wants me there."

"Henry's probably just being a grump, and anyway it's not his decision," I said warmly. "Come on, there will be loads of us, so you don't have to sit near him, and if he sends you even the hint of some stink eye, I'll jab him in the hand with a fork."

"Ok, sounds like a plan." She smiled gratefully.

We formed a long procession on our way to the restaurant, looking not too dissimilar to a pre-school outing, only minus the yellow high-vis tabards, and holding hands was not compulsory. Naomi and I had paired up and we ambled along at the back, largely in silence.

"Despite what Henry thinks, I just want him to be happy, you know," she said eventually, giving me a curious glance.

"That's good." She seemed to be genuinely sincere and, despite her own obvious unhappiness about the situation, I could sense that she harboured no ill feelings towards Henry. It left me wondering again what could have gone so badly wrong between them. Because, even if the green-eyed monster within me didn't want to admit it, they seemed perfect for each other.

"Was it a surprise when he turned up in Oxford again?"

Her question jolted me out of my pondering, and my mind wandered back to that day when he'd walked into my office, only a few weeks ago. "Yes, it was a bit. We didn't stay in touch after he returned to the US when we were students, so I'm glad we have been able to meet up again. I'd forgotten what a good friend he is."

"Have you ever wondered why he cut contact, Clara?"

"I think a few thousand miles and our busy respective graduate programmes just got in the way," I answered cautiously, unsure what she was insinuating.

"You really should ask him about it sometime."

The rest of the group had moved a little way ahead of us, and Naomi pulled her coat tightly around herself and quickened her pace slightly, so I had to jog for a few strides to catch up.

"It was a good meeting yesterday, this new trial is pretty awesome isn't it?" she said brightly, obviously keen to change the subject and not bothering to hide the fact.

"Yes, it is. I'm sorry if it ended up being a bit awkward for you, I didn't know that you were Henry's ex-wife when we met."

Naomi huffed a little sigh. "That's ok, it's not your fault. Things have always been kind of off between us since we broke up."

A cool sea breeze buffeted us as we walked in silence, ruffling my hair so that it blew across my face, the strands catching in my mouth, coated by the tangy taste of the ocean. As we neared the restaurant, I turned back towards Naomi, stopping her lightly with a touch to her arm. "This really is none of my business, and tell me to get lost if you want, but what actually happened between you two?"

Did I really want to know about this? If I found out something unpleasant, would it taint my friendship with Henry? Would I view him in a different light? Curiosity killed the cat and all that.

"He hasn't told you anything?" she murmured, looking at me in surprise.

"Err, no not really, just that you were married briefly, and it didn't end well."

"Yeah, that's true, at least. In reality, there was another person in our marriage, and neither of us were ever able to get past it." There was a quaver in her voice, despite a valiant attempt at breeziness.

Oh. I wondered who had had the affair. I struggled to think

that Henry would be unfaithful, but I didn't really know that part of him. He said he hadn't been proud of himself, and it wasn't like he wouldn't have had a lot of offers if he'd actually gone looking for a bit on the side.

"I'm sorry that things didn't work out." I paused and regarded my companion in the gloom of the streetlights. "I just want Henry to be happy too."

"I sometimes think that he's determined to sabotage his own happiness," she muttered, considering me intently.

"Oh? Why do you say that?"

"I thought our marriage was pretty good, at least from my side. I wished he'd fought for us, hoped he'd be able to get over his past. Then who knows, maybe we could both have been happy." Naomi's voice was tinged with the bitterness of loss.

"Nothing in life ever turns out quite as we'd hoped, does it?" I knew better than most that trusting other people with your own happiness was a catastrophic mistake.

"Things seem to have worked out pretty well for you though, haven't they?" In the shadowed halo of light, it was hard to decipher her expression, and she quickly looked away. "I'm sorry, that was mean of me. None of this is really your fault. I'm just finding it hard seeing him again."

"It's ok." That comment was a bit of a slap in the face, but I could sympathise with her. Lately being around Henry seemed to have knocked me off balance too. "I'm sorry that you went through a messy break up, and I'm really sorry that you got hurt. But Henry and I are friends and I'll do whatever I can to support him, because I really don't want to lose him from my life again," I added, deciding to nail my colours most definitely to Henry's mast at this point in the conversation.

"Good, I'm glad that you're going to stick around and that he's got you looking out for him." Naomi paused and took a deep breath. "But it seems that you've been blind to a lot of what's been going on with Henry, so you should probably have a talk with him, and soon." But before I could question her further, we were being ushered into the restaurant and to a long table under the window with a spectacular view of the city lights.

In the scrum for seats, I was quickly separated from Naomi and found myself between Henry and Richard, and most unluckily, directly across from Dominic who was already necking the wine at an alarming rate and eyeing me speculatively from under lowered brows.

This was going to be a fun night of epic awfulness. Excellent.

Chapter Twenty-One

T he conversation had been pretty lively all evening, although I kept my head down, avoiding the unwelcome stares that I was getting from Dominic across the table. Marina had positioned herself next to Henry, and I found him leaning further and further towards me, until he was practically sat on my lap.

"Do you want to use your own chair, because I think you're a little big to be sharing with me?" I whispered in his ear.

"She's *touching* me, Clara," he hissed back, pressing himself even more firmly against me.

"Tell her to stop then, Henry." Looking around him, I was met with Marina's lop-sided and slightly unfocused, gin-induced grin.

"Hey, Marina, how are you doing over there?" I asked.

"Ooooh, I'm good." She winked and licked her lips, running her hand up and down Henry's arm. Good god, she really was insatiable.

Henry shot me a hopeless expression. "Help me," he mouthed.

"Erm, I think Richard wants to talk to you," I said loudly, tapping Dick Dastardly on the shoulder and simultaneously standing up, allowing a grateful Henry to slide over into my chair.

Marina slumped slightly in her seat, but quickly turned her attention to Derek who was sat on her other side. I sent a silent mental apology to him and his wife, deciding a trip to the ladies' room was in order, as Henry gestured with a not-so-subtle thumbs up. The Wonder Woman theme tune popped into my head, which I hummed on my way down the stairs, congratulating myself on yet another successful rescue mission.

The restaurant was in an old building in San Francisco's financial district, set over quite a few sprawling floors. Its atmospheric lighting and old wood interiors were cosy but were proving quite difficult to navigate. With a little help from a perky waitress, I finally found the loos in a dark corridor on the ground floor, where the clatter and noise of the kitchen could be heard nearby.

Today had been a strange day, to say the least.

Whilst washing my hands and staring into the mirror, I recounted the difficult morning on the booth with Dominic and the weird conversation on the walk over with Naomi. In each situation I had been made to feel as if I was missing a part of the puzzle. Was there something I should have seen? Could have done differently? Was Dominic really a crazed stalker, or had I actually hurt him? Or worse, was Naomi suggesting that I had hurt Henry all those years ago? Playing the conversations over and over in my mind was exhausting, and not really getting me anywhere, but I didn't seem to be able to stop.

My reflection gazed morosely back at me, a familiar expression of regret and disappointment etched on my face. The uncertain face of an abandoned, blue-eyed, blonde-haired, eight-year-old girl. Unable to see past the hurt and rejection that festered like an insidious infection. Unable to get to a place where there wasn't the continuous echo of fear and self-blame raging inside.

Some days I could pretend, convince myself, that my hard work had paid off and that all that self-doubt was ridiculous and unfounded. That I wasn't really a clueless imposter trying to make my way through a world that I was definitely not worthy of being in. But today was not that day. No, today these conversations were enough that a little chink in my carefully constructed fortifications had opened up just a fraction more.

My hair was beginning to come loose from its up-do, and the grips were hurting my head. Carefully, I teased out the wavy ends, running my fingers through it until I was happy I didn't look entirely like I'd been dragged through a hedge backwards. Head down, hair across my face, suddenly tired and ready for bed, I exited the bathroom when my wrist was immediately gripped forcefully, and I was hurried off down the corridor and away from the stairs, to a corner where the light was even more sketchy.

"Christ, Henry, what is it now?" I grumbled, not bothering to look up or work out where we were going.

"Not this time, Clara," Hannibal Lecter muttered darkly, bruising fingers tightening on my arm as I pulled away in horror.

"Dominic?" I gasped, a warning siren going off somewhere

deep in the recesses of my mind. "What are you doing? Where are we going?"

But he ignored my questions, tugging me along forcefully. He was frighteningly strong, and despite putting all my efforts into resisting him, he just carried on like I was an errant toddler who needed to be taken home for having a tantrum.

"Dominic, stop, you're hurting me!" I wailed desperately, trying to get him to see sense.

When he finally halted and spun around to face me, his expression was lecherous and cold. "This is what you like, isn't it, Clara? Clandestine sexual liaisons in public places? So, let's do it."

"What?"

He stepped closer and I backed up, hitting the wall behind me with a bump. And this is the moment when the actual real-life terror began to bubble inside me, flooding my body with adrenaline, my sympathetic nervous system firing off signals in every direction. I glanced to either side, looking for an escape, but it was almost as if Dominic was surrounding me, and the dark corridor offered no refuge or chance of rescue, the sounds of the kitchen now distant and unreachable.

"Come on, Clara, I know you and Simmy have talked about what I might be like under my clothes," he said with a humourless laugh. "And I've wondered the same about you, so now is our chance to find out."

My brain backfired in my skull. How was this even happening? "Dominic, we weren't talking about—"

But he cut me off with a shake of his head. "You've got to admit that you've been teasing me for a long time now," he whispered, tilting his head to the side and closing the gap between us still further, before running his knuckles down the side of my face. "We both want this."

"I don't know what you're talking about, Dominic. But I don't want this, please."

He was now so close that I could smell the sour aroma of wine on his breath and the strong, astringent, almost medical scent of his aftershave. I turned my head to the side to try and gain some space. But icy fingers gripped my chin painfully and not-so-gently pulled my head back round to the front.

This unwelcome contact kicked my fight-flight response up to nuclear proportions, his shadowed face coming into focus as his gaze flickered frostily over me. I had never seen such soulless eyes up close, black pupils large and lustful, but no affection or desire warmed them. This was not about romance or love, no, this was to prove a point, I was a conquest, merely something that he needed to possess and control, rather than there being any kind of feelings that were driving his actions.

"Please stop, Dominic, I don't want to do this," I whispered, fear stealing my voice as he angled his head down towards mine.

"Don't be shy, Clara. I'll make sure it's red hot, just as you like it," he sneered, licking his lips, his snake-like tongue just millimetres from my face.

"I said stop, Dominic." My voice louder this time. But he kept on coming, caging me with his body, pressing me against the wall with all his strength so that I could barely breathe from the crushing force against my ribcage. And when he brought his lips down to cover my mouth, kissing me forcefully, with far too much saliva for it to ever be pleasant, my inner kung-fu ninja eventually awoke. Raising my knee as hard as I could, I connected with his groin eliciting a particularly satisfying grunt of pain from him, and he pulled back briefly, allowing me to suck in a gasping breath and try to wriggle free.

"Stop! Get off me and leave me alone!" I screeched, bashing his chest with my fist and stamping on one of his feet with the spiked heel of my shoe.

"You bitch," he snarled, raising his hand to slap me and I cowered instinctively, braced for impact.

"You will get the hell away from her, Dominic, or I will kill you." Henry's voice was deadly and seemed to stop the intended violence in its tracks.

"Ah, here he is," Dominic spat down into my face, and keeping his eyes trained on mine, he carried on, "I wondered how long it would be before your pretty boyfriend showed up, like some kind of bespectacled superhero."

"Let her go, she clearly told you to stop," Henry said authoritatively, he sounded closer now, although I couldn't see anything other than Dominic's twisted expression.

"I definitely told you to stop," I croaked, voice shuddering.

"You are a dirty little cock tease, and not worthy of my attention," Dominic growled, wiping the back of his hand over his mouth as if I had been the one to spread unwelcome saliva onto his face.

"Right, that's it, I should have done this fucking weeks ago," Henry roared. And the next thing I knew, Dominic had been ripped away, the punch that Henry landed throwing him against the wall on the opposite side of the hallway. He slithered to the floor in a comedy villain way, landing in a very angry, writhing heap, spluttering obscenities in my direction.

"Are you ok?" Henry turned towards me, running his hands gently over my face, touching with warm, soft fingers, concerned eyes searching every inch of me. I supposed that he was merely checking for injuries but even though I was still shaking, this contact between us was reassuring, soothing. Safe.

"Yes," I whispered.

Dominic had stood up and was straightening his usually perfectly slicked hair, and wiping at a trickle of blood that was running from his nose. "I'm going to sue you for assault, but you're welcome to her. She's just a common slag, leading us all on."

"That's enough, Dominic," Richard ordered curtly, and I looked around to see a small group of onlookers watching intently. "Come on, I think it's time that you went back to the hotel. The company will be informed of your gross misconduct in the morning."

Henry wrapped his arms around me, and I buried my face into his chest. "Thanks for rescuing me again, Superman, I really hoped you'd show up."

"I will always show up for you, Clara, you're my Lois Lane." He breathed softly into my hair.

Chapter Twenty-Two

"Get your hands off me. She was leading me on, she's been flirting with me for months," Dominic raged, as Richard tried to escort him away and up the stairs.

Henry still had his arms around me, and I hadn't realised that I was crying until I sobbed noisily into his chest.

"I should probably help Richard get him into a taxi," he murmured gently, "but I don't want to leave you here alone."

"I'll be ok," I replied, backing out of his grasp, examining the tear-stained patch of snot and mascara that I had left on his pristine white shirt. "I've left a version of the Turin Shroud on your chest. Sorry about that."

"Are you sure?"

"Yes, it's definitely an imprint of my face," I answered nasally.

"No, you loon, are you sure you'll be ok if I leave you for a minute? I'll be back as soon as I can," he said with a slight laugh, casually flexing the fingers on his hand as if they were troubling him after his impromptu boxing debut.

"Yes, go, go." I waved him away, even though my lip was trembling slightly. "I need to go back into the loo and sort out my gloopy eyes."

"I can stay with her," Naomi said, appearing from the small crowd, while Richard still wrestled with a belligerent Dominic.

Henry looked hesitant, glancing between the two of us. "Are you sure that's ok with you, Clara?"

I nodded and whispered, "Yes, Henry, I'll be fine."

Naomi placed an arm around my shoulder and lightly guided me back up the corridor and towards the toilets again. Henry's gaze seemed to linger on us for a few moments, a solemn expression on his face, before he finally joined Richard at the foot of the stairs.

"Come on, you absolute piece of shit, let's get you out of here," he said, and between them they practically lifted Dominic off the floor, carrying his angry form out of sight.

Inside the bathroom I examined my puffy panda eyes staring wildly from my pale face, while Naomi fished in her handbag for makeup remover wipes and handed me a couple.

"These might help," she said.

"Thanks." I began dabbing at the black goo that was running down my face like a Salvador Dali painting.

"You're welcome." Naomi was watching me carefully, as if I might bolt at any moment. "Henry was really concerned when you didn't appear back at the table, especially when he noticed that Dominic had also gone."

Thank heavens he had been keeping an eye on things. The possibilities of what could have happened otherwise, of how this could have ended, did not bear thinking about. Could I have really saved myself this time without his help? I didn't actually know the answer to this, so best to bury it and never think of it again. Default ostrich setting engaged.

Naomi was regarding her reflection and absently fiddling with her immaculate hair. She gave me a sympathetic sideways glance in the mirror. "Dominic's a piece of work, isn't he?"

"Yes, he's a grade A arsehole, but I didn't think he'd ever resort to physical violence," I muttered shakily. Rifling through the travel case of make up in my bag, I started to reapply some foundation and mascara to my now swollen and blotchy face, but soon gave up when it seemed to be making no difference at all.

"Lucky that Henry turned up when he did then really."

"Yes, although I had already kneed Dominic in the balls to weaken him and give Henry a chance at being a hero," I joked, before blowing out a long sigh. "He's made rescuing me a bit of a habit recently, it's rather annoying."

"Yeah, he's the perfect hero, isn't he?" There was a sorrow to her voice, which made me pause and observe. Her face had a pinched look to it, even if you ignored her pout as she reapplied some lipstick, tension creased her perfectly manicured brows, and there was a distinct tightness to her shoulders and jerkiness to her movements.

"There's a reason I call him Superman," I murmured, and she smiled sadly in return. "Naomi, can I ask you something?"

"Sure, what is it?"

"What did you mean earlier when you said I was blind to what's been going on?"

She looked indecisive for a minute, then squaring her shoulders and facing me, she said with a soft sigh, "Henry's going to be mad at me for saying anything, but I really don't think he could hate me any more than he already does, so here goes." She paused, looking briefly up at the ceiling, then turning back to me, she let out a long sigh. "The reason we broke up was because of you."

Completely unconsciously, I did a comedy double take, but her expression was sincere. "Me? How can it have anything to do with me? I haven't had any contact with Henry since he left Oxford!"

She continued as if I hadn't even spoken. "We just clicked; you know? He's funny and kind and attentive, and so completely gorgeous," she said, "and I was so desperate to keep him, determined to make him want me as much as I wanted him. So, I tried really hard to make him happy. Really hard, Clara. But I knew that there was something he wasn't telling me."

I stared at her in complete confusion.

"Derek had warned me to stay away from him, told me he was pining for someone, a tragic case of unrequited love. But when a guy like Henry asks you out, who in their right mind would say no?" She laughed, but it sounded hollow and echoey.

Naomi leant back against the wash basins and looked down at the floor. "We dated for a while and things were going great, he was really sweet and caring. Although, he could be quite distant sometimes, but I figured that it was just his repressed Britishness that stopped him opening up. I was so in love with him that I thought if I kept pushing for more, he'd eventually show me that he loved me back, right?" She paused again, picking some invisible fluff from her sleeve before continuing. "There was a conference in Vegas, and the whole lab was going. I persuaded him to stay a few extra days with me afterwards and we had a really fun time. On the last night when we'd had a lot to drink in one of the casinos, I suggested that we go and watch one of those drive-thru weddings with Elvis. Funny really, except it wasn't, because when we got there and watched other people in the chapel all loved up and happy, he jokingly suggested we do one too, and I was so desperate to be his wife that I agreed straight away. Pathetic, huh?" She gave me a sad look. "He was so drunk and didn't know what he was doing, but I knew and should never have gone through with it, because the next morning he was full of regrets, distraught at what we'd done. But I felt like if he'd just give us a chance, we could be happy together and I know now it was stupid, but at the time I felt like I'd finally got him, you know? Won myself the perfect husband, and eventually he'd realise I was his perfect wife too, and we'd live happily ever after."

It was both ridiculous and amusing to think of Henry being married by an Elvis impersonator, and a story such as this would normally have led to a lot of leg pulling, but I knew that there was more to this story, so I resisted making any quips. "What happened?"

"He slowly became more and more disinterested, and we barely spoke anymore. I loved him so much and didn't want to see what was happening, but he was slipping further and further away. Believe me, Clara, I tried everything to seduce him and get him to come back to me, fancy dinners, romantic weekends away, sexy lingerie, the works. But nothing seemed to get through to him. He was so distant, and seemed to be working away more than he was at home, avoiding being alone with me, I suppose. So I did something stupid, really, really stupid." She stopped talking for a beat and looked stricken. "I tried to make him jealous, make him realise what he was losing, so I slept with someone else."

Oof, no wonder he was angry with her. A bit of my heart turned against her then. How could she have hurt him like that? "Naomi, I—"

She cut me off with a wave of her hand. "I'm not proud of myself, Clara, at all. And I know that I ruined whatever chance I had for us staying together. But the thing is, that unrequited love of his? Yeah, well Derek was right to warn me, because it never left him," she carried on sadly, then turned an accusatory glare at me. "*You* never left him. You were there, in our relationship, the whole time. He didn't admit it at first, but when he found out about my affair he broke down and told me that he had never loved me. He said that in the beginning I had reminded him a bit of you, and that was why he'd asked me out, but he'd never meant it to go so far. He could never love me because he loved someone else." She paused and shook her head. "He loved you, Clara, and from the way he is acting now, he still loves you, perhaps even more than he did before."

"But we're just..." I trailed off. My heart seemed to have stopped dead in my chest. A ringing in my ears. A crushing panic rising up from my toes as I processed her words, my brain refusing to accept the absurd possibility of what she was saying. Of what some other people had said recently, knowledge that I had completely disregarded. Because I couldn't possibly let myself believe that any part of this was true.

"Just friends?" Naomi looked me straight in the eye. "Listen, Clara, maybe you think you're just friends, but I've got to tell you that you're stringing him along, again. Basking in his attention but not giving him anything back, just like you did in your grad school days. You're messing him up and it's really shit. He deserves better than that. Better than you."

No. No, this was not true. I'd have known. He'd have told me. We'd have chatted about it and laughed, and he'd have admitted that he was being ridiculous and we'd have moved on with just being friends. Because that's all we ever could be. Naomi was right, I would never be good enough for Henry. He should be with someone who could love him in the way that he deserved to be loved. Someone capable and whole-hearted. Definitely not someone like me.

"You're wrong, it must be someone else, we've only ever been friends," I whispered. But something was stirring and fluttering in that bleak place inside of me, something warm and hopeful and distinctly uncomfortable tugging away in my chest. A worm-like niggle of all the 'could have beens' and 'what ifs'. This was dangerous territory, and I knew better than to let myself go there.

"I'm not wrong. And even though I hate to admit it, it's you he loves, Clara, it's always been you."

Chapter Twenty-Three

I was a chicken. A yellow-bellied and despicable coward.

I had told Naomi that I would go back to the table in a minute, and would be fine, that I just needed a pee and a moment to myself, and she reluctantly left me alone, agreeing to tell Henry that I would meet him upstairs.

When she left, I waited in my cubicle for five minutes and then I snuck out into the corridor and down to the kitchen area, where I bumped into the perky waitress again.

"I've split up with my boyfriend and he's really angry," I told her. "Please could you phone for a taxi and let me out the back so I don't run into him again?"

Looking at my blotchy face and panicky expression, she clearly believed me and ushered me through into the 'staff only' corridor and out towards the bins at the back. "Wait here, our chef, Rodriguez, is going home now and he's dropping one of the other waitresses off too, I'm sure he'll take you wherever you need to go."

I shivered in the darkness of the alleyway, until a burly guy with tattoos and a ponytail came through the doorway, followed by a small dark-haired woman in her twenties.

"You ok, sweetheart?" he asked.

"Yes, fine. I'm staying at the Marriott, is that far out of your way?"

The waitress grabbed my hand and looked up at Rodriguez hopefully, "We can take her there, can't we?"

The big chap nodded.

"Thank you so much," I murmured, my voice choking a little as we walked over to a parked car, hidden in the dark outside the back of the restaurant.

———

After a warm shower, I got into my pyjamas and made myself a hotel room special hot chocolate (which was a bit gritty, but at least something warm to hold on to), and settled down in the chair by the window. This day had been too much for my poor brain, I felt frazzled and unable to make sense of anything that had happened since I had got up, sixteen hours earlier. So instead, I sat gazing out at the flickering city lights laid out below, not yet ready for sleep, until a knock at the door roused me from my spiralling thoughts.

"Clara, are you in there? It's Henry, you're not answering your phone and I just want to know that you're safe." his voice was muffled, but I could still hear it was laced with panic.

"I'm ok, Henry," I replied, padding over to the door, pressing my hand to the thick wood between us, and peeking through the peep hole. Even to my fish-eye perspective, he looked thoroughly miserable.

"Can I see you?" he asked.

My heart rate leapt, could I handle speaking to him now? Naomi's words resounded in my head: 'You're messing him up and it's really shit. He deserves better than that. Better than you.'

"I don't know if that's such a good idea, Henry," I answered truthfully.

"Please, after everything that's happened today, I just need to see you with my own eyes so that I know you're ok, Clara. Please."

He was right, I owed him that. Slowly I slid back the security chain and unlocked the door, opening it wide and moving backwards to let him in.

"Thank you," he murmured, stepping warily inside. "Are you really, ok? I've been so worried about you."

"Yes, it's been a hell of a day, full of character assassinations, unwelcome attention, and big revelations." I sighed, returning to my chair and curling up in it again. "The kettle has just boiled if you want a gritty hot chocolate or some revolting tea substitute."

Henry smiled, but it didn't reach his eyes. "You make it sound so tempting, but I think I'll pass."

He followed me back to my seat and folded himself into the chair opposite, taking off his glasses, he rubbed his hands over his face. "Richard told me that Dominic has been suspended, he won't be allowed back in the office or anywhere near you, until a full tribunal has been conducted. He wants to know if you'll press criminal charges."

"No, I don't think so."

"He assaulted you, Clara," Henry growled.

"He tried to kiss me, that's all." My voice broke a little as the terror that I'd felt in that moment resurfaced and I swallowed it back down with a gulp of my drink.

"That's not all, Clara. If I hadn't found you, who knows what would have happened." Henry's hands were shaking slightly as he gripped the wooden armrests of his chair.

With sad resignation I stared back out into the night. He was right, who knows what would have happened and how much worse I could be feeling right now. Superman to the rescue again. I suddenly recalled his words to me: *'I will always show up for you, Clara, you're my Lois Lane'*. My heart swelled for a moment before shrivelling again.

This was all too much.

"I don't know, Henry," I murmured against the windowpane.

"It's your decision. You know that I'd support you if you wanted to go for it, I can give a witness statement about how he harassed and intimidated you in the workplace," he said.

I just nodded absently, still locked in my own mind. "Maybe Dominic was right, maybe I led him on," I muttered, barely registering what Henry had said.

"What? You mustn't ever think that, that fucking creep who can't take no for an answer is to blame, not you," Henry cried in frustration, leaning towards me and reaching out across the small round table between us.

"I tried to tell him that I wasn't interested at the company away day, Henry, but I ended up babbling and talking about sex in the office. It was horrific. Then he saw us coming out of that cupboard and me smoothing down your hair, wearing your jacket. He assumed that we'd been at it like rabbits and that I was some kind of nymphomaniac who gets off on having sex in public places." I laughed humourlessly. "So, you can sort of see why he might think that I was up for it tonight."

Henry dropped down to his knees by my feet, taking my trembling hands in his, placing my mug on the table. "No, Clara, all that stuff is irrelevant, you told him to stop, and he didn't. He's in the wrong here. End of."

Staring at the knuckles on his right hand, which were reddened and starting to bruise, I gently brushed my thumb over the discoloured skin, and felt him wince, fingers gripping onto me tighter for a moment. Taking a chance, I looked deeply into his familiar blue-grey eyes, but it was difficult to decipher what I saw there. Was it pity? Was it love? Whatever it was, the soul of a beautiful human being, inside and out, gazed back at me, unflinching.

"Don't look at me like that, not unless you mean it, Clara," Henry whispered bleakly.

I turned away, Naomi's words echoing again. 'He deserves better than that. Better than you.'

"Why did you and Naomi break up?" I needed to hear this from him, needed to turn off my own emotions for a moment, so I didn't do something we both regretted.

Henry dropped my hands again and went back to his chair, a disappointed slant to his shoulders. "What do you know already?"

"I'd like to hear your version, Henry," I replied quietly.

He bent his head low and blew out a long sigh. "I'm not really sure where to begin."

"The beginning is usually a good place."

"Right. Well, I was born on the sixth of May, nineteen…" he began, and I threw a cushion at his head.

"The abridged version, you idiot," I groaned but couldn't help the small smile from spreading over my face.

Henry looked up at me with a lop-sided and slightly apologetic grin. "Sorry."

"Get to the good stuff, Fraser, I'm tired."

"The good stuff? Ok, here goes." He paused and took a deep breath. "As a PhD student I was sent to work in a lab in Oxford to do some cell culture, and I met someone there. I knew instantly that she was really special and that we were going to get on, but I got the feeling that she wasn't as keen on me, at least to start with, anyway." He stopped and looked up.

"You're not wrong. Continue."

"Why though? I know I ruined your experiment, but even before that you were a bit off with me for ages, what did I do?"

"I was annoyed at having to babysit a PhD student from MIT. And you were entirely too perfect, Christ, even the female professors were ridiculous around you."

"Not this again," Henry sighed.

"Maybe you never saw it, but it's true! I found it highly irritating. Anyway, you won me over with your charming personality and ability to remember my drinks order," I said with a small smile.

"Oh, ok," he replied, a little puzzled.

"Continue."

"Right. So, I won her over with my charming personality and ability to remember her drinks order, until she finally stopped hating me and agreed to hang out sometimes."

"Accurate."

Henry chuckled then put his head in his hands. "The thing was, I didn't want her to hate me, I wanted her to like me. In fact, I wanted her to want me the same way I wanted her. I loved her from the very first moment I saw her, but she didn't seem to feel the same," he said softly, and looked up with pain dancing in his eyes.

Chapter Twenty-Four

"Are we really talking about Jo? You know that she was seeing that postdoc the whole time, right?" I asked, trying to mitigate my unease with humour. My usual go-to tactic when icky grown-up feelings were involved and I had to step up and face them.

"No, Clara, you know it wasn't Jo, it was you. Always you," Henry admitted, his voice raw and tinged with hurt.

We both stared at each other, unspeaking, the air thick with emotion, our friendship hanging on a knife edge of uncertainty.

"Have I got something on my face?" Henry whispered hoarsely, breaking the silence.

Shaking my head, I shifted in my seat and reached for the mug, holding it like a shield, its small, solid form clasped in my hands, trying to protect my heart, a relentless ache starting inside.

"Why did you never say anything, Henry?" I asked, still reeling from his confession.

"Because I thought you didn't feel the same. I tried a few times to ask you out in the beginning, but you either invited everyone else in the lab, or turned up and told me off about something. You made it abundantly clear that friends was as much as I was going to get, and I wasn't sure if I could handle the inevitable rejection on the off chance that you weren't bluffing."

Letting my mind wander back to those first few weeks when he arrived in our lab, I recalled his easy-going nature, his quick, shy smiles and gentle humour, and how hard I'd tried not to notice any of it. But it started to come back to me, the times when he'd just happened to pop into my office with a coffee with no other reason than he was passing. Or how he'd stopped by to chat to me while I was isolating cells or running a proteomics analysis late into the evening, on the pretence of learning about what I was doing, even though he never needed to know for his own projects. Sitting together in the lab, pouring over protocols, easy in each other's company and finding solutions to issues that neither one of us could have come up with alone. The times we'd gone to the pub and chatted and laughed, our 'in jokes' bizarre and unknown to everyone but us, and then how quiet and withdrawn he would become when everyone else arrived.

"Oh shit. *Chats and drinks*." He had loved me all along, after all. Why had I been so blind? Jo and Simmy had been right, and were going to be insufferable when I told them.

Henry looked up from the floor. "What?"

"Never mind, why didn't you stay in touch when you left though? I sent you emails, and you never replied."

"I never received any emails from you, Clara, what did they say?"

"Oh, just chit chat. Wondering what you were up to, how you were doing. I missed you. Missed being friends with you." My voice was barely audible, soft and sad at how badly I had misread things between us.

"Oh. I didn't get them." He paused and swallowed, before continuing, "I'm sorry Clara, my Oxford email account was shut down shortly after going back to Boston, I would have replied if I'd seen them, believe me."

"Why did you never try to contact me, though? You knew where I was. Why did you end our friendship so abruptly?"

Henry gazed at me for a moment, his expression raw and painful to observe. "You don't know it, but every look that you ever gave me is burnt on to my memory, every touch like a small electrocution, even when it was just accidental. I just couldn't cope any longer, and it had come to the point where I was struggling to be around you, so for my own sanity I decided to leave and try to move on. Shit, I sound so pathetic..." His voice trailed off.

I moved awkwardly in my seat, putting my mug back on the table, the hot chocolate now cold and completely unappealing. The small ceramic cup not proving to be any sort of defence against the feelings that were bombarding my heart.

"This still doesn't tell me what happened with Naomi," I said, her accusation and blame ringing in my ears, cementing this newly acquired feeling of guilt at being the reason that their marriage was doomed from the outset.

"Oh right. Sorry." Henry rubbed his hand over his face. "I didn't intend to get married. Naomi was fun and pretty, and we had socialised in a group quite often. She made it clear that she was attracted to me—"

"Oh, you saw *her* interest, but the rest of the female

population is invisible?" I interrupted, trying to be jokey, to get back to our normal equilibrium.

Henry frowned. "Let me finish my tale of woe, then you can take the piss if you want to."

"Sorry," I replied, sufficiently chastised into silence.

Henry leant right back in his seat, hands laced together behind his head, staring up at the ceiling before he continued.

"We'd been seeing each other for about six months when she had an abstract accepted at a major international conference and was so excited. She suggested that I join her on her trip to Las Vegas to celebrate after the congress was over, to have some fun." Henry rolled his shoulders uncomfortably and shifted in his seat. "She organised the whole thing, and after we'd been to a few casinos and got really, really drunk, we ended up in a taxi at a drive-thru wedding place." He looked back at me, clearly expecting a comment on this.

"But Elvis though? Really?" The humiliated expression that greeted me was enough to make me sign that I was zipping my lips shut.

"I regretted it, of course, and don't really know why I did it, but I had been feeling so lonely, and Naomi was there and wanted me, and I guess I didn't want to be on my own anymore. So, we gave it a go. But it became clear that the relationship was becoming more and more one sided and I tried to end things with her. But it was difficult, and she was so upset about it. I really never intended to hurt her," he said sadly. "The divorce came through pretty quickly, luckily, as it had become clear to me that I wasn't, and never would be, in love with her."

"Because she cheated on you?"

He looked up in surprise. "She started seeing one of the

other research fellows, but at that point I already knew the relationship was dead in the water, so I don't really blame her."

"So, that's not why you're angry with her still?"

Henry gave me a slightly sorrowful look. "I'm not angry with her. I found that if I was even remotely attentive, she'd assume that we were going to get back together, and I'd have to go through the whole break up scenario again. It was exhausting and it felt like I was just upsetting her over and over again. I left Stanford a few months after the divorce was finalised, but we move in similar academic circles, and it was easiest just to be standoffish with her and not let her think I wanted to give it another go."

"Oh. How did she know about me?"

"I had confided in Derek one evening over a few whiskies at his house. He was trying to persuade me to take a more permanent post at Stanford, so I explained that I thought I'd like to head back to the UK. He probed me further, and it all came out, all about you and how much I had loved you and why I had left Oxford early to return to Boston. How much I regretted it. He was her supervisor and he told her I think, trying to warn her not to get too attached to me," he replied. "I didn't talk about you with Naomi because I was trying not to think about you too much day to day. But when it ended, I told her that I loved someone else, and she guessed that it was you."

"She said that she reminded you of me, is that true?"

"A little, physically I suppose, but as I got to know her, I realised that you and she couldn't be more different," he answered wearily, removing his glasses and rubbing the heel of his hands into his eyes.

I sat quietly and contemplated his confession, guilt surfaced over everything else, the uncomfortable surge of other emotions was easy to squash, I'd been hiding from them for years.

"I'm so sorry. I genuinely didn't know, I would never have done anything if I'd thought for one minute I was hurting you, or stringing you along."

"I know you wouldn't. And you have never strung me along, Clara, you have been crystal clear in your intentions," he said with a sigh. "The thing is though, you're still entirely oblivious, aren't you?"

"Oblivious to what?" I asked distractedly, knowing that I had, in fact, not been crystal clear at all, but in reality, had buried my real feelings and intentions so deep that I'd managed to even fool myself.

"To how I still feel about you."

"I…" Gazing back up into his eyes, his expression so open and vulnerable that my heart lurched, until I remembered my conversation with Jo, a few weeks back: *'Maybe when you can have anyone you want, you end up wanting the person who doesn't want you.'*

"I still love you, Clara. I wasn't sure how I would feel seeing you again, but these last few weeks have been amazing. Being around you has lit me up inside, I felt as though a piece of me has been missing since I left Oxford, and since seeing you again it has been restored," he whispered and reached for me.

"I'm very tired, Henry, it's been a long day and I need to sleep," I said in a small voice, pulling my hand away. This was too much to take in, and I couldn't possibly deal with it on top of everything else that was whirring around in my overloaded brain.

"Oh, ok," Henry murmured, his face a picture of sorrow and rejection. I couldn't stand to see him like this because of me, leaning forward I placed my hands over his where they were now clasped tightly together on the tabletop.

"I am so sorry, but I don't know how I feel, Henry. I am worried that you only want me because I've been the only woman never to have shown any romantic interest in you. I wonder if you're just wanting something that you think you can't have."

"That's not it, Clara, not for me."

"But what if it is? What if we got together and you realise that the person you have imagined me to be all this time is a long way short of the person I really am?" I cried desperately. "Maybe you think you're ordering a full-fat latte with a hazelnut shot, but what you end up with is a really teeny, tiny, cold and bitter espresso?"

"Clara…"

"Or what if someone really beautiful or intelligent comes along, all wanton and beautiful and says, '*Oh Dr Fraser, look at how gorgeous you are, please can we get naked on a lab bench*', and you feel the same? What will happen to me then?"

"What?! Clara that's not—"

"I wasn't joking when I said I'm damaged and broken. I will take everything that you offer and then not give anything back because I don't know if I can trust anyone with my heart, Henry, not even you," I admitted, wary when he'd already cut contact with me once before, an echo of what my father had done. "I'm just not sure I'd ever be good enough for you—"

"Clara, stop!" he almost shouted, then more gently. "Just

stop talking. You're right, it's been a long day and I shouldn't have heaped all these feelings onto you. I know that you struggle with talking about this stuff, and I get it that you're nervous about commitment. Please, just think about what it is that you really want. If it's not me, I can live with that, I'll be gutted and it will be hard, but I've put all my cards on the table and it's now up to you to figure out what you want."

Henry stood up and kissed me lightly on the cheek. "Just know that you are enough, exactly as you are, and that I will always love you for being you, and not for any other reason."

Chapter Twenty-Five

I slept poorly that night, my anxious mind spooling through all the events and revelations of that day. In particular, I had gone backwards and forwards about what to do about Henry and whether I wanted to risk the friendship we had by trying a relationship with him. I was still convinced that he had created a fantasy Clara, and I would never live up to that expectation. Maybe we should just carry on as we were because that was great and more than I had ever thought possible after he'd left Oxford. But then there was the niggly, little voice that reminded me of how it felt to be close to him, how delicious he smelled and how when he looked at me in a certain way, I felt as if I might just burst into flames on the spot. But mostly, it was how fucking wonderful he was, in general, so funny and patient and kind and generous. I seemed to have a video montage of all his best bits flicking through my mind on a loop, which was mightily distracting and really not helping with the 'we should just be friends' mantra I was trying to convince myself with.

But after an exhausting night of restless indecision, when I got up the next morning, I had made up my mind.

Richard met me at breakfast and gravely took me to one side. "I am so very sorry about what happened with Dominic last night, Clara. I feel responsible and should have noticed his nefarious intentions towards you."

"It's not your fault, Richard, honestly."

"It is kind of you to say, but as your manager and the head of the department, your welfare is my responsibility. If you want to press charges, we will all support you. Unfortunately, there will have to be a disciplinary procedure at work, and we will need you to provide evidence. Henry has already made a statement about how you spent much of your time at work avoiding running into Dominic." Richard sighed wearily and pinched the bridge of his nose between his fingers. "Why didn't you come and tell me about it, Clara?"

I shuffled uncomfortably. Like I would ever confide this sort of thing in Dick Dastardly. "I never imagined that he would do anything like that, I thought I could handle it by avoiding him. But that didn't work out so well."

"No, it didn't. In the future, let's not bury our heads in the sand, much better to face things head on, hey?" He smiled at me in a fatherly, kindly and not at all dastardly way, awkwardly patting me on the shoulder as I nodded in agreement.

It was our last day on-site, and I had a few meetings to attend and posters to take down. When I finally found Henry at one of the many conference centre cafes, I gave him a small wave

214

and he immediately raised his coffee cup in the air and mouthed "I've got one already", with a little embarrassed thumbs up, saving me from performing any lewd hand gestures for his benefit. Such a gentleman.

"Morning, Mr Darcy, how are you today?" I asked casually as I slid into the seat opposite him, placing my cup on the table.

"Very well, Miss Bennett, you?"

"Absolutely bloody knackered and looking forward to sleeping in my own bed, but otherwise good."

"That's a relief," he said warmly.

"Listen, Henry, about last night, I want to apologise," I began.

"You have nothing to apologise for, Clara."

"Ok, well the thing is… You see, here is the thing," I stuttered. Crap balls, this was going to be bloody hard, and all the lines that I had practised in front of the mirror had disappeared out of my head the moment I was looking at real-life Henry, who, himself, seemed a little tired.

Clark Kent raised an eyebrow above the dark rim of his glasses, not helping me out at all. If he'd come as Superman, maybe he would have been able to read my mind and I could have kept quiet, and all would be well. Oh no, wait, Superman didn't read minds, did he? He had that weird red laser death vision. Not helpful. Focus Clara.

"I think we should just stay friends," I blurted, and his face fell. "What I mean to say is that I love being your friend, I love spending time with you, you're funny and kind and considerate, you're quite possibly the best friend that I've ever had. In all probability the best person I've ever known. And I don't want to risk losing that."

"You love being my friend, but you don't love me?" he whispered. His complexion was suddenly ashen, the light gone from his eyes.

"I do love you…"

"But just as a friend," he finished for me, no longer looking me in the eye but focussing on twisting the wooden coffee stirrer in his fingers, bending and flexing it increasingly forcefully, until it finally snapped.

"No, Henry. I don't know!" This was not going at all like I'd planned it in my head. In my head, he had agreed that we should keep things exactly how they were, and we'd have a laugh about some inane thing and then carry on with our lives. But I'd not counted on how much he was hurting, and it was killing me to know I was the cause. Naomi was right, he did deserve someone better than me. "I think you only want me because—"

"Not this again, Clara, you can't possibly know what I'm feeling inside, so do not try to project your insecurities onto me," he cut me off curtly.

Ouch, that stung, and was so very close to the actual mark. He knew me so well, and could absolutely see through my bullshit, which was making this even more difficult.

"But I think that you deserve better…" I tried again, cringing slightly at the cliche. But Henry held up a hand.

"Stop, just stop," he said, angry now. "I think I am the best person to judge what I do or do not want, or what I do or do not deserve. If you don't have feelings for me, then be brave enough to say it to my face."

"Henry, please," I tried again, but he shook his head sadly.

"I don't think that I can carry on just as friends, it's not enough and it's too painful for me. I'm sorry if it's selfish, but I want more."

"But it's been ok up until now. Why do things have to change?" I tried desperately.

"I'm sorry, Clara, but I think perhaps it would be best that we go our separate ways, and don't see each other again," he continued, like he hadn't even heard me.

No, not this. He can't leave me, despair bubbled like toxic gas in my brain. Make this better, Clara, for fuck's sake.

"Henry, I am so sorry, I don't know what I can do to make this ok, but please don't leave, I need you in my life, need you as my friend," I pleaded with him. Feeling my eyes begin to burn, I reached out across the table, fingers brushing the back of his hand, but he recoiled at my touch.

"And I need more than that. There are two people with feelings and needs here, Clara, not just you, and I can't carry on pretending that everything is ok and will remain the same," he said in stinging retribution.

"I don't think I can be what you want me to be, Henry. I don't think I can ever be more than friends, I am too damaged, and incapable of loving you like you want me to," I whispered, bleakness clouding my tone. Tears were running freely down my face now, and his expression was as desolate as I felt.

"I am trying really hard to understand how you're feeling, Clara. I would give anything to be able to make this ok and take away what your father did to make you so afraid of loving someone. But if you won't let me in, if you won't trust me, how can I help you?"

Taking off his glasses, Henry ran shaky hands over his face, rubbing his red-rimmed eyes, before replacing them and continuing, "I cannot sit idly by and watch you be so much less than you could be, so closed off to the world because of things that happened in the past, Clara. And I cannot be the one who is always yearning for you, always hurting because you do not feel the same. It's too difficult for me."

"I'm so sorry," I answered, not knowing what else to say. My body no longer felt like my own. I sat there numbly, seemingly unable to do anything remotely practical or helpful, and hopelessness leached through my whole being.

"I can't … it's just… I'm so sorry too," Henry stammered unsteadily, and with one last devastated glance at me, he stood quickly, knocking the table and sloshing coffee everywhere. Cursing in frustration, he hastily mopped up the spillage and threw his unfinished coffee and breakfast paraphernalia into the bin before storming away across the concourse, not once looking back.

Large, fat tears rolled down my cheeks. This was not what I wanted, but I felt powerless to do a thing about the disastrous trainwreck that I had just caused. I was too cowardly to take that leap and give him my heart, it was precious and had been stamped on and wounded before, rejected by the one man who was meant to love me unconditionally and who hadn't been able to do it. I needed to keep it locked up, safe from more damage, lest it be hurt anymore and irrevocably broken.

It seemed ridiculous, but I couldn't risk the same thing happening with Henry, couldn't risk him being another man that I allowed myself to love and trust with all my being who eventually let me down. Someone who I let in, someone who I let see what I had known all along: that I was worthless and completely unlovable. I knew that if I opened my heart up to him fully, I would totally and absolutely fall for Henry Fraser, and wouldn't be able to come back from it. Better that I kept him high on the friendship pedestal that I had put him on. Safer that I never let myself know just how wonderful loving him could be. Because I couldn't see how it would possibly be better for me to have loved and lost him than to have never loved him at all.

The deity in charge of horrible coincidences chose that moment to beam a blinding light down upon me, I thought bitterly, as Naomi slid into the seat that Henry had just vacated.

"Are you ok, Clara? We were worried when we couldn't find you last night," she said, handing me a tissue from her bag. She was like Mary bloody Poppins with that bag. I wondered if she had a hat stand in there as well.

"I'm fine. I just headed straight back to the hotel, it had been a long night," I muttered, blowing my nose with an elephant-like sound.

"Was that Henry I just saw leaving?" she asked, looking intently at her nails.

"Yes."

"Are you two ok?"

"No, we're not, but thanks for asking," I muttered tightly.

"Oh, do you want to talk about it?"

I really didn't want to talk about it. Didn't want to relive the last five minutes of my life ever again. But the idea of being alone at this precise moment in time suddenly seemed infinitely worse. With a large sigh, I looked up into Naomi's face, surprised and heartened to see compassion and recognition burning brightly in her eyes.

"I took what you said onboard, and I had a long chat with Henry."

"Oh." She dropped her gaze. "I really shouldn't have said

anything to you, not after everything else that had happened last night…"

"Yesterday was a bit of a shocker all round, really." I hiccoughed softly and scrunched the tissue into a soggy little ball in my fist.

"I am sorry, Clara. I hadn't intended to say anything, but I was pretty mad at you both, especially you." She smoothed a lock of hair that had bounced over her shoulder, and then her voice turned soft and wistful. "You had Henry in the palm of your hand all that time and you couldn't even see it."

I shuffled uncomfortably in my seat, not knowing what to say.

"But it was wrong of me to have said those things to you. I'm sorry," she said again.

"You were right though," I whispered, "I'm not good enough for him, and I've just told him that we can only be friends. But now, on balance, I don't know if it was the right thing to do at all, because I'm worried that I've hurt him really badly." I let out a juddering sigh. "I'm just trying to do the best thing for him and for me, so why do I feel really, really shitty?"

"If you don't want to be with him, then you did the right thing, Clara, believe me. It will be better for you both in the long run," she said in a commiserating voice. She was at least trying not to be too awful about this, and the sad and resigned look on her face told me that this was bringing up some difficult feelings for her too.

"Are you still in love with him?" I asked quietly, wiping my nose again.

Her startled eyes met mine briefly, hurt singing brightly in her sharp gaze, and she nodded. "Yeah. But I know that he doesn't love me back and he never will. I know I have to accept it and move on, but actually doing it really sucks, doesn't it?"

Despite my own mixed emotions warring inside, a surge of pity and empathy hit me in the chest. Leaning forward, I covered her hand in mine, feeling the tremor that was bouncing under her skin. "Grown up feelings are pretty bloody crappy, aren't they?"

Naomi smiled faintly and nodded again. "Being around him again really hurts, and seeing the two of you together last night was like being stabbed through the heart." She paused and chewed her lip. "Please, Clara, just do what's right for him, that's all I ask. I couldn't bear to think of him unhappy for the rest of his life."

I contemplated the sad and broken-hearted woman in front of me, someone who had been willing to put her whole self on the line, someone brave enough to chase her happily ever after, even if it hadn't worked out. "I know it probably doesn't help, but you should know that Henry doesn't hate you and has never once spoken badly of you."

She smiled weakly in reply. "That's good to hear."

"He never meant to hurt you, and he's told me how much he regrets that he did. It's why he's so awkward and distant when he sees you, he's desperately trying not to upset you again. Even if he is doing a monumentally shit job of it." I paused and observed a multitude of emotions skim over her features. "I hope that you find someone who loves you for who you are," I finished sadly.

"Thank you," she replied, tears now rolling down her face as well.

"What a pair of sad sacks we are," I said snottily, and Naomi chuckled, taking a tissue from the packet on the table.

"This is not going to help my membership of the women's liberation movement is it, Clara?" Her nose blowing was loud and trumpeting, and not at all ladylike, which endeared me to her further.

"Absolutely not, but the Hot Henry Effect seems to have a way of bypassing feminism in a most alarming way."

"The *Hot Henry Effect*?" Naomi's brow wrinkled in bemusement.

"It is a bone fide biological phenomenon," I replied, in all seriousness.

"I believe you. I think I've been a victim of its impact first hand," she said, crumpling her tissue and getting to her feet. "I should go, my presentation is in the next session."

"Thanks for stopping by to check on me, I appreciate it." I was genuinely grateful to have had this time to clear the air with her.

"You're welcome." She paused and looked away briefly. "Hey, Clara, I know I don't know you that well, but I'm starting to see why Henry loves you so much; maybe you should take a leaf out of his book, and love yourself a little bit more too?"

After a gentle hug, Naomi wandered off and out of sight, leaving me alone and utterly confused and distraught. Not really caring who could see me, I burst into howling sobs in the middle of an international medical conference, parting the crowds of delegates like a modern-day, snotty-nosed, emotionally unstable Moses.

Chapter Twenty-Six

From: AH.Fraser@frasertech.com

To: clara.clancy@pharmavoltis.com

Subject: Travel arrangements

Hi Clara,

I have decided to stay on in San Francisco for a bit and have changed my flight. I'm sorry, but you'll need to organise a taxi home from Heathrow for tomorrow.

Kind regards

Henry

From: clara.clancy@pharmavoltis.com

To: AH.Fraser@frasertech.com

Subject: Re: Travel arrangements

Hi Henry,

Thanks for letting me know, that's no problem at all. I hope you have an enjoyable time on your extended trip.

Clara

The flight back to London was uneventful and a lot more lonely and less enjoyable than the flight out. When the taxi finally dropped me off at my house, I was exhausted and fell into bed curled around an ecstatic Spencer, who purred loudly in my ear all night long. At least there was one male in the whole world who loved me unconditionally and whom I knew would never leave. Not while I was the keeper of the tin opener, at least.

The next morning, I woke at 4am and couldn't get back to sleep. Cursing the jet lag, I turned on the light and caught sight of my packed suitcase at the foot of my bed and was instantly reminded of the rollercoaster that had been my San Francisco trip. Worst of all, I had been left feeling like there was a piece of me missing, just as Henry had described it, and his absence was like a dark hole in my chest. Lying back down, I silently stared at the wardrobe door, largely unseeing, until Spencer jumped up and licked my eyes in an attempt to coerce me from my bed. Groaning and swatting at him, I tried to turn over and hide under the covers, but he was a persistent – and hungry – little blighter, who was now kneading the side of my head with his claws out and meowing loudly in my ear.

"Alright, alright, you demanding little git, I'm getting up," I muttered, lifting him from my pillow and placing him on the carpet. He swiped haphazardly at my bare arms, claws partially sheathed, and gave a little growl, his displeasure at being man-handled evident. "I'm not sure that you actually deserve my devotion, you grumpy little horror-bag."

The heating hadn't yet kicked in, so dressed up like a granny in the blitz, bobble hat on and wrapped in numerous layers, an enormous saggy jumper and cosy slippers, I trudged downstairs and into the kitchen. Spencer yowled his approval while I busied myself preparing his breakfast, winding himself around my legs so that we performed a little cat agility dance across the floor, and I attempted not to fall flat on my face.

"There you go, my gorgeous boy," I crooned fondly, now that he was no longer growling and was actually purring, all animosity forgotten in the name of food. I'd hardly got the dish down on the floor when he attacked it like he hadn't been fed since I left five days ago. I checked the recycling bin, and there were, as I expected, a number of empty cans of cat food in there, proving that Mrs Boswell from next door had come in each day as promised.

"You are a dramatic cat," I chuckled.

Still in a sleepy fug, my mind not quite working at full capacity, I grabbed the kettle to make a cup of tea, pottering across the kitchen towards the sink, firmly in old lady mode, absently looking out of the window into the still darkness of early morning, when something fluttered to the floor by my feet. The unexpected article was a large, bright yellow sticky note that lay face down on the tiles. Picking it up and turning it over, my insides lurched at the sight of Henry's familiar messy handwriting.

A joke for with your next cup of tea:

Three cannibals survive a plane crash and are trapped on a mountain, one was a biologist, one was a chemist, and one was an engineer. On the third day, they found a human thigh bone.

The biologist examined it for signs of disease and assessed the age and sex of the donor before trying to extract the marrow.

The chemist put it in various solutions of differing concentrations to try and dissolve it.

The engineer took it, whacked the other two over the head with it, and ate them.

Snorting with laughter at his terrible joke, I placed the note on the side and filled the kettle, setting it to boil. The tea and coffee cannisters were in a high-level wall cupboard next to the sink. The door had always been a bit rickety, so as cautiously as ever, I opened it, never quite sure if it would finally come adrift and bash me over the head. But to my surprise it opened smoothly and didn't even creak.

Curious now, I stood on tiptoes and peered in. All my cups were ordered, by colour and size, all handles facing the same way. My numerous types of fruit teas had been grouped and boxes stacked neatly, coffee jars lined up like soldiers on parade, and all decaffeinated items (that were largely out of date and unused) were placed together. I smiled to myself, Dr Neat Freak had been in here; he must have mended the door as well while he waited for me before we went to the airport.

Thinking of that happier time made my heart hurt, and trying to push the pain away, I reached up for a mug as the kettle whistle blew noisily.

To my surprise, inside the mug was another, smaller sticky note:

Mess makes me crazy and so do you
(in a good way)

I felt tears start to well up. Staring blurrily at the letters and not wanting to soil the mug he had selected for this note, I reached up and pulled another one down. Only to find that it too had a note inside.

I think your face is beautiful, even
when you have 'sambuca lips'

And so did the next.

Your coffee cup mime was the highlight of
my year, but I'm glad that you're a
scientist and not a children's entertainer…

As I took them out of the cupboard, I found that the whole first row of mugs had sticky notes in them.

Rulers rule.
My favourite one just did it better.

You are the absolute best hiding partner.
When can we hang out in
a cupboard again?

I hope you know that:
Science + engineering = the perfect match

In fact, he'd filled all my mugs with notes. I greedily pulled every one out and sat on the floor surrounded by positive, funny little messages, lovingly hand written by Henry.

I coveted them all. I sat there in tears overwhelmed by the devastation that all this time he'd been trying to tell me that he loved me, in subtle ways that I had studiously ignored, too self-absorbed to see that this kind and wonderful man was sincere. So broken and distrustful of intimacy that I let the gnawing and persistent feeling of self-doubt and unworthiness cloud my every interaction with him. I thought back to all my jibes about him getting a girlfriend, how he had seemed so down when I mentioned it. His tender smiles, his thoughtful actions and how he always seemed to know how to make me laugh or say the right thing at the right time. Shit, I was such an insensitive, hopeless idiot.

Spencer sat in the middle of the sticky note snowstorm that I had created on the kitchen tiles, fastidiously cleaning himself.

"I'm so stupid, Spence," I said, resulting in a curious look and a confirmatory chirrup, which suggested that he was likely in full agreement.

"Fuck it, I've got to tell him, haven't I?" Spencer licked his backside in reply.

"Are you even listening to me?" Studious ignoration ensued.

"I need to call Jo," I said suddenly.

And, I thought wryly, I need to stop having conversations with my cat.

Chapter Twenty-Seven

"Hi Prof, how's it hanging?"

"Hello Dr Clancy, good to hear from you at a more reasonable hour, at my end anyway, what are you doing up at four thirty in the morning?" Jo replied.

"Jet lag." I yawned. "Are you busy?"

"My postdoc is off sick and I'm trying to prevent a student from breaking the new half-a-million-dollar confocal microscope. Hang on a minute, will you?" She sounded distracted.

I sniggered as she muffled the phone handset. "Don't touch that bit, Steven, just the controls I showed you. For Christ's sake."

"So, what can I do for you? Or am I the only person you thought would be awake for a chat?" She returned to full volume in my ear.

"I wanted to tell you that you were right," I said quietly.

"Right about what exactly? There are many things that I am sure I'm right about, including my theory on neuronal development and repair, but no bugger believes me about that yet," she grumbled.

"You were right about Hot Henry, Jo," I said with a shaky sigh.

"Oh. Ok. Hang on, I'll be right back." She covered the handset again. "I am stepping out for a moment. Do not touch anything other than the touch pad, and do not break anything in here, or I will fail your ass. In fact, just count the green and red dots on the screen and don't touch anything, Steven, ok?"

There was the sound of a door being opened in an echoey corridor and a thump of it closing again. "Right, where were we?"

"I was telling you that you were right, Henry Fraser loves me," I said quickly and gulped. It was hard to even hear myself saying it because the words sounded so preposterous, I was sure she was about to fall down laughing.

"He told you that?" she asked calmly, like I had just told her I was having a tuna sandwich for lunch and not the most ridiculous thing I had ever uttered, in the history of the world, ever.

"Yes?" I said uncertainly.

"And how does that make you feel?"

"A bit bloody terrified, if I'm being honest."

"Why?"

"Alright, Sigmond Freud, this is not the conversation I was expecting from you, where is the 'I told you so'? Or some inappropriate reference to getting naked with him?" I muttered.

"Ok, we'll get to the subject of nakedness in a minute, first I'm trying to gauge how panicky you are on a scale from mill-pond calm to monsoon-level frantic."

"Like a windmill in a category five hurricane is probably closest to how I'm feeling on the inside."

"Right. So, what did you do when he told you? Did you really freak the hell out in front of him?" Jo was never one to mince her words.

"In a manner of speaking, yes," I reluctantly answered.

A large sigh filtered its way to me from many thousands of miles away. "Are you still speaking to each other?"

"No, he doesn't want to see me," I whispered miserably.

"So, what are you going to do about it?"

"I don't know." Anguish and guilt piled into my brain in avalanche-like proportions.

"Do you want to see him again, or would it be better for you to have some space and time to think about it?" She was being far too rational and caring, and this was not like her at all.

"Jo, I've really hurt him, and I don't know what I can do to make it better, but I miss him so much already and it's not even been twenty-four hours." I sniffled, the tears starting again.

"Right. You're going to give me fifteen minutes to sort out this bloody student, and then I'm going to call you back and you're going to tell me everything that went on, in detail, and then we're going to get the two of you married off like you should have been seven sodding years ago," she ordered decisively, and hung up, allowing no room for negotiation on this.

An hour later, Jo was brought up to speed on everything that had happened in San Francisco. She needed to take a few calming breaths after I told her about Dominic, and while she did threaten to send him anthrax through the post, she largely remained silent when I relayed to her all the Henry-related bits. She did give in to some heavy breathing when I told her about the sticky notes I'd found this morning, though. But I could forgive her for that, I was feeling a bit breathless every time I looked at them myself.

"Damn it, how can someone who looks like that, be so bloody nice, Clara?" she moaned. "It's like he won the genetic lottery or something."

"I know, which is why—"

"If you are about to tell me that you are not good enough for him, then the anthrax is coming to you," she stated bluntly.

"Right, ok, sorry."

"Do you love him, Clara? Be honest with yourself. You can't lead him on, if there is any doubt in your mind, but you owe it to both of you to give it a chance if you do have feelings for him," she said gently.

"I love him, I think I probably always have," I groaned. It was like the fog of denial had finally lifted.

"Ha! I knew it! I bloody well knew it!" I could tell she was doing a little dance around her office.

"Are you actually doing a celebratory dance, Jo?"

"Yes! This is too good to sit still! Imagine the beautiful babies you'll have!"

I choked a little, a cold sweat beginning to form on my top lip. "Hold your horses there, cowgirl, I'm not sure that's on the cards."

"Pfft. He loves you Clara, of course he's going to want to put a mini version of himself in you," she said, sniggering like a dirty old man.

I held my head in my hands, trying to ignore her not-so-subtle inuendo. "But what if what you said is true?"

"Which bit of what I said?" she asked, now a little out of breath from her jig.

"The bit where you said he's probably only interested in someone who isn't interested in him back, you know, wanting what you can't have? What if we got together and all that mystery has gone and there's nothing left but an empty husk of nothingness..." I trailed off back into my lonely pit of despair.

"He told you that he loved you from the first moment, didn't he? So, ignore what I said. If he really was a shallow arsehole that simply pursued unobtainable women for his kicks, he would have moved on to someone else eventually. He'd be a serial offender and he's not. He stuck with you at the detriment to his own happiness, it seems. He's totally one hundred per cent into you. Poor deluded chap."

"Jo! That's not helping," I cried.

"Sorry, I just can't get over the fact that he pined for you for so long. Or that he had an Elvis-themed wedding, but I'll try to let that one slide," she muttered.

"What if after all these years, he's built up a fantasy in his head of what I'm really like, and I can't live up to it? What if he realises how truly hopeless I am, and he doesn't want me after all?" I whispered morosely.

Jo was one of the very few people who knew the true extent of my brokenness due to my father's rejection. She had been there when I'd discovered where he was, due to the all-seeing eyes of social media, and had held my hand as I wrote an email, asking him to meet me. But he never replied, even though I knew it had been delivered and read. She had coached me through that angst, helped me to pick myself up and move ahead with my life, focus on my research and doctorate. But she also knew it still plagued me, the fear of further rejection often stopping me from doing so many things.

"Stop this self-doubt, Clara. I know where your brain is going with this, and it's beyond ridiculous; he's not anything like the sort of man your father is. He's spent a lot of time with you recently and got to know you all over again, and it's made him realise that he really can't live without you. Trust that what he's feeling is real, there is no reason on Earth why he would be putting himself through this if he wasn't totally sure about you, is there?"

"No," I agreed. She was right, I just had to be brave and take a risk, this was Henry after all, and he was good and kind. And in love with me. Who'd have thought it?

"Good, now we just have to work out how the hell you can convince him to give you another chance," she said thoughtfully.

One of the sticky note messages was stuck to Spencer's leg as he got up and walked past me, heading for the cat flap. I plucked it from his fur, eliciting an angry feline scowl and a half-hearted swipe in my general direction.

My coat is always available for covert
operations, whenever you need it

"I think I've got an idea, speak to you soon," I murmured and hung up the phone.

Chapter Twenty-Eight

"FraserTech, Janice speaking, how can I help you?"

"Hi Janice, its Clara Clancy from Pharmavoltis," I said cheerfully down the phone, spinning around on my office chair.

"Hi, Clara, how are you, dear?" Janice replied in her lovely grandmotherly tone.

"I'm alright thanks, you? When do you go in for your hip op?" I asked.

"Next month, it'll be a godsend when it's done. Now what can I do for you? Henry's not here at the moment," she said kindly.

"I know, when is he back? I was hoping to pop over, as I've got some bits and pieces that I'd like to run through with him in person," I said, stretching the truth a little.

"He flies in this afternoon, he has a meeting early tomorrow, free from about ten-thirty until eleven, but is then in back-to-back meetings for the rest of the day."

"Right, ok." This could be tight, but definitely doable.

"Do you want me to put a meeting in his diary with you at ten-thirty?"

"No, thanks, Janice. Do you know what, my day is pretty busy tomorrow, if I can get time away, I'll pop over then, but don't mention anything to him as I might not make it."

"Of course, Clara, I'll be sure not to put anything else in that slot though, just in case," she whispered conspiratorially.

I laughed. "Thanks, that would be great."

"See you tomorrow, I hope, bye."

"Bye."

I sat back in my chair, gripping my coffee tightly, until the plan came together in my mind. I was going to do this, and either make a right tit of myself or bag Oxford's answer to Superman as my boyfriend.

"Welcome back, I've missed you and I want to know all the gossip from San Francisco," Simmy said, coming into the office and hanging her coat on the coat rack, before placing a muffin in front of me as I spun my chair gently around again. With an appraising glance she asked, "What bonkers scheme are you concocting now, Dr Weirdo?"

"So, you know that thing you said about Henry being in love with me?"

Simmy's eyes went wide as she nodded, perching on the edge of my desk.

"He admitted it."

"About bloody time. And...?" she queried, flapping her hands wildly for me to continue.

"Well, I'm putting my big girl pants on and going to tell him I feel the same."

Her squeal was so loud that the medical team admin assistant, Gemma, popped her head around the door in anxious horror, but Simmy absent-mindedly waved her away. "Tell me everything."

So I did. The whole story of what happened in San Francisco. She was insistent that she was going to castrate Dominic if she ever saw him again and would support me through the tribunal, and that I definitely needed a frontal lobotomy for not leaping on Henry when he confessed his feelings in my hotel room.

But when I got to the notes I'd found in my cups, and my cunning plan to win him back, she let out a long sigh, chinked coffee cups with mine and whispered, "If this doesn't work, he's the one who needs a lobotomy, Clara."

The next morning, I was in a right bloody tizzy. I'd texted Jo with a brief outline of my Hooking Hot Henry plan (as she'd named it) and she had sent me a good luck message this morning and told me to put on my sexiest underwear, as I was clearly going to be divesting of my clothes in front of him at some point today. I wasn't so sure about that, but decided that it couldn't hurt as a little confidence boost, so I had donned the matching black and pink set that I rarely ever wore because it made me feel a little bit like a stripper in disguise.

Dressed head to toe in black (trouser suit and silk blouse), coupled with killer heels and my trusty oversized handbag, I was ready for some covert action, hoping that I could actually pull this off.

When I flashed my Pharmavoltis badge at the front desk of the FraserTech offices, I was let through quite quickly, and made my way up to the top floor where Henry's private office was. Janice was seated in the open-plan area outside and beamed at me as I alighted the top step. She'd been in a few of our meetings, taking notes and organising things, so her familiar and friendly face was a welcome sight.

"Ah, you're a bit early but I'm glad you made it. Henry will be so pleased to see you," she said warmly, giving me a hug.

I really bloody hoped so, otherwise she'd be calling security and having me dragged out and sent straight to the loony bin, with what I had planned.

"Is it ok if I wait in his office? I've got some charts and things that I could do with pulling up on my computer and checking before he gets here," I lied.

Janice looked confused at my request for a moment, before shrugging. "I'm sure he won't mind, dear, it's you after all."

I wasn't quite sure what she meant by that, but decided not to probe, in case she changed her mind. "Oh, and you know how I like to tease him, Janice?"

"Yes, you two do like to have your little jokes, don't you?" she replied, eyes twinkling. I wondered with alarm how many of our conversations she had actually been privy to, but decided to plough on, regardless.

"Oh, we do! Well, please can you not let on that I'm here, I want to surprise him!" I winked.

She cackled and tapped the side of her nose. "Mum's the word."

I gave her a double thumbs up and slipped inside his office and cased the room, rubbing my hands in glee as I noticed the coat stand over by the window, and the familiar and very welcome sight of his navy wool overcoat hanging from it. I quickly scribbled a note and placed it on his keyboard, then hid my bag behind the door. Slipping my secret weapon into my trouser pocket and wrapping myself in his coat, I lay in wait like a sneaky woollen-chrysalis-clad spy.

I had become a jiggling bag of nerves and was struggling to keep a lid on my anxiety, but luckily, I didn't have to hang about too long before I heard his voice as he came down the corridor.

"Show them straight in, when they get here, please, Janice," he said, the smooth, deep tones carried on as he opened the door and came into the office, his phone held between his ear and his shoulder, glasses slightly askew as he placed his laptop and a coffee cup on the desk. He was a sight for sore eyes, and my heart rate ratcheted up another notch, thundering loudly in my ears, a heady mixture of attraction, panic and tachycardia. Shit, get a grip, Wonder Woman.

"Sorry about that. Yeah, yep, I'll do that…" he said into his phone. It was then that he noticed the notepad and with a puzzled expression looked up towards the coat stand, his eyes widening in total shock as he saw just my face peeking out between his lapels and I silently mouthed 'hi' at him. "I'll um, well. Yeah. I'd better call you back. Just hold off on that for a bit. No, yeah, everything's fine, I think. Gotta go. Bye."

I stared at him, and he stared at me. It went on for some time, both of us barely blinking.

"Is there something on my face?" I eventually asked from within my cocoon.

"Err, not that I can see from here," he replied quietly, before adding quizzically, "What are you doing in my coat, Clara?"

"It's my safe place, remember?"

"Yes, I remember. Who are you hiding from?"

"I was waiting for you, and it seemed like as good a spot as any," I said and gave him a hopeful smile.

"Oh." Henry looked conflicted. "I don't think it's such a good idea for us to see each other, I've got a day full of meetings and things..." His voice drifted off sadly.

"I know, I won't be long, I just have some stuff I need to say to you, but because I'm a bit shit at anything to do with grown up feelings, I've written it down and thought maybe you could read them out and I'll stay here, in my safe place, where I feel safest," I rattled off quickly, trying hard to hide the nerves. Reaching into my pocket I pulled out the stack of sticky notes and threw them to him.

He caught the little yellow block and looked at the first one and then at me. "You want me to read them out loud to you?"

"Yeah, and then you know, you can throw them away or stick them on something. Sticky notes are a handy way to communicate, I've recently found," I said with a small smile.

Despite his obvious misgivings, Henry smiled too, and sighed, coming around to the side of his desk nearest the coat stand and perching on its edge, long legs stretched out in front of him, crossed at the ankles.

"Ok, here's the first one. 'Hi Clark (I knew you'd be Clark today). I just wanted to say hi and sorry'." Henry looked up at me with a raised eyebrow, peeled off the first leaf and stuck it to the thumb on his left hand.

"This one's an interesting one," he murmured. "'Just to let you know that I've forgiven you for killing all my stem cells'. I'm glad to see that you're not prone to exaggeration and that you've been able to move on during the last seven years, Clara."

I nodded. "I am a paragon of forgiveness. It's a good way to be, FYI. Read the next one."

"So bossy." He huffed, sticking the note to his index finger. "Ok, 'Have I already told you that I'm really, really sorry?'."

He looked up at me again. "You know you could just say this to my face?"

"I'm really, really sorry," I mouthed, and then shrugged helplessly.

"Chicken." He peeled off this one and stuck it to the tip of his middle finger. "'I'm a million times sorry', 'Sorry that I hurt you and sorry that I didn't tell you the truth'," his voice trailed off and he stuck these two notes to his ring and little fingers.

"'I was too frightened to tell you that I loved you, and not just as a friend'," he said this slowly and reread it a few times before he looked back up at me. Confusion and disbelief flitted over his handsome features, my chest constricting at how unsure he seemed in this moment.

"There are more," I whispered, when he didn't say anything.

"What am I going to do with these, I've run out of fingers?" he said hoarsely, waving his note-adorned digits.

"Put them in a little box and keep them forever?" I suggested helpfully.

Henry pushed off from the desk and stalked towards me, reaching forward he tugged at the lapel of his coat and it fell open, revealing the front of me in my top-to-toe black outfit. "Are you hiding in my coat dressed as a business-attired, office-based ninja?"

"I wanted to blend in, be stealthy and unobserved," I said, a bit breathlessly. He was really quite close to me now. "I opted not to wear my balaclava though, I wasn't sure security would let me in with it on."

"Probably not. Although, I think you have pulled off this

very niche look spectacularly, and with a panache that only you possess." He stuck the first sticky note to my chin, with a smirk. Then stuck the others at various points on my shoulders, pressing the last one lightly against my shirt, just below my collar bone. Suspiciously close to the swell of my right breast where it was pushed artificially upwards by the Wonderbra I was wearing. And it was his turn to get a little breathless.

My confidence was bolstered significantly.

He read the next one silently and looked up at me questioningly. "Do you really mean this?"

"Yes, Henry, I mean all of them."

He cleared his throat. "'I know that you have a good heart and I trust you with my broken one'."

He stuck that one above my heart.

"'Have I told you that I actually really love your face, and your smell? You're really rather swoony, in fact'." He laughed and stuck that one to my cheek. "I really love your face and your smell too, Clara, but swoony?"

"I couldn't think how else to describe it, so I channelled my intimate knowledge of romantic fiction and it was the best I could come up with. Don't take the piss."

Henry shrugged, still smiling, and looked down at the next note. "'Your hair is like something out of a shampoo advert, and I loved running my fingers through it.' I loved that too," he whispered close to my ear, his lips brushing the sensitive skin on the lobe as he placed this note on the top of my head.

My legs felt a bit weak, I won't lie, and I was in real danger of losing my strong, independent woman street cred at this point. What would Wonder Woman do? I channelled my inner superhero and stood tall.

Henry read the next one, and his expression turned incredulous. "Are these the opening lyrics to the well-known eighties pop-rock ballad, 'If I Could Turn Back Time'?"

I nodded. "Indeed, they are. Cher can say it so much more eloquently than I can."

He shook his head before sticking the note to my forehead and examining the next one. "It goes on? Of course, it does." He read silently, lips twitching. "The full chorus. Wow."

"I was really sure you'd sing those ones to me," I grumbled, as his fingers pressed the two lyrically inspired notes next to each other above my eyebrows.

"I cannot believe you quoted a Cher song," he replied, still shaking his head slightly.

"Your taste in eighties pop rock music is legendary, Henry, so do not pretend that you're not humming that tune in your head right now."

"You're correct, it will be stuck on a loop in my brain all day. Thanks for that," he muttered drily.

"You're welcome. Do you still listen to your Bon Jovi playlist when you're working?"

"Absolutely, Jon Bon Jovi is a god amongst men, Clara, have you not realised this yet?"

I snorted and rolled my eyes. "Whatever you say, Henry." I paused, before adding quietly, "The next note is the last one."

"Are there any dubious song lyrics involved?" he asked, amusement lighting him up from the inside.

"No, this one's straight from the cold dead place where my heart should be," I quipped. Despite everything, I was still readying myself for imminent rejection and total crushing cardiac failure.

Henry looked down at the note and chewed his lip, then in

a soft voice he read out my words. "'Henry, I love you with all my heart, no matter how damaged it may be. I want to spend the rest of forever trying to be enough for you, trying to make you as happy as possible. All I ask is that you continue to be you. Because, I have finally realised, it's always been you'."

Looking deep into my eyes, he reached up and stuck the final note on my lips. "My turn to speak now, in my own words, Clara, ok?"

I nodded.

"Good." He hesitated and took a deep, steadying breath. "You are enough, you've always been enough, and I want you, I love you, just like you are. You're crazy and funny and kind and beautiful, and so bright and intelligent that it makes my brain hurt just trying to keep up with you. Please don't ever feel that you need to be anything other than yourself," Henry finished quietly, using the soft pad of his thumbs to brush away the tears that were rolling down my cheeks.

I stared intently at this most fantastic of human beings and thanked my lucky stars that our paths had crossed more than once in our lives. I was teetering forward, hoping to lean in for a big old snog, when there was a knock at the door, and in walked Janice, followed by Claus Baumann and Richard Holmes.

And my entire digestive tract fell onto the floor in dismay.

They all gawped at me like I was a business-attired, office-based ninja, covered in sticky notes, partially hiding inside Henry Fraser's coat. So, no snogging for me, just an uncomfortable staring contest with Dick Dastardly and grumpy Father Christmas.

Chapter Twenty-Nine

I stood there like a rabbit in the headlights, Henry's hand frozen on my cheek as we turned as one to look at the intruders on our private, strange little rendezvous.

Henry was the first to react, dropping his hand to the side and taking a step around me to shield my body slightly from view.

"We are brainstorming some publications ideas," he said rather unconvincingly, while I frantically pulled the sticky notes off my face and clothes. "We'll just finish off and I'll be with you shortly. Janice, please can you show Richard and Claus to the coffee facilities."

"Yes, yes, of course. This way, gentleman," she bustled, and I heard the door close.

"Oh god," I moaned.

"It's not that bad," Henry murmured, turning back to me and plucking the last sticky note from my hair. "They probably didn't even notice anything."

"Brainstorming ideas by sticking notes to a member of their

medical team? I think they're going to have noticed, Henry," I said, waving the little pile of yellow papers at him.

"Mmmm, maybe," he agreed and caught my hand, taking the sticky notes from me and putting them securely in the breast pocket of his shirt.

"What are you going to do with those?"

"Find a little box and keep them forever," he said with a small smile. "Now where were we, when we were so rudely interrupted?" His eyes had turned impossibly dark, pupils large and a faint blush coloured his cheekbones.

"Well, I don't know about you, Superman, but Wonder Woman here was hoping for a little snogging action," I said, my words belying a confidence that I didn't really feel, hoping I had read the situation correctly, a small part of me always waiting for devastating rejection to strike me down.

"Wonder Woman, hmmm?"

"Yeah, I reckon all the times that I rescued you from Marina Montgomery, I could definitely be Wonder Woman."

Henry nodded thoughtfully. "Wonder Woman's outfit was pretty hot, but I think you're more Cat Woman. And that tight black suit really does it for me."

He'd moved in very close now and my breath was coming out in funny little gasps.

"Does it now? Tsk, what would Lois say?" I murmured shaking my head in mock consternation.

"I think, Lois, that while you may have designs on being Wonder Woman, in reality maybe you just like wearing distractingly impractical outfits at inopportune moments?" Henry replied, his eyes glazing over for a second. "I seem to recall some particularly good taste in underwear."

My mind leapt to my current lingerie situation, and I let my lips curl up seductively. "Oh, poor sweet Clark, you have no idea as to the full extent of my knicker drawer."

Closing his eyes briefly, he let out a little groan. "Who knew that scientists could be so sexy?"

Who knew engineers could make such seductive sounds? Cripes it was like he'd just hotwired my libido.

"Ah, you should never make assumptions about what goes on underneath a person's lab coat," I said waggling my eyebrows and making him grin stupidly.

"And for the record," I continued, "I never knew that engineers could be so..." I struggled for a moment with a word beginning with 'E' and finally settled on, "Erotic."

Henry chuckled and wrapped an arm around my waist, pulling me in closer, so that now our bodies were pressed flush up against each other. My drunken assessment in San Francisco had been right, he was most definitely firm under his clothes. *Everywhere*. Holy moly.

"I am not sure that the majority of engineers could be described as erotic, but I am going to take that compliment," he said quietly, his gaze now focussed on my mouth.

"You should," I practically panted as he angled his head towards mine.

"You seem to be getting a little breathless on me here, Miss Bennet, you ok?" Henry asked with amusement, sliding his palm along the edge of my jaw before gently cupping the back of my head.

"Finally, he notices," I whispered against his lips feeling his returning smile, before running my fingers up and over his broad shoulders and into his hair.

Then he was kissing me. And it was most definitely Superman and not Clark Kent who had stepped up for this part. I had truly never been kissed like this. His mouth was warm and soft, a steady pressure then release, leaving me yearning and pushing for more, his skilful lips and tongue whispering of hot, dark, forbidden pleasures, which soon had me gasping and moaning against him. When he deepened the kiss, like a starved man at a banquet, taking and possessing, nipping and exploring with more force, pulling me ever more urgently into him, I fervently matched his desperation with a greedy mouth and grasping hands.

"Dr Fraser." A distant voice came from somewhere, perhaps another planet, I couldn't have cared less at this point, but Henry had clearly heard it too and pulled away.

"Shit, Clara." He sounded husky and his eyes were huge, lipstick smeared on his face, and hair standing delightfully on end where I had mussed it, rather violently it would seem. "I have a meeting with Richard and Claus."

"Oh, yes, I'd totally forgotten," I whispered in a daze, leaning against him for support.

"Henry, it's ten past eleven and your guests are eager to get going with the meeting," Janice said, her kindly, sing-song voice muffled through the wooden door.

"Yeah, we're almost done here," Henry said loudly, then looked back down at me, and grinning wickedly, he whispered, "Almost."

Then he was kissing me again so passionately that my knees buckled, and I actually collapsed into his arms, like a Regency debutante at her first soiree.

I was grinning like a loon when Simmy walked in after lunch.

"How did it go? You look a little deranged, so I'm assuming it went well?" she quipped, dropping her bag on the floor and sitting heavily behind her desk.

"Nope, better than well," I replied dreamily.

"Better? You've married him and already having his baby? And then won the lottery and given Dick Dastardly your resignation?"

"Close, but no cigar," I sniggered.

"At least tell me you have a more intimate knowledge of Henry Fraser's mouth, now, please?"

"I do." I winked. Not sure about this newly found penchant for winking, but it felt right, so I was going with it.

"Don't leave out any details, Clara, *any*, do you hear me?"

And after I'd given her an account of this morning's shenanigans, culminating in the office-based kiss-a-thon, Simmy sat back with a satisfied smile, fanning herself dramatically. Although, I decided to leave out the bit about Richard and Claus walking in on us, that was a private mortification for me and Henry alone.

"Woooaah, well, I can totally see why your face looks like that," she gushed. "You've done well in your quest for true love, my young Padawan."

"Thank you, Obi-Wan, it was a rocky road," I replied, laughing.

"Oh, and by the way, Richard popped in to see you first thing, said to tell you to stop work on the FraserTech project for now, as Claus is trying to organise an acquisition or something," she said breezily, opening up her laptop.

"Oh, ok." That would explain why Richard and Claus had been in Henry's office then. But surely Henry would have told me if he was going to sell his company? Maybe there was another explanation.

Plugging in my earbuds and selecting an eighties rock ballad playlist, I fired up my emails, feeling that I should try and do something productive today. I hadn't properly checked my inbox since I had returned from San Francisco, and scrolling through the list of usual replies, internal company notices and spam, one message stood out, one to Henry that I was copied into from Derek Smith a little way down, which included a forwarded message from Henry below it.

From: dsmith@stanford.edu

> *To: AH.Fraser@frasertech.com*
>
> *CC: clara.clancy@pharmavoltis.com; nporter@stanford.edu*
>
> *Subject: Fwd: Clinical trial next steps*
>
> *Hi Henry,*
>
> *It was great to get some extra time with you over the last few days and I'm so glad that you've decided to accept the tenured professorship position in the bioengineering department. It will be fantastic to have you back in California with us.*
>
> *I've copied Clara into this as the point of contact for the heart valve trial now, and also Naomi as she will be the key liaison from my group, to make sure that everyone is kept in the loop.*
>
> *Best regards*
>
> *Derek*

> *---------- Forwarded message ---------*
>
> *From: AH.Fraser@frasertech.com*
>
> *To: dsmith@stanford.edu*
>
> *Subject: Tenured professorship position*
>
> *Hi Derek,*

Thanks for letting me know about the position coming up in the Bioengineering department. Just to let you know that they've offered me the post and I'm in the process of organising things at my end.

I'm hoping for a quick turnaround, with the aim to be in Stanford relatively quickly. Probably best to liaise with Clara at Pharmavoltis re: the clinical trial.

I'll keep you informed.

Kind regards

Henry

I felt all the colour drain from my face. I wish I could unsee all of this, unknow it. I wish I'd attempted to scoop my own eyeballs out with a spoon instead of opening my emails. It would have been infinitely less shocking and painful.

The gentle hand on my shoulder made me look up with a start, and I pulled out my earbuds.

"Clara, what's happened, you look devastated?" Simmy was standing close by, and I gestured for her to read the screen. When she'd finished, she turned a concerned face to mine. "Don't over-react, it might not be what you're thinking."

"What else could it be, Simmy? He's going back to the States," I whispered morosely.

"There could be a number of things going on that you don't know about. Give him a chance to explain." She squeezed my arm gently.

But it was too late for that, the rush of hurt and loss was already burning through my brain, the unmistakable niggly little 'I told you so' voice had started in earnest, pummelling my self-confidence down a narrow hole of darkness, telling me over and over that I wasn't worth staying for, totally blinded to any other possibility.

I honestly couldn't see a way out of this, couldn't see how I wasn't going to be left all over again, despite what had happened with Henry this morning or Simmy's warning to hear the full story. He was going back to America, leaving Oxford behind. Like history repeating itself.

And I was completely consumed by the indescribable feeling of the newly healed fractures in my heart shattering into a million pieces.

Chapter Thirty

I hadn't heard anything from Henry all day, and I finally turned off my laptop and headed for home at 7pm. It was a cold, clear evening and stars sparkled brightly in the sky, twinkling magically overhead as I left the warmth of the Pharmavoltis office behind.

It was a prickle of awareness that made me turn around in the company car park, a feeling of unease that heightened my senses the moment before Hannibal Lecter got out of his car.

I let out an involuntary screech, glad I had my trainers on as I geared myself up for a Usain Bolt-like sprint back into the safety of the security-controlled building.

"Clara, wait!" Dominic called out, "I just want to talk to you."

"I don't think we have anything to talk about," I hissed, while simultaneously rummaging in my bag for my keys, finding the pointiest one to grip between my fingers. Ninja Clara was quicker on the uptake nowadays.

"Please, just hear me out," he pleaded, hands held up in a supplicative gesture in front of him.

Adrenaline was coursing through my body, the images of him pressed against me in the gloomy corridor still haunting if I let myself think of them, his cold and undeterred advances sitting like lead in my stomach.

"Say what you have to say, then leave me alone," I muttered, edging back towards the soft glow of the doorway, in full view of the security camera on the front of the building.

"I'm sorry that I upset you in San Francisco," he mumbled, putting his hands in his pockets, shoulders hunched. "I honestly thought you were interested, Clara, I just misread the whole situation. I'm a nice guy, honestly."

"How had I ever given you reason to think I was interested, Dominic?" I said aghast. My brain screaming that he was as close to being a 'nice guy' as I was to being a purple turtle.

"You talked about having sex with me, Clara, isn't that reason enough?" He seemed genuinely to believe what he was saying. And the self-satisfied smirk was back. See? Not even a hint of a nice guy. Urgh.

"No! Christ, Dominic, I was trying to let you know that I wasn't interested, and I panicked when I said that. But not once did I actually say that I wanted to have sex with you!" I cried out. "Did you not realise that I kept running away from you, avoiding you? I even hid under Henry's desk so you wouldn't see me."

"Ha! I knew you were in there!"

"This is not something to be proud of," I muttered, shaking my head. "You made me uncomfortable, and I was trying to be kind to you and not disrupt our working relationship, but you frightened me, intimidated me. I thought if I kept out of your way, you'd eventually leave me alone."

"I thought you were just playing hard to get."

"Women don't do that. No means no. Even maybe does not mean yes. Saying the word 'sex' is not an invitation to stick your tongue down someone else's throat," I said more forcefully, "and, while we're at it, lurking in corridors, hiding behind pot plants, and jumping out at lone women in dark car parks are all *not* ok either, Dominic!"

"Sorry," he replied through gritted teeth. "Although, really you should see it as a compliment that I find you attractive."

I think that my eyes might have actually fallen out of their sockets. "A *compliment*?"

"Yeah." He smiled smarmily. "I think you're very pretty."

I stared at him in disbelief, the half-light of the lamp post illuminating his smug expression. "Just. Stop. Talking, Dominic. It's not helping your cause, at all."

"What is it with women in this day and age, unable to accept some well-meaning flattery."

"I don't need you to comment on how attractive you think I am, Dominic, we are work colleagues. An appropriate compliment might be, I don't know, you're really good at your job, or something, rather than accusing me of sleeping around to further my career." I gave an exasperated huff. "Why am I even needing to spell this out to you?"

He let loose a long sigh and leant back against his car. "I'm sorry, I've acted like a dickhead, what more can I say to get you to stop this stupid disciplinary hearing, so things can go back to normal, and I can get back to work?"

Oh. Right. He was not sorry, not in the slightest. In his mind he had done nothing wrong. He just didn't want to lose his job, and he thought that a quick apology in the car park would suffice, and he could have it all neatly swept under the carpet. And everything would go back to how it was before. Not on my watch, Hannibal. People-pleaser Clara had most definitely left the building.

I took another step back towards the office door, the metal key in my grasp reassuring, but not enough to stop the anxiety creeping back into my chest. "I won't be stopping the disciplinary hearing."

His body noticeably stiffened, his face turning angry. "What do you want? Money? A pay off?" he sneered, "Because despite what you think, Clara, you did lead me on, and I'll make it clear in the hearing just how much of a prick tease you really are."

It's funny how the sympathetic nervous system works. One minute I was absolutely on the path of flight, preparing to run like a chuffing gazelle, the next, a rage so fiery rose up and obliterated all rational thought, erupting like a volcano and propelling me towards a definitely (maybe) serial killer to firmly poke him in the chest.

"No, I don't want your money, I don't want anything from you other than to never see you ever again. So, I'm going to do everything in my power to make sure that you are sacked." I glared at him, proud of myself for not backing down, for facing this head-on and telling it to him straight. His answering glare withered and died on his face, replaced by a closed-off resignation.

"You have to know that I would never have forced myself on you, Clara, it was only a kiss. I just want to get my life back," he said, his tone now whiny and pathetic.

"You already did though, Dominic, dragging me down that

corridor and kissing me when I clearly told you no: that's forcing yourself on me. And it's not ok, what you did was not ok," I whispered a bit shakily, knocked slightly off kilter by his change of tone. Come on brave pants, do not desert me now.

"Fine, so there's nothing at all that I can say to make you change your mind?"

"No, nothing," I replied, the fire in me dimming, the fight dying away, the need to curl up in a ball on my sofa all-consuming.

Dominic lurched forward and I pulled out my stabby little key hand, waving it in warning. But he just snorted and opened his car door, sliding into the front seat with an ominous glare, before starting the engine and racing away.

I slumped back against a concrete bollard, my legs giving out as I found my phone to type a message to Richard, to tell him what had happened and ask him to check the security cameras from this evening.

The twenty-minute walk home suddenly felt like a terrifying ordeal, and I stared at my phone, willing Henry to call me, or to magically appear again and make everything alright. But it was clear that this wasn't going to happen, and I'd need to get used to not relying on his rescue missions anymore. Scrolling through my contacts, I hit call when I came to Jo's number, keeping my fingers tightly crossed that she would answer.

"Hello, Dr Clancy, or should it be Dr Clancy-Soon-To-Be-Fraser?"

"Clara will suffice," I replied sadly.

"Oh. Shit. Do we need to go and get a litre of supermarket gin?"

I sighed. "Just keep me company on my walk home?"

"Of course, everything ok?"

"I bumped into Dominic in the car park, and I'm still a tiny bit scared," I admitted.

"Call a taxi! Don't mess about with this, Clara!" she yelped into my ear.

"No, honestly, I'm fine, he's gone, and I think definitely got the message not to harass me anymore."

"What about Henry – can you call him to come and get you?" she said, clearly agitated.

"He's in meetings, so not answering his phone." I didn't tell her that I'd not tried him just now. That I couldn't bear to see him at this moment, not until I'd got things straight in my head again.

"How did the sticky note plan go this morning then?" she asked warily, sensing something was off.

"Oh, well, we snogged, which was nice."

"Just nice? Or like knicker-wettingly nice?"

Laughing and continuing to walk whilst staying under the reassuring light of the lamp posts, I murmured, "It was really nice, Jo."

"Soooo, what aren't you telling me?"

"He's accepted a tenured position at Stanford. He'll be heading out to the States again as soon as he can," I replied. Saying it out loud made my heart break all over again.

"Are you certain? Has he told you this for definite?"

"I was copied in on an email where it's all laid out, so, yeah, pretty certain."

Jo was silent for a moment. "Before or after your meeting today?"

"What?"

"When did the emails get sent?"

"I don't know."

"Ok, little Miss Jump-To-Conclusion, forward me the emails and get yourself off the panic train, right now."

"I'm not jumping to conclusions, Jo. I know he's selling his company, probably to Pharmavoltis as Claus and Richard met with him today, and Simmy told me they were at an acquisition meeting this morning. He wouldn't be selling up if he wasn't totally sure about moving, would he?" I paused and gulped a deep breath. "What is wrong with me?"

"Clara. Don't be a moron, there is nothing wrong with you."

"Then why do the men I love leave me, and the ones that actually want me end up being weirdos?" I moaned.

"Firstly, I refuse to believe that Henry has left you. You need to talk to him, give him a chance to explain before you fall into a pit of eternal despair. And secondly, name one weirdo, other than Henry, who you think you might have loved eventually?"

"The phantom knicker nabber, Paul?" I suggested helpfully.

"Oh yeah, he was weird," she agreed, "but I don't think he was ever cut out to be Mr Clara Clancy."

I humphed gloomily down the phone. "Tell me something nice to cheer me up, Jo."

"I'm sat on the balcony looking out over the sea, having my morning coffee and it's already bright sunshine and roasting hot here. Is that helping?"

I shivered as a chilly wind blew my coat against my legs. "No, not really."

"Ok. Ooh! Did I tell you that my neuronal modelling study was accepted by *Nature* last week? And I've been asked for an interview by *New Scientist*!" she exclaimed excitedly.

"No! That's amazing! Jo, I'm so happy for you!"

"Yeah, I'm totally blown away, and it's definitely going to help me secure that grant I desperately need for the new development study I want to do."

We settled into easy conversation, our shared love of science and her infectious enthusiasm helping to keep me grounded and suitably distracted as I made my way home.

Chapter Thirty-One

Despite my uplifting pep talk with Jo, I struggled to process the barrage of shitty, bastardly emotions I was feeling after I got home. A small part of my brain knew I was being overdramatic, knew that I should wait to hear Henry's side of the story before condemning him quite so vehemently. But that was the quiet voice, and it was being drowned out by the deafening screaming voice of rejection, which was most definitely the loudest noise in my head.

Heating some soup on the hob, I stirred mechanically, pouring it into a bowl and then allowing it to go cold while I stared at its orangey red hue without even having one spoonful. I had forwarded the emails to Jo as she'd asked me to, then turned off all my electrical devices, not wanting to discuss it anymore with anyone. Preferring instead to snuggle down into a lonely black hole of self-pity and regret.

Spencer, who was not known for being much of a cuddler (except at night when he was just after my body heat), mournfully curled up alongside me on the sofa, his tabby fur mottled in the soft lamp light, his little body pressed against my leg the only warmth I could feel. I don't know how long I sat there, not even crying, just staring into space, numb, not sure what to do or how to be. I was sad, yes, but I was also angry; annoyed at myself for letting down my guard and annoyed at Henry for letting me down after everything that I'd told him.

The ringing of the doorbell woke me from my daze, and zombie like and unseeing I rose to answer it.

"I've brought a takeaway." Henry beamed down at me from the doorstep, shaking a bag proudly. "And, never one to forget a drinks order, I brought Sauvignon Blanc as well."

I think my eyes must have looked like saucers. I know my skin was devoid of all colour. The ancient and bobbled penguin onesie I was wearing was the least flattering garment I owned, and now had a fetching orange stain where I had sloshed tomato soup onto it. I looked a fright.

"Clara, are you ok?" Henry asked, his previously joyous expression falling away. "What has happened?"

"I don't think I should see you," I stated flatly.

"What's happened?" he asked again, his voice turning dark and gravelly, a deep crease forming between his eyebrows.

"You were right, going our separate ways is probably best for both of us," I whispered, moving to close the door before I began to cry. My heart hurting just to look at him.

"Clara, wait." Henry's shoulder against the wood, stopped me in my tracks. "Please tell me what's going on?"

"You're leaving me," I murmured, tears finally beginning to fall.

"I'm not leaving you, what are you on about? Please let me in and we can talk about it," Henry begged, his voice wobbling with emotion. The usual easy-going face that I knew so well, was now pinched and frustrated. "Please, Clara."

After the evening I'd had, I was too tired to fight him, so I let go of the handle and walked through into the kitchen, pulling out a chair at my small table and sitting down. Henry had followed, and was now leaning back against the counter, unbuttoning his coat while placing his culinary offerings on the worktop next to him.

"Start at the beginning and tell me everything."

I blew out a sigh. "I was born on the twelfth of September nineteen–"

"Clara," Henry warned.

"Sorry, I was just trying to lighten the mood," I said humourlessly.

The soup from earlier sat cold and congealing in its bowl, an undrunk mug of tea its sad little companion on the tabletop, surrounded by all the lovely teacup notes Henry had written. I could smell the curry that he had brought, chicken tikka masala if I wasn't mistaken, a favourite of mine from way back, but the thought of eating anything made bile rise in my throat.

"Clara, speak to me, please," Henry pleaded.

"Have you checked your emails today?" I asked, staring at the swirling patterned grain of the wooden tabletop.

"Not since this morning, no, I've been in a million boring meetings," he replied, "Why?"

"Oh. Just that I was copied in on a message from Derek, you know, from Stanford?" I began picking at a knot in the surface of the table, scratching at the imperfection with my fingernail. My heart breaking all over again as I thought about him being thousands of miles away, the soul-shattering realisation that my declaration of love had not been enough to keep him here. I had not been enough. Yet again.

"Yes, I know who you mean. What did it say?"

My brain was in overdrive, negative thoughts flitting around like the dry husks of autumn leaves fluttering haphazardly in the wind. Crushing humiliation and rejection was surfacing, and I couldn't bring myself to look up, couldn't bear to see the truth in his eyes when he told me that he was leaving, and that maybe we could hook up occasionally when he was this way with work. Wondering if the kisses that we had shared had just been empty and meaningless to him, when I had put myself out there, allowed my vulnerability to be seen.

"Umm, well, Derek was congratulating you on your new tenured professorship and that he was looking forward to having you back in California. You really should read it, it's a nice message," I choked out.

"Clara, I—" he started, but I cut him off.

"He kindly forwarded your message too, the one where you talk about wrapping up your life here quickly to be able to move out to California as soon as possible," I said sourly, standing up from the table abruptly and turning to face him. "Then Simmy told me how Claus is planning to acquire FraserTech, so I guess that's what your meeting was about this morning. So now everything is neatly sorted and ready for you to leave, nothing stopping you, right?"

"Clara, hang on, let me explain—"

"I think that you should go, Henry."

"No, you don't get to do this to me, Clara," he growled, his tone low and furious, the whites of his knuckles showing as he gripped the edge of the worktop forcibly. "You don't get to kick me out and reject me again, not when you haven't got the full story."

How exactly did he have the right to be cross with me? I glared right back.

"I trusted you, I opened myself up and gave you my heart, and you've stamped on it already, despite everything that I told you, Henry, and I want you to leave," I said, scrubbing my hands at the stubborn tears that had dampened my cheeks.

"No, not until you bloody well hear what I have to say first," he countered angrily.

He seemed to have grown bigger. Had I mistaken my superhero, was he actually Bruce Banner? Was he about to go green and burst out of his shirt all Incredible Hulk? My newly awakened libido perked up at the possibility of Henry ripping his clothing off, and it took a great deal of stern internal dialogue to silence these thoughts and remember that he was leaving, and I was mad with him. Really, Clara, fantasizing about him was not helpful at this point.

"Fine, say what you have to say and then get out," I said, walking up to him in a show of bravado and jabbing him in the chest (poking angry men was the theme of this evening it seemed).

Henry looked down at our one small point of contact, then back up into my face, eyes narrowed until I stepped back again, realising that a bit of distance would be good here, and that prodding the Hulk was maybe not the best plan. To his credit, Henry didn't move, he carried on with his death grip on my kitchen worktop, and I wasn't sure, but I think I saw the oak boards begin to bend under his hands.

Finally, when he eventually spoke, his tone was rough, still angry. But his sharp gaze couldn't hide the hurt that was lurking not far beneath the surface. "When you told me in San Francisco that you didn't love me, that you only wanted to be friends, I was destroyed, Clara. I needed to find a place to go, away from here, away from any chance of bumping into you. Derek had told me at the faculty dinner about the tenured position coming up in the Bioengineering Department, so I stayed on for an extra day to meet with the board. They were prepared to offer me the job on the spot, but I told them I needed to think about it."

He paused and I scowled angrily up into his face and gestured for him to continue.

"I needed to make it clear to Derek that *if* I took up the job at Stanford, I would be selling my company and no longer be involved in any of the heart valve projects but that they would continue without me. I owed him that explanation, which is why I emailed him yesterday."

I stepped forward and poked him again, with a little less conviction this time. "Derek's message said that you have already accepted the post."

Henry reached for my jabby finger and wrapped his hand around my wrist, pulling me towards him. "He is mistaken. I had planned to accept it, but then I found this beautiful, crazy, Wonder Woman wannabe, hiding in my coat this morning, and my entire focus changed."

"What?" I whispered in disbelief.

"I had geared myself up to sell FraserTech to Claus today and accept the position at Stanford. But you turned up in the nick of time and persuaded me that there was a reason to stay in Oxford, the best reason to stay," he murmured, tugging my hand again so I was now flush against his body, his other hand still holding onto the worktop, like he was using it as a life raft to keep himself afloat.

"I did?"

"You know how in superhero films there is always a countdown, and usually the hero succeeds with mere seconds to spare? Well, you performed that feat in real life today. I was on the phone to my lawyers to draw up the conditions of sale when I walked back into my office and saw you. I'd just written the acceptance email to Stanford, but hadn't yet hit send, and you already know that you got to me before I could meet with Claus and sell away my life's work," he said, a small smile starting to play over his lips. "So, on balance, I think you may actually be a really good candidate for Wonder Woman. Although Cat Woman is definitely sexier."

"So, you're not leaving me?" I asked, not daring to hope. The sharp ache that had been present all afternoon, dulling a little.

"No, you crazy lunatic of a person, I am definitely not. I have it in writing that you love me and that you want to spend forever with me. A very formal and binding sticky note contract between us," Henry said, his tone becoming quiet and intense.

"What else is in this contract?" I murmured, barely audibly, fighting my lips so that they didn't spread into the broadest smile known to man. I could almost physically feel the gaping chasm that had appeared behind my ribs starting to close, the pain lessening with each breath.

"It says that the two parties, Dr Henry Fraser and Dr Clara Clancy, henceforth to be known as boyfriend and girlfriend, are to mutually love, trust and respect each other, and to have red hot sex as often as is humanly possible, in perpetuity."

Henry's expression was gloriously adorable, enhanced all the more by the trying-not-to-smile smile.

"Urgh, oh my god! W-w-who told you?" I stammered, my face turning beetroot at the mention of my Dominic-related mental guff, those little words continuing to haunt me.

"About the fact you alluded to '*red hot monkey sex*' when trying to persuade your ex-work colleague and a certifiable homicidal maniac to stop stalking you?"

"Yes, that," I groaned burying my head into his shoulder.

"Simmy Anand," he answered, laughing.

"What? Why would Simmy tell you that?" I asked, looking back up into his face, horrified.

"Because, Clara, she was worried about you, I think, either that or she is trying to devise some sort of real-life soap opera for her own entertainment," he muttered, clearly undecided on her actual motives. "Anyway, she came to talk to me with some very specific requests, and I'm going to use her terms here. She said I had to '*stop dicking around and get on with asking you out*', because '*Dominic was being a creepy little git*' and you were '*incapable of effectively telling him to get lost on your own*', and also '*clearly head over heels in love with me*'," he finished with a grin.

"You met with her before our trip to San Francisco?" I really was going to kill her. Slowly. With only the stationery contained in her desk drawer.

"She first came to me before the company away day actually, but then I bumped into her again before we flew out, and she told me everything that had gone on with Dominic and threatened to castrate me if I didn't sort it out soon," he replied, cringing. Her willingness to neuter the male members of our office was alarming.

"Oh. So, were you planning to ask me out at any point?"

"Well, I was just looking for the right opportunity, but in usual Clara Clancy style, you have managed to thwart quite a few of my attempts, until somehow my ex-wife managed to tell you everything that I have been unable to say in the last seven years, and then all my feelings came out in a great big brain dump, at a really bad time, which totally freaked you out." He winced. "Sorry about that."

"It did freak me out."

"I know, and I never meant for it to happen the way it did," he said, gazing down at me and pushing my hair from my face, smoothing away a stray tear that still lingered. "I guess I should be a bit grateful to Dominic and his unwelcome advances for pushing me into action. Although, I still feel a bit murdery when I think of what he did."

"He was waiting for me outside work today," I whispered.

"What?! Are you ok?" His grip on my body tightened. "Why didn't you call me? Did he touch you? Fuck it, I am definitely going to kill him!"

"No, he didn't touch me. He wants me to stop the disciplinary hearing so he can keep his job."

"I wish you'd called me, I would have dropped everything and found you and kicked his arse for even looking at you." His eyes were luminous, jaw muscle tense, nostrils flared and breathing ragged, a pot of simmering anger that he was struggling to keep a lid on.

"I didn't call you because I was mad and hurt, because I thought you were leaving, and I wanted to deal with this my way, Henry," I murmured.

"What did you do?"

"I told him that I wouldn't call off the hearing and that

what he did was wrong. But he showed no remorse, as expected, really. I made sure I stayed in front of the CCTV camera, and I sent the time to Richard so he can use the video as more evidence."

Henry hugged me tightly into his body, chin on top of my head. "If you ask me to, I will absolutely punch him again, even if my knuckles still hurt a bit from the last time."

"My poor brave Superman, but that's really not necessary." I relaxed a fraction more against his chest. "Thanks for being on my side, though."

"Always."

We clung to each other in silence for a few moments before I asked the thing that had been playing on my mind for a while now. "I just don't understand why everyone else knew that you loved me before I did?"

"Because, Clara, you are totally oblivious to the trail of devastation and broken hearts that you leave in your wake. The sheer amount of inane gestures designed to impress you that I have employed is embarrassing," he said in an exasperated voice.

"What are you talking about, Henry?" I asked, baffled, leaning backwards to look into his face.

"I'm talking about the macho posturing that happens continuously in your presence, and not just from me," he replied.

"That clearly does not happen," I snorted.

"As a not-so-impartial observer, I can tell you that it does happen. *All* the time in fact, and it's really rather irritating," he said with a small frown.

Chapter Thirty-Two

"Whatever," I muttered and leaned back in against him, my nose pressed to that small dent at the base of his neck where his collar bones ended, the place where his shirt lay open, and where he smelled at his most delicious. Washing powder, clean, warm male skin, and that woodsy, outdoorsy scent that was totally Henry.

I nuzzled in a little more and I felt his body shift, arms pulling us even tighter together, closing the millimetres of distance so that every part of me was touching a bit of him. I had never felt so comfortable, so at home, ever before.

But then the cave woman in me began to stir, her primal urges awakened. The desire to kiss Henry's skin was all I could think about. Resisting, I tamped down on it, trying to keep myself satisfied with sniffing him instead. But the need to taste him was now burning a hole in my limbic system.

Was I going to do this? My tongue darted out but didn't make contact, a reptile testing the air.

No, nope, I couldn't do it.

But I wanted to. I really, really wanted to.

But it might be a little weird. To just kiss his neck, with no other preamble, when we were just having a little cuddle.

Or maybe he'd really like it?

As if sensing the war that was waging inside me, Henry dipped his head and murmured, "Are you alright down there?"

"Mmmm, hmmmm," I mumbled, keeping myself buried tightly in this heavenly little nook.

My tongue darted out again, of its own volition, and this time it made contact, and Henry went completely still.

I'd started and now I couldn't stop myself.

I was doing this, really actually doing this.

His skin tasted faintly salty, divine, and as I began my slow lingual perusal, lips gentle against the corded muscles of his neck, which were bunched tightly, his pulse began to thrum under my touch. When I reached his Adam's apple, which bobbed beneath my tongue, my cave woman was fully awake. And she was feisty.

"Clara, what are you, Christ, ahhhh," Henry mumbled, his voice turning a bit strangled and then incoherent, as my confidence grew, and I increased the pressure that I was applying.

Gently, at first, I nibbled my way along his stubbled jawline, nipping his ear and then returning to his chin, kissing the little dimple by the corner of his mouth. And he was definitely getting breathless.

"Bedroom, now," he growled, dipping his head against my cheek. Clearly his inner caveman was taking the lead too, fully formed sentences no longer achievable.

"Yes, please." I had barely had a chance to form the words

when he scooped me off the floor and slung me over his shoulder in a fireman's lift, striding purposefully towards the stairs. Arm clasped tightly around the back of my thighs.

Affable Henry was gone, Alpha Henry was here. And he was sexy as hell.

"Bathroom." I gesticulated when we got to the first door on the landing. He grunted beneath me in acknowledgement.

"Spare room," I whispered at the second door. This was a weird way to show someone my house, but not wholly unpleasant I thought as I stared down, bumping against his broad back.

"Your room?" he asked, tone gravelly, pushing the final door open and striding inside.

"Yes."

I'd absently left the bedside light on earlier, the soft glow lighting the space, my case from San Francisco, which was still packed, untouched, clean washing piled in the basket, not yet put away, my black ninja clothes from earlier strewn on the bed haphazardly. Spencer was now curled up happily amid the chaos, right in the middle of the duvet.

"Sorry about the mess, Henry," I apologised, still upside down, addressing his lumbar region and thinking that Dr Neat Freak must be breaking out into a cold sweat at the state of the room he was in.

In response, he slowly slid my body back down the length of his front, eyes big and dark, murmuring, "What mess?"

Taking a step back Henry removed his coat and laid it out on the chair by the window, then, he turned to the bed and carefully and considerately picked up Spencer. "Now then, mate, I bet there is a particularly good spot on the sofa with your name on it. Be a decent chap and head off there."

I fully expected for Spencer to shred Henry's arms to pieces and then launch at his face savagely, akin to the larval stage of the alien in the film 'Alien'. But he didn't. Instead, he just gazed adoringly up at him, and began to purr. Even purring when Henry gently deposited him outside the bedroom door and shut it behind him. For crying out loud, even my cat wasn't immune to the Hot Henry Effect. Traitorous feline.

With his back to the door, Henry began to slowly unbutton his shirt, his attention focused on me. Each twist of his fingers revealing more and more of his body, until he finally was able to shrug the shirt off his shoulders and place it, neatly folded, with his coat, on the chair. Henry was now standing before me, naked from the waist up, and despite him being at least six feet away, the air between us simmered with heat and tension, an almost palpable haze of lust, which was dizzying and intoxicating.

Mute and in a state of shock, I was rooted to the spot, not quite able to comprehend what I was seeing, but desperately trying to process the images that were being lasered onto my retinas. His face was gorgeous, dreamy, totally breathtaking. I knew this from all the time I had looked at it. But his upper body was a work of art. Ridges and furrows, flat planes and hard angles, enough of a covering of dark hair to be totally masculine, but not so furry that there was a worry you might find small creatures living in the wilderness of his chest.

"Now, if only you were in a cotton shift and I was in a kilt, we could recreate some of that magic," Henry murmured, placing his glasses on top of the book that was lit up by the lamp next to my bed.

"Hmmm, you did once promise me that you'd wear some tartan, don't back out on me now, Fraser," I replied.

"Och aye, I am definitely up for that little role-playing activity," he said in the worst Scottish accent I had ever heard, before stepping closer. "But for now, I'm just wondering what you could possibly have on under this sexy garment."

"Are you sure you can see what you're doing, without your glasses, Clark? Need me to fetch your guide dog?"

"I think I'll manage, thanks," he replied, trying to hide his amusement, by rubbing a finger over his lips. "It just might mean I have to get *really* close to be able to see you properly."

"Ok." I shivered with anticipation at the intonation he'd put into that comment, just as he reached under my chin for the zip of my onesie, and slowly, so tortuously slowly, began sliding it down, revealing the black and pink stripper underwear that I had not yet taken off.

I could see his throat working as he gave a sizable gulp, which boosted my ego intensely.

"Holy shit," he groaned, "one must never assume to know what this scientist is wearing under a penguin onesie, as well as her lab coat."

A determinedly fascinated expression stole across his face as he eased the fleece arms over my shoulders and helped me to step out of the one-piece pyjama suit, folding it carefully, almost reverently, and placing it on the chair with his coat and shirt.

I gestured down my body. "This is my preferred outfit for answering the door, just so you know."

"In that case, you are never answering the door to anyone but me, ever again," he said with a grin and, reaching for his fly, he swiftly divested of his trousers, socks and shoes, standing there in just his boxers. Except, they weren't just any boxer shorts. They were royal blue with red binding, and a large red and yellow 'S' motif adorned the corner of one leg.

"Superman underwear?" I laughed incredulously, not quite believing what I was seeing.

"Yes, they are new and have recently become my favourite pair." Henry waggled his eyebrows and gave me a twirl (and a brief, tantalising glimpse of his extraordinarily tight backside). "In fact, you have no idea how hard it is to find adult-sized Superman underwear."

"I can only imagine." I giggled, putting my hands over my eyes in mock embarrassment. "I am quickly learning to never assume to know what this engineer wears under his business suit, either."

A sudden increase in temperature alerted me to his close proximity, and when I uncovered my eyes, he was stood in front of me, close and intense, tentatively reaching out to sweep his hands slowly up and down my sides.

"You are so incredibly beautiful, and I have wanted to touch you like this for so long." Henry's tone had gone from playful to awestruck, and the feel of his hands on my skin reawakened the cave woman who was quite ready to hit him over the head and tie him to the bed.

"I think I can probably manage to see past your obvious physical imperfections too," I murmured, hesitantly running my fingers over his firm, contoured stomach muscles and shuddering with pleasure at how he felt under my hands. Allowing my fingertips to trace the line of hair that disappeared beneath the waistband of his underwear, before I hooked them into the elastic and gave it a quick twang.

"That's very charitable," he whispered, leaning his head

down towards me, his knuckle grazing under my chin to tilt my mouth up to meet his.

"Isn't it? Practically care in the community." I smirked against his lips.

"Right, that's it," he growled, and with lithe, sure movements, he picked me up and threw me on the bed, where I bounced a couple of times, still laughing. Quickly, he was on top of me, crawling up my body, running his nose up from the junction of my thighs and all the way up my midline, pausing at my sternum to study the Wonderbra more closely. An almost pained expression crossed his face before he started to taste my skin, using his lips and tongue to explore my collar bone and up my neck, feathering my jaw with light kisses, until we were, at last, face to face.

"Did I ever tell you just how much I love your smell, and your face, Clara?" he whispered, smiling and bending down to kiss me on the mouth.

Chapter Thirty-Three

The thing is … what was the thing? Right, yes, the thing is… Nope it was impossible to concentrate on the thing with the feel of Henry's mouth and hands on me.

His incoherent moans, punctuated with the odd comment such as "How can your skin be so soft and taste like strawberries?" and "I always knew you'd be incredible" and "Clara, these sounds you are making are really doing it for me" and "we're definitely making this last all night long", were enough to completely liquify my entire body. Even Angus the Highlander and his dirty talk hadn't made me feel this turned on.

Yes, back to the thing. Well, the thing is, it turns out that foreplay with Oxford's answer to Superman has only gone and ruined me for any other man, ever. Not that I could have even thought about anyone or anything else at that point, my brain about ready to explode with the sensations that were flooding in. Taste, smell, colours, sounds and touch all started and ended with Henry, and the delicious things that he was doing to me.

And he definitely knew what he was doing to me – holy crap-balls of fire, if this wasn't the hottest thing I had ever experienced.

Cool, delicate kisses fluttering down my neck, a huff of warm breath over skin, firm fingertips skimming the lace and silk of my bra, brushing pebbled nipples through the fabric so that goose pimples littered my chest, and I was willingly arching upwards in response.

"Yes, that's it," he murmured seductively, smiling against the curve of my breasts, and I grasped his hair quite forcefully, anchoring myself to him, a primal response to his insistent and sensual fingers that were encouraging me to groan and move against him. Toes curling with the pleasure that was being unleashed on me, my body now quivering, hips rocking and tilting rhythmically, his hand slipping into the top of my underwear, until I could feel the spasm starting.

Oh no, oh crap, not now.

"Owww, shit, owww! Get off! Get off!" In a totally unplanned and mood-killing manoeuvre, I was suddenly leaping upwards like a scalded cat, and jumping around the bedroom in a jerky, uncoordinated Irish jig, hopping up and down and starting to laugh like a maniac, as the pain built and built.

"Have I hurt you? What did I do? I'm so sorry! Shit, Clara, what's wrong?" Henry was sat up, his hair pleasingly messy and on end, a look of horror and confusion on his face as he watched me from the bed.

"Sorry, no, not you. Owww!" I tried doing little stretches, nope not working. "It's cramp, I've got cramp! And it shitting-well-bloody-hurts-like-a-bastard!" I swore, between laughs, now hopping up and down on the afflicted limb.

"You've got cramp?" Henry replied sceptically. "Then why are you laughing? Like an actual crazy person?"

"Because it hurts," I cried, still snorting with pain-induced mirth and bouncing on one leg.

"You're laughing because it hurts?" He was now starting to smile, clearly relieved that he hadn't been the one to inflict the pain on me. "This is not how I was expecting this to go, Clara. Where is the cramp?"

"In my foot, look I've even got a sticky out little toe," I moaned, showing him my deformed, claw-like foot, before quickly stomping it down into the carpet as a new wave of muscular convulsions started.

"Let me see," he said, scooting to the edge of the bed and placing his feet on the floor. "Trust me, I'm a doctor."

"You're a doctor of engineering, Henry, I don't think it qualifies you to treat my twisted metatarsals," I said, dramatically, hopping away from him.

"Much as I'm enjoying watching you do a stripper-esque version of *River Dance* in your underwear, Clara, don't be such a baby, and let me have a look. Maybe I can rub it better?" he suggested.

"You are NOT touching my foot," I shot back.

"Why? I've touched quite a lot of your body already, and I really, *really* want to touch quite a lot more," he replied, now smirking, the dark lustful look back in his eyes, making my insides clench a little.

"Yes, well, I'd like that too, anywhere but my feet."

"Why can't I touch your feet? I'd like to, even if your freakish sticky-out toe is grossing me out a bit."

I threw a balled-up pair of socks from the pile of clean

washing, aiming vengefully for his head. "Hey! My feet are not gross!"

He caught the sock missile easily, before it could inflict any damage to his amused face, throwing it in the air and catching it again like a cricket ball. Then, narrowing his eyes in contemplation, he asked, "Are you ticklish?"

I gave him a mulish look and leaned back against the dresser, pointing my toes and trying to curl them upwards to relieve the spasm.

"Ah, that's it! You have ticklish feet," he said triumphantly when I didn't answer. "I promise I won't tickle your foot, Scout's honour."

He was back to being a boy scout and his funny little salute begrudgingly wrenched a smile from me. "Promise?"

"Promise," he said seriously, then patted his knee and in a soft crooning voice carried on, "Let Dr Fraser see your poorly foot and make it all better, Clara."

Cautiously I raised my leg and placed my still cramping foot on his lap, my bottom resting on the edge of the dressing table for support.

"There we are." Henry's hands were so warm as they wrapped firmly around my ankle before sliding down and cupping the arch firmly. I flinched, and he tutted. "I'm not going to tickle you, stay still."

I nodded, but remained tense, watching his long fingers knead at the sore muscle underneath, his face steeped in concentration, tongue poking out of the side a little. He looked adorable and I felt myself start to relax, the tension easing from my lower leg, pain dissipating under his deft strokes. This was actually really nice, making me hum appreciatively as he worked his way down to my toes, gently manipulating each one, before sweeping back up again.

"So, you like this, huh?" Henry murmured looking up at me, biting his lip.

"Dr Fraser's magic touch," I whispered, and he smiled in return. "You're the only person in the whole world who I have ever let touch my foot."

"I feel honoured," he replied, his hand starting to slide up my leg, now that the cramping in my foot had subsided.

"You should." My head began to swim a little, a fug of hazy lust building as his fingers massaged my calf, heading steadily upwards. "You do know that if it had been the other way round, I would have definitely tickled you, don't you?"

"Yes, without a shadow of a doubt," he said with a soft chuckle, and I was momentarily disappointed when he gently pushed my leg from his lap and stood up. "Any other areas that require Dr Fraser's magic touch?"

"Umm, how about here?" I held my hand out and waggled the tip of my little finger, which he kissed lightly.

"That particular body part looks ok to me," he said, his tone turning deep and husky.

"Oh really? In your professional opinion, where do you think needs your attention then, Dr Fraser?" My heartrate was now skipping along again, anticipation and excitement at his obviously seductive intention roiling through me.

Henry stepped forward and reached around behind me, slipping his hands down my back and caressing the waistband of my knickers, giving the elastic a little snap, before palming my backside firmly through the lace, drawing me towards him. "I think, based on many hours of study, that this particular bit of your anatomy may be unusually tense and definitely requires my ministrations."

"Many hours of study?" I queried, wiggling in his grasp, and raising myself up on to my tiptoes to whisper against the corner of his mouth.

"Many, many hours," he confirmed, grinning and kissing me.

Kissing Henry was, I imagined, like taking part in an Olympic sport; it required complete dedication, was all-consuming and intoxicating, and most definitely left you out of breath and deserving of a gold medal and a good lie down. I felt as though I could go without eating or sleeping, or breathing really, if he just kept kissing me this way.

Henry's hands were not so gently cupping my backside, the material of my pants bunched up to allow him free access, thumbs caressing the skin of this body part that he seemed to have stared at quite studiously, unbeknownst to me.

The feel of his body under my own hands was mind-altering and I was greedy to touch him, taste him. Every part revealed something so different and new, the warm soft skin of his back, the ridged, firm muscles of his stomach, rough chest hair scratching deliciously against me.

"As a keen researcher, Henry, how many … hours … of study … are needed … to fully … acquaint oneself … with the delights … of the human gluteals?" I asked between kisses, slipping my hands into the back of his shorts and squeezing the firm curved muscles packed snugly inside.

"I would say that it could be a person's whole life's work, Clara," he replied gruffly, one hand now trailing up my back to expertly undo my bra. "But I am very thorough when it comes to examining my topic of study, and I never want it to be said that I only focussed on one anatomical region."

Henry pulled back and reverentially pushed the bra straps down my arms, letting it fall to the floor and gazing at me unabashed. "You are so beautiful, every single bit of you, I could never have imagined this," he whispered.

Then he smiled. But this was a new one, one that I had never seen before, one that was dark and secretive, and so full of delicious promises that it made my brain melt into a puddle. One that was reserved for this moment right here, a time when it was just the two of us, totally vulnerable and exposed, but so utterly focussed on each other, that it was as though the rest of the world was entirely inconsequential.

His large hands covered my breasts, palms cupping the undersides gently, thumbs brushing rhythmically, maddeningly, against my sensitive flesh. When I bowed my back and pushed forward firmly into his hands, he groaned, bending his head to kiss my fevered skin, and I increased the grip I had on his arms, moaning against his shoulder and biting down gently.

I wasn't really sure what I'd done specifically, but it seemed as though his control snapped at that moment, and Alpha Henry took over again, lifting me off my feet and pushing me against the wall behind me, all the air from my lungs huffed out against his neck. Trapped between his body and the cold plaster at my back, his mouth and hands everywhere, seemingly all at once, I groaned and writhed against him, desperate for some friction. Wantonly like a hussy if I'm really being honest. But he responded equally enthusiastically. And, while I will agree that the material of my underwear was of quite flimsy construction, the point when he actually ripped my pants completely off, totally caveman style, was quite possibly one of the defining moments of my love life thus far.

"I think perhaps your manhood might be straining in those shorts, Henry," I whispered, grazing the shell of his ear with my teeth, but he just growled in response. Dropping me back on the bed and stepping out of his underwear, his large frame caging me in as he crawled back up my body. The feel of so much warm skin had me wrapping my arms and legs around him like some sort of primate (or maybe a sloth clinging to a branch) and left me consumed with the need to pull closer, to feel every inch of him, dragging him on top of me so that his heat and length was now pressed against my stomach. And let me tell you, there is absolutely nothing small about Henry Fraser.

Sliding my hands down his abdomen and tentatively grasping him with both hands, his breath hissed, and he ground out a rather desperate sounding, "Fuck, Clara," in response to my hasty fumbling.

"Well, this is impressive, not sure we even need your favourite ruler as a guide," I muttered huskily, unintentionally saying it out loud, a little concerned as to the physics of him. And me. And him in me. "Will it even fit?"

"I see that you've been working on your motivational speeches," Henry said with a chuckle. Then grazing my nipple with his teeth, his hand travelled over my hip and down between my legs, stroking me with a long, firm motion, before sliding a finger inside and then another, and whispering heatedly, roughly, "But don't worry, I think that we can definitely make this work."

The slip and slide of his fingers, the firm circular movements of his thumb over my bud of highly tuned nerve endings, coupled with increasingly fervent kisses and groans against my mouth was beyond anything I had ever felt before. And when his breathing became noticeably more ragged, his timbre more hoarse, the heady realisation of how I was affecting him was almost too much for my heated brain and over-sensitised body. There was no room for self-consciousness, no time for my usual doubts or hesitations, the thoughts that often plagued me during sex, that evil little voice inside that stopped me from just enjoying the moment, gone, just like that. Just from being with Henry.

"Fuck, you feel amazing, Clara, so warm and soft," he continued, the deep vibration rumbling through his chest, shuddering over my body. His voice was hypnotising, wonderous and resonant. I'd not been one for real-life bedroom talk before, those men who'd tried it had been terrible. But this was definitely working, his husky words washing over and taking me along with their rich mellow sound.

In the past, I'd usually had to work quite hard for every orgasm I'd ever had, desperately concentrating on the bodily sensations while simultaneously telling my brain to be quiet. And yet, just a few more of Dr Fraser's magic touches sent me spiralling over the edge, bright lights flashing behind my eyelids as I practically levitated off the mattress against his hand. Before I knew it, I was calling out his name into his shoulder as he held me close, still stroking me through the tremors, knowing exactly where to apply pressure to prolong the pleasure.

"Do you have any protection?" he managed to mumble against my cheek.

"I have the contraceptive implant," I replied, my voice

sounding very far away as the aftershocks still coursed through my body.

"Ahhh, thank god, I don't think I can wait any longer. I want to be inside you, is that ok?" he whispered into my hair.

"Yes, I want this, I want you, I trust you, Henry."

And I did. I trusted him not to hurt or use me, trusted him to be there for me.

Trusted him to love me.

Kissing like a man who'd been celibate for a century, large hands cupping my backside, he slowly slid into me, filling my now soft and compliant body, reigniting my desire as I stretched to accommodate him. The raspy hiss of his breath fanned over my skin as he began to move, slowly and cautiously at first, eyes firmly fixed on mine. His gaze observant and curious, filled with wonder and passion. Unflinchingly determined and yet vulnerable at the same time, and I reached up in awe to trace the familiar contours of his face.

I can't explain it, but it was as though our bodies had been made for one another. A cliché perhaps, but we fit exactly right and completed each other like no one else could. There was no fumbling or apologies, and just a few squelchy noises that were only a little bit off putting. The usual sense of disappointment never came, you know, that moment when the other person is concentrating so fully on getting themself off, that they forget that you are even involved. No, not this time. Henry was resolutely fixed on my every response. Like he was studying the Clara Clancy satisfaction instruction manual and committing it to memory.

As we moved together, like we had always known where to touch each other and how to angle our hips for maximum pleasure, it wasn't long before the pressure was building inside me again. Henry's attentiveness deserved a very large and shiny gold star as he recognised the signs, increasing his cadence and upping the power of his thrusting to meet me exactly right, sparks now shooting under my skin, whole body trembling. And when he placed a hand under my lower back, lifting me up to seat himself more completely, he quickly sent us both soaring into a mutually noisy, slightly squelchy, and hugely satisfying simultaneous climax.

Did the earth move? It could well have done; this was superhero sex after all. And while it seems that the Hot Henry Effect can result in skyrocketing oestrogen levels in the general female population, the ultimate culmination of this phenomenon can be measured according to the number of orgasms achieved by this one scientist.

As any good researcher knows, experiments must be conducted in multiples to ensure that outliers and bias are mitigated for, and results are meaningful, and as an ex-Oxford academic, I am nothing if not methodical. And luckily so was Henry.

Chapter Thirty-Four

Henry was back in his Superman boxer shorts and one of my dressing gowns, which wouldn't quite do up across his broad chest, the arms tight around his fairly large biceps. I sat on the edge of the work surface wearing his blue striped shirt and a new pair of non-shredded pants, swinging my legs and ogling him as he scooped out the curry into microwavable bowls.

"Is it funny that we are wearing each other's clothes?" I asked, taking a mouthful of wine, thinking he definitely looked funny in my things.

"I like seeing you in my clothes," he replied, putting the curry into the microwave and studying the dials diligently until the machine started its wizardry and began heating up the lukewarm food. "Is it creepy that I have not yet had the tux jacket you wore at the away day dry cleaned, because it still smells of your perfume?" he said with a wince as he leant back against the work surface.

I nodded thoughtfully. "Yep, totally creepy and weird."

"Oh."

"But you could salvage this situation by telling me how you sniff it every night before you go to sleep, just to be constantly reminded of me."

"Of course. I keep it with me at all times for sniffing purposes," he chuckled, "although, I don't actually need anything to remind me of you, Clara, you're in the very forefront of my mind all the time anyway."

Wow, he was good at this. Grade A boyfriend material.

Henry's expression quickly settled into his shy smile, the one that he had used to great effect when we were in the lab, the one that could pretty much get me to do anything for him. I felt like I was drowning in his gaze, when I was hit with a sudden clarity, like a bus running over my head: this had never been the manipulative or coercive look that I had thought it to be. It was, in fact, a genuine and unintentional manifestation of what he was feeling deep inside. It was the look of love (and now that song was in my head), and something that I had become very familiar with the entire time I'd known him but had never been able to decipher before.

I really was as blind as a bat, and I silently thanked my lucky stars that Henry had been blessed with infinite patience. Sliding off the worktop, I padded over to where he stood, his face now amused as I pretended to sidle up to him in a comedy villain way, and then wrap my arms around his neck, leaning up on my tiptoes to kiss him.

Our make out session was getting pretty steamy, and I had practically climbed his body like a squirrel up a garden bird feeder, fully prepared to straddle him on the kitchen work surface if necessary, when we were disturbed by the ding of the microwave, signalling hot food, and the very timely rumble of Henry's stomach.

"Woah there, Wonder Woman, Even Superman needs to refuel at some point," Henry said with a slightly reluctant groan, and put me down on the ground, patting my bottom affectionately before dishing out the food.

We'd shared a number of meals together, sometimes just the two of us, but this reheated takeaway around my tiny, cramped dining table, was more intimate and memorable than anything else we had ever done. I couldn't help staring at him as he ate, totally consumed by an entirely new emotion, one that seemed to be fizzing inside me, as if I'd uncorked a shaken Champagne bottle and the bubbles were spewing out everywhere.

"Have I got curry on my face?" Henry asked, still concentrating on the last bits of his food, not looking at me, lips quirking in amusement.

"Nope. I just really like looking at your face. It's definitely grown on me recently."

"Is that so?"

"Mmm hmm."

"And why is that?" Henry had finished eating now, and was studying me intently, while I swept up the last bits of tikka sauce with my naan bread.

"Well, you're not unattractive," I began, looking up at him through my eyelashes, thrilled when his gaze darkened, and his jaw clenched as I licked some residual curry from my fingers.

"Strong start, carry on."

"And you're pretty great at kissing, and you know, *other things*, so that's definitely upped your appeal somewhat."

"Good to hear," –he was trying hard not to smile– "likewise, you're really great at kissing and *other things* too, just so you know."

I preened a little inside at this comment, who doesn't want to be told that they're good in bed?

"And sometimes the way you look at me, and definitely when you touch me, well, it makes me feel…" I trailed off, blushing and not really knowing how to describe it sufficiently.

"A bit swoony, perhaps?" he suggested with a raised eyebrow, choosing to repeat my embarrassingly twee turn of phrase from my earlier sticky notes.

"Maybe just a bit," I replied, using my fingers to indicate a tiny amount. "Mostly though, I feel like I have no bones, a bit how I imagine it must be to live life as a box jellyfish." There was a pause while Henry processed what I'd said and I realised how ridiculous that analogy sounded, adding, "Which is a good thing, just so you know."

Finally, Henry lost the battle with his face and grinned stupidly across the table. "Listen to you, talking about how you're feeling, almost like a real grown up."

"Hmmph. Very funny. How do you feel when I look at you or touch you, then?" I muttered petulantly.

Henry stood up quickly, knocking over the chair, which clattered noisily on the tiled kitchen floor behind him. Reaching down and pulling me to my feet, he swept me up into a bridal hold and murmured, "When you look at me, and especially when you touch me, Clara, I feel like I'm an actual fucking superhero."

I awoke to Spencer stood on my pillow; his backside close to my face.

"Urgh, your cat is trying to lick my eyeballs, Clara," Henry grumbled sleepily.

"It's just because he's hungry and he likes you," I mumbled, diving under the duvet again and away from the cat-engineer love-in that was occurring above my head, back to the blissful unawareness of sleep.

But Henry followed me under the safety of the covers, feathering my shoulder with kisses, his large hands almost encircling my waist and pulling me towards his warmth, murmuring huskily, "Good morning."

Twisting in his grip to face him, hair charmingly ruffled and gaze dancing with something dangerously primal and hot, he didn't give me a moment to even think about morning breath before he dived on me, and we were kissing passionately. And he didn't taste of anything other than Henry. How was this even possible? I wondered if we'd expended so much saliva with our kissing marathon (which had lasted most of the night), that the inherent antimicrobial properties of spit had, in actual fact, fully cleaned our mouths of all bacteria. An entire doctoral thesis could be dedicated to this phenomenon, without a shadow of a doubt.

The sound of a phone ringing, and the intensely disgruntled meowing of a cat, penetrated the fog of my mind, and reluctantly I pushed Henry away, who seemed entirely oblivious. "Is that your phone, Henry?"

"Mmmm?" he murmured still kissing my throat, when Spencer appeared under the covers and yowled loudly, worming his way down between us and purposefully turning his backside in my direction again.

"Argh, fine I'm getting up!" I disentangled myself from Henry and slid out of bed and onto the floor with a bump. "That's definitely not my phone ringing, shouldn't you answer it?"

"It can wait," Henry replied, he'd found his glasses and was peering at me over the edge of the bed, while I ferreted about on the floor for my discarded bathrobe. "Why don't we get your persistent cat his breakfast, then we can get some coffee and come back to bed?"

"Insatiable much, Dr Fraser?" I muttered, and, whilst I was a tiny bit sore from such a lot of unaccustomed nocturnal activity, I was also more than a little victorious that he was clearly completely obsessed with my womanly attributes.

"I think insatiable is a fair approximation of how I'm feeling at the moment. I've waited over seven years, Dr Clancy, so we've got a lot of catching up to do," he murmured seductively.

"Mmmm, and how's this going to manifest at work, Dr Fraser? Quickies in the stationery cupboard? Blowjobs under your desk?" I teased, but he was looking a bit feral now and I was starting to wonder if he didn't just mean to keep me locked in my bedroom forever. Which actually might be ok with me… No. Nope. Remember that you're a feminist, Clara.

"Those sound like excellent options, I'll send you some meeting requests." He smirked darkly. The phone started ringing again and with a huff of frustration, Henry turned over and retrieved it from his coat pocket on the chair. "Shit, it's my mother."

"Why is your mother calling you first thing on a Saturday?" I griped, pulling on my dressing gown and slippers.

"It's actually after 10am, and I'd totally forgotten that it's my brother's birthday and I said I'd be there for lunch," Henry replied, swiping the screen to answer. "Hi, Mum."

This was weird and uncomfortable, and a little disappointing that I wasn't going to be able to spend the day with him, but I would cope.

"No, I haven't forgotten… No, that's fine, I'll get the cake… Don't worry, I'll be there." Henry turned to watch me as I padded towards the door, Spencer curling excitedly around my legs. "Is it ok if I bring someone?"

I stopped dead and stared at him. Bring someone? As in me? To a family party?

"Yeah, she's a she." He smiled, keeping eye contact with me, quietly and patiently listening to the high-pitched chattering that was now coming out of the speaker. "That's a lot of questions, Mum, why don't you save them for when you meet her?" He was nodding his head, amused at my slowly shaking head.

I was no longer a jellyfish, more like a panicked sardine caught in the deadly tentacles of a poisonous anemone.

His expression turned soft and intense. "Yes, it's serious."

Oh my.

"She's called Clara, and I met her at Oxford when we were PhD students. We've recently caught up again." He was now asking me to come with his eyes. "Please," he mouthed at me while still vaguely paying attention to his mother.

And I felt myself begin to nod, even though my brain was screaming to abort all head movements.

"She's right here if you want to talk to her?" His grin had turned mischievous. "You do? Excellent, I'll hand you over."

Numb with shock, wondering how to kill him in the most painful way possible, I took the phone and held it up against my ear. Professional Clara appeared in the nick of time, dispelled all my flustering and spoke as if she was addressing an important professor who needed impressing.

"Hello, Mrs Fraser, how are you?"

"Hello, Clara, please call me Fiona. I'm so excited to meet you, Henry has kept you very quiet." Her voice was soft, her accent faintly French, and a little bit admonishing, as if she should know all the ins and outs (so to speak) of her son's sex life.

"Oh, well, Fiona, it's still pretty early days so I'm not surprised he hasn't mentioned me to you," I answered breezily.

"If you say so, but Henry has never brought anyone home to meet us, not even that American girl, so you must be incredibly special and important to him," Fiona gushed, sounding not unlike an enthusiastic puppy being told 'walkies'. "I hope that he is being a gentleman, Clara?"

This question brought up a lot of erotic flashbacks of activities that he had performed fairly recently that would probably (definitely) not be considered entirely gentlemanly, flooding my brain with X-rated material so that a furious blush stole over my skin. Henry was watching me with amused bafflement, and when I answered, "Yes, Fiona, a total gentleman." He burst out laughing and then blew me a kiss.

"So, you have a PhD too? In engineering as well?" Fiona was still questioning me. Focus.

"Yes, but not in engineering. I am a scientist and work for a pharmaceutical company," I replied, just as Spencer gave his biggest yowl yet, and reached up to dig his claws into my knee. "Ouch, oww! I really should go!"

"Is that a cat?" Fiona asked in surprise.

"Yep, mine, and he's a bit hungry. I'll hand you back to Henry – see you later!"

I practically chucked Henry's mobile at his head and unhooked Spencer's razor-sharp needles from my leg, nipping out of the door at lightning speed, just as I heard Henry saying, "Yes, I'm at her place, no I've not asked her to marry me yet, Mum…"

Chapter Thirty-Five

My toe was tapping on the drive over to Henry's, nerves jangling as we made our way through the outskirts of Oxford and turned into Summertown where large, elegant townhouses lined the leafy streets. Henry's house was a three-story redbrick Edwardian semi, set back from the road, with an obscenely neat garden and driveway to the front.

"I'll just change, then we should go," Henry murmured, sweeping us both over the threshold and kissing me lightly on the cheek as we entered the hallway. We were running late, having fallen back into bed after breakfast, followed by a highly pornographic shower. Which was still making me want to fan myself repeatedly every time I looked at Henry's mouth, causing my brain to replay all the wicked things he had done with it this morning. "I won't be a minute, make yourself at home."

He disappeared up the stairs, and I began my snoop of the immaculate modern kitchen, complete with a huge range cooker and real stone flooring. An antique crystal decanter was nestled, somewhat out of place, amongst lots of very shiny and expensive-looking appliances meticulously arranged on the worktop. I couldn't help but snigger when I opened a cupboard and found matching coffee mugs lined up like soldiers on parade. Reaching into my handbag, I grabbed a sticky note and scribbled a quick (filthy) message and stuck it in the first one, putting it back, upside down and out of alignment.

Off the kitchen was a utility room and laundry. Here, clean clothes were hung to dry, the scent of his washing powder triggering memories of snuggling against his chest and hiding in his coat, making me sigh a little more breathily than I would really care to admit.

A tatty and ancient-looking Bon Jovi tee-shirt draped on the clothes airer caught my eye, and I crushed the incredibly soft grey material to my nose and inhaled deeply as if I were a junkie having a fix. A mischievous idea popped into my brain, and feeling like a sneaky cat burglar, I quickly stuffed it into my handbag and carried on my perusal of Henry's house. In every room, the décor was minimalist with stripped floorboards and neutral greys, all the furniture was stylish and grand, and very different from my cosy, cluttered cottage.

"Henry, are you ready?" I called up the stairs, when I had poked around the entire ground floor, finding nothing of particular interest, other than confirming his extraordinarily mess-averse tendencies.

"Almost, come on up," he shouted back down.

Henry's bedroom was a picture postcard of masculinity. A huge bed dominated the space with a large piece of monochrome modern art hung above it, and very little else adorning the sparsely furnished room. I was just running my hands over the cool, crisp white bedding and trying to work out what the grey and black splodges on the canvas were, when Henry appeared from a doorway, freshly showered, buttoning up a checked shirt and tucking it into dark blue jeans.

"Another shower?" He looked like a yummy, newly washed lumberjack.

"I smelled of strawberries, like your body wash, which although delightful, was making it hard for me to concentrate and not end up with an embarrassing trouser tent situation." He smirked. "Probably not entirely family appropriate."

His usual, woodsy fresh scent was filling my nose as he sauntered over. I gulped in a lungful as he wrapped his arms around me. "Probably not, but your smell is pretty delightful too, by the way."

"I'm glad you think so." He placed a soft kiss in my hair, and we stood quiet and comfortable for a moment, holding each other tenderly.

"I've just picked up quite a weird voicemail that came in early this morning, I wonder if you can help me decipher it?" he said quietly, after a beat.

"Ok?" I answered, puzzled.

He pulled out the phone from his pocket and pressed the screen, and Jo's voice filled the room, her tone cross and a little bit grating.

"Hello, Henry? Bloody hell pick up, will you? Shit. Where are you? Right, well hopefully Clara has totally got the wrong end of the stick, and you two are kissing each other all over, or something, and, if so, you can disregard this message. But if you have bloody well disappeared back off to America and left her behind, I will come over and personally drag you back to

Oxford. You may not know how emotionally stunted she is, but, well, she is, and she doesn't need another man dropping her like a hot sausage at a faculty barbeque. So, you know, just sort it out, will you? Right. Good. Excellent. Bye."

"Was that Jo Harrison?" Henry asked quietly, turning the phone off.

I nodded; I couldn't believe that she'd told him I was emotionally stunted. His arms squeezed me tighter when I said, "I'm sorry, I didn't know that she was going to call you."

"It's ok, I'm glad that you've got friends like Simmy and Jo looking out for you."

"Yeah, well they're both firmly on Team Henry," I admitted with a flush.

"How about you, I'm really hoping that you are now firmly on Team Henry too?" he asked, seemingly unsure for a moment.

I nodded again, pressing my cheek firmly against his solid chest wall. My eyes unexpectedly began to burn. I couldn't really trust myself to speak, the fizzing champagne of emotions was threatening to spill over again, and I wasn't sure how to clumsily say these big feelings out loud.

"Good." Henry paused for a moment, stroking his fingers in lazy circles on my back. "And while I agree that you probably are a bit emotionally stunted—"

"Hey, I am not!" I cut him off with indignation.

"You really are, Clara. But I love you, and I hope that by now you know I'm not going to drop you like a hot sausage. Because it seems I am entirely incapable of doing so, no matter how badly I may have been burnt in the past," he said softly and a little sadly into my hair.

"I'm so sorry about what happened in San Francisco, and

for every awful thing I have ever done to you." Shame and guilt were bubbling uncomfortably close to the surface at the hurt in his words.

"You don't have to keep apologising."

"I do, Henry. I am so appalled at myself for hurting you." I paused and tried to order my thoughts into coherent sentences, while he clutched me a little tighter. "It's just that I'd put such a high value on our friendship, and I couldn't bear it if you thought less of me because I feel so little self-worth myself. Then, when you told me that you loved me, it was really hard to hear, because I couldn't have coped with it if you became another person who I let myself love, who just let me down eventually." I paused again, before continuing in a small voice, "But, I know now that you won't drop me like a hot sausage at a faculty barbeque just because I'm emotionally stunted." I swallowed drily. "I know this because I trust and love you with all my heart."

Henry didn't say anything. Taking my upper arms, he gently moved away so he could gaze at me, his expression reverent and patient.

"Is there something on my face?" I whispered, feeling my skin prickling under the intensity of the moment.

"Yes." He reached up to brush away the solitary tear that had unknowingly leaked onto my cheek. Then, slowly, he leaned in and touched a butterfly light kiss to my lips. And just like in a Richard Curtis rom com, an uplifting pop song started to play. Was it *Always* by Bon Jovi? Might have been.

"Can you hear music?" Henry asked, pulling away in confusion.

Damn, I thought that had just been in my head, but I now realised (with not an insignificant amount of mortification) that it was actually coming from my handbag and not my subconscious mind. "Shit."

I fumbled around until I found my phone and quickly turned it off, the ring tone alerting me to an incoming call from Jo.

"Was that a Bon Jovi song?" Henry's eyes had narrowed.

"Yes. It's Jo's ring tone, she programmed it into my phone many years ago and I haven't bothered to change it." She had in actual fact put many different ones on my phone over the years, this had been the one she'd selected just before she moved to Australia, the day she left me bereft and sobbing at Heathrow.

"Shouldn't you answer it?"

"No, I'll text her later." Knowing she would just quiz me about last night and I didn't want to have the Spanish sex inquisition levelled at me with Henry in actual earshot.

He looked at me thoughtfully for a moment. "What ring tone are you going to assign for me?"

"I don't know."

"Can I select my own one then?" he said with a mischievous look in his eye.

"Nothing embarrassing, Henry."

"Would I?"

With a huff, I unlocked my phone and handed it over, while he fiddled about with the screen for a few moments, grinning ridiculously.

"There."

"What is it?"

"Hang on, I'll call you."

My phone began to vibrate, and the haunting, nerve-jangling sound of bagpipes filled the air. "What the hell is that?"

"The Highland Fling."

"Why would you put that on my phone?"

"Och aye, Clara, I'm from the clan Fraser remember?" His pleased face was hilarious.

"Alright, Laird Fraser, but maybe drop the accent?" I winced. He really was dreadful at being Scottish.

"Oh." He looked a little crushed.

"Your own voice is way sexier. You must know how much I love an upper-class Cotswold accent."

"Mmmm. Well, you'd better strap yourself in and get ready for the barbaric attentions of Henry the Hopeful Highlander, from Oxfordshire, then."

I couldn't help it, I started to laugh. "How do you do this?"

"Do what?"

"Know exactly what to do to make me feel better? Know just what to say to make me laugh?"

"This is going to sound soppy, and probably a bit pathetic." Henry paused and cleared his throat uncomfortably. "You are the love of my life, the only woman that I will ever love. I think that we were actually made just for one another."

I stared up at him for a moment. "You're absolutely correct, I couldn't have put it better myself…" Henry smiled, his brows raised, clearly expecting that I had more to say. He was right. "That really was soppy and pathetic…"

"That's it, you've had it now, Clancy, I'm bringing out the big guns!" He hoisted me up onto the top of an antique chest of drawers by his bed. Slowly, he slid his hand down my leg seductively, long fingers exploring my denim-clad limb, massaging as he went.

"What are you doing?" I giggled in anticipation.

"Sit still and you'll see."

Carefully he slipped my ankle boot off, cupping my heel gently, his strong fingers working out the tension in the muscles, deft strokes relaxing and turning my body to jelly, so that I leaned against him for support, humming lightly in my throat.

"Now, what was it you were saying again? Ah yes, I remember, soppy and pathetic, right?" he growled in my ear, as he curled his free arm around my back to hold me in place, before suddenly tickling my instep until I was squirming and screeching with laughter and begging him to stop.

Chapter Thirty-Six

"Just let go, I promise they're going to love you," Henry murmured softly against my cheek, as he reached around behind me and tried to pry my vice-like grip off the car door handle, which I was holding onto for dear life.

"What if they don't, Henry?" I knew my eyes were a little wild and it was fairly obvious that I was freaking the hell out. There was a real chance that I was going to bolt like a feral animal to live in the wilderness of the Cotswolds countryside.

"They will love you, because you are brilliant, and funny and kind. But they'll also love you because I love you, and they'll see how happy you make me." His tone was reassuring, fingers slowly loosening my hold, his body now sandwiching me between him and the cool red metal of the car at my back. Delicious heat lit up inside me as he nibbled my neck and huffed gentle warm breaths over my skin. I couldn't help but moan and press myself against him, burying my face in his shoulder. "But if we carry on our PDA in this highly gratuitous fashion, my mother is going to demand that I marry you this very second, Clara."

"What?" My eyes snapped open, remembering that we were up against his car, which was parked in the palatial circular drive of his parents very grand house, and I was practically dry humping him in broad daylight. Feral was the right word for me at this moment in time.

"Yeah, my whole family are on the doorstep and watching us," he murmured, as he eventually freed my hands and brought them round and up to his mouth, where he kissed my knuckles lightly.

"Really?" I groaned.

"Yes, really. Now, are you ready?"

"Yes." No, I bloody wasn't ready, I needed about fifty flaming sambucas and then I might be a little bit more on the actual same page as ready. But Henry had already grabbed the cake off the car roof (where he'd momentarily put it while he talked me down off a cliff edge), and keeping a tight hold on my hand, he marched me around the car and towards the front of the giant Cotswold mansion that his parents lived in.

The view that greeted me was a bit like something you'd see in *Hello!* magazine. The most beautiful family in the world on the steps of a grand, honey-coloured house, gorgeous dark-haired men (four of them), two effortlessly chic women, and one very cute little boy, all smiling and staring intently at me.

"You can do this, Wonder Woman," Henry whispered, squeezing my hand.

"One of those men looks very like you, Henry," I replied out of the corner of my mouth as we walked what felt like five hundred miles from the car to the front door. I mean, they all looked similar, and I recalled he'd once told me that he had some brothers, but the one on the end with the very smug-looking grin, really did look like him, impossibly so.

"Yes, that's my twin brother, Ted. I'm older by three minutes." He seemed absurdly proud of this miniscule age difference.

"You never told me you had an identical twin."

"Well, you never asked. And we're actually not totally identical."

"Is he the better looking one?"

"If you think that, then I will legitimately have to kill him in a jealous rage."

I laughed and returned the hand squeeze. "Nah, don't worry, I think I like your pretty face the best."

Henry's answering smile was dazzling, and as we got near to his family, I could have sworn I heard his mother let out a gusty sigh. But it was not directed at Henry, it was most definitely directed at me.

"Hello, darling," Fiona said, sweeping down the steps towards us and enveloping Henry in a hug, while his father (I assumed that's who he was, he looked very like Henry too, but with a smattering of grey at his temples), rescued the enormous cake box from being squashed. "I'm so glad you could make it."

Henry kissed her lightly on the cheek. "Hi, Mum. This is Clara, my girlfriend."

Girlfriend. This sounded weird, but not unpleasant, coming from Henry.

"Oh, let me look at you." Fiona turned her attention to me and reached out a hand, taking my free one in a brief handclasp (my other was busy crushing Henry's metacarpals into dust). "It is so nice to meet you, Clara."

"Nice to meet you too. Thank you for letting me gate-crash your family party," I replied with a small smile. Stop freaking out Clara, she's just a person, just like you. Although, actually not at all like me, because she was impossibly glamourous and had quite clearly got her shit together. So, the actual antithesis of me, clearly.

Henry tried to stretch his fingers in my death grasp, but reflexively I clung harder, and he flinched. Casually leaning in towards me, he made to gently kiss my hairline, whispering, "I am simultaneously aroused by, and afraid of, your impressive grip strength."

Sincerely hoping that Fiona had not heard any of that, and unable to voice the witty retort that I had lined up in my brain, I just returned a soft peck on Henry's cheek with another strong squeeze of his digits, until he bit his lip and his eyes watered.

Luckily, Fiona just stared between us with a misty expression and a sort of awestruck admiration, focussing on me like I'd just cured world hunger right in front of her. "Oh, Clara, you are more than welcome in our home, any time. We are just so surprised and delighted to meet you."

"Now, now, Froggie, let's not overwhelm the poor girl too much, she's not even got in the front door yet." Henry's father had reappeared, sans cake, and was smiling down at me, his arm affectionately draped around his wife's shoulders. He had round glasses, kind crinkly eyes and a very firm handshake. His accent was unmistakably New York, but clearly softened by many years in England. "I'm Henry's dad, Jim."

"Hi," I murmured shyly.

"And this is Edward," he carried on, pointing to Henry's twin, who's arrogant grin widened further when he gave me a little wave. Then Jim pointed to the others. "This is Daniel and his wife Rebecca, and little Milo. And then that's Thomas, whose birthday it is today."

Everyone greeted me warmly. "Happy birthday, Thomas."

"Thanks. You can call me Tom, only my parents call me Thomas," he replied, walking forwards and enveloping me in a hug. Followed by Daniel and Rebecca, and Milo who leapt into Henry's arms with delight.

"Nice to meet you," Rebecca said brightly, her wavy auburn hair and hazel eyes giving her a natural Celtic beauty. Her hug was delicate and graceful, and I caught the adoring glance from Daniel when she stepped away, before he gave me a little nod and hugged me too, then extricated Milo from around Henry's neck.

Right, a family of cuddlers, I'd need to get more relaxed with this, sharpish.

Finally, Ted came over as the rest of the family started to make their way inside.

"Hello, Clara," he said in a deep voice, then he too went in for an embrace. Weirdly, being held by him felt hugely familiar and similar to Henry, and yet totally wrong at the same time.

"Put my girlfriend down, Ted," Henry grumbled, breaking up his brother's bear hug, and tucking me firmly into his side, arm protectively around my waist.

"Keep your hair on, Henry, I'm sure your girlfriend won't even be bothered that she didn't pick the better-looking twin," Ted said with a wink. Now, here was a man who knew how attractive he was, and how to use his charms for maximum effect.

"Nice to meet you, Ted. I'm not sure who told you that you were the better looking one, but as long as you believe it and it helps you to cope with your obvious physical afflictions, then that's the main thing," I replied in a slightly condescending tone, and patted his arm in a conciliatory fashion.

Henry burst out laughing next to me, and luckily after a moment, so did Ted.

"I like her, Henry, don't screw it up. Or actually, maybe do, then I could come over and be the one to comfort you." He waggled his eyebrows comically at me.

"Back off, you lecherous git," Henry muttered, stepping away from me and pushing his twin ahead of us and in through the front door.

As I followed the Fraser clan into the sumptuousness of their family home, I caught a glimpse of my reflection in the hall mirror. There was something noticeably different about the woman who stared back at me. She seemed radiant (like an advert for some expensive face cream), and strangely content. Her eyes were a bit sparkly, her cheeks a bit rosy. And she couldn't stop smiling.

"Well, you're an annoying cow," I said under my breath at my likeness, and she grinned widely in return.

It was strange to acknowledge that I was, for the first time in my life, in love with an actual real-life person. Openly and without reservation, with the added bonus that the object of my affections hadn't run away screaming at the thought of me clinging to him like a sucker fish to the face. No, he loved me back with such wonderful and absurd intensity, that my brain was dissolving at the prospect of this being part of my life from now on.

Those painful parts of me that I had held onto for so long, which had ruled so many aspects of my life, they were definitely still there, but they now no longer took up the majority of the space in my head. With a little (big) push from some wonderful friends (and with the help of my new favourite pair of lacy brave pants), I had faced my insecurities head on, finally allowing myself to follow the gentle and insistent tugs of my fragile glass heart. And despite my worries, it had not shattered like an antique crystal decanter dropped on immaculate, real-stone flooring. Instead, it had healed until the fissures were no longer in danger of exploding, so that just a mere crackle glaze on my pericardium was left.

My phone vibrated in my bag, and I dug it out quickly, glancing at the message on the screen.

Professor Jo: Are you still alive? Have you drunk all the supermarket gin? Or are you participating in some sort of Clark Kent sex-a-thon which is why you have been ignoring me?

Laughing, I quickly typed back.

Clara: Superman sex-a-thon over, you'll be glad to hear. But was DEFINITELY worth the seven-year wait. Now meeting the whole Kent family.

The answering ding, had me smiling.

Professor Jo: Go get 'em tiger.

The sound of Henry's familiar, heartwarming laughter filtered through from the kitchen, and a rush of love and happiness bloomed under my skin, soothing my soul and calming my overactive brain cells. I glanced up at the mirror again and Wonder Woman gave me a quick 'you've-got-this' salute.

Is this what it's like to be a superhero with a bunch of superhero accomplices and the confidence to take on the world, one dastardly villain at a time? Yeah, I reckon it probably is.

And it feels pretty bloody amazing actually.

Epilogue

As I opened the bathroom door on my way to Henry's childhood bedroom, large warm hands were placed over my eyes from behind. What was it about being accosted as soon as I set foot out of washroom facilities these days?

With a sigh, I muttered, "Ted, I know it's you, what are you doing?"

"How? How do you know it's me? Even with their eyes open and looking straight at us, most people can't tell us apart." His hands dropped away, and he walked around and faced me.

"You're not totally identical. Plus, anyway, you smell wrong."

Ted gave a spluttering little laugh. "I *smell* wrong?"

"Yep, weird, if I'm being honest." I shrugged apologetically.

"I smell *weird*?"

"You definitely smell weird, you git, now leave her alone." Henry's voice rumbled from somewhere behind me.

"Alright, alright. I'm going. But it was worth a try." Ted smiled wickedly at me. "I can't believe you think I smell weird though, we've only just met, and my ego has taken a real battering already."

"I think your ego will survive," Henry muttered, stepping between us and giving Ted a little shove.

Leaving the twins to have their macho standoff, I slipped into Henry's room and got ready for bed, donning a pair of pretty racy black pants and the tee-shirt that I had stolen from Henry's house earlier in the day, the sheer size of it swamping me, neckline falling over one shoulder and the hem brushing my legs at mid-thigh.

When Henry returned, a pair of dark blue pyjama bottoms slung loosely around his waist, he found me standing on his bed playing air guitar like a boss.

"What are you doing, you maniac?" He laughed, before adding, "Is that my Bon Jovi tee-shirt you're wearing?"

"Yes, it is. Stolen from your house this morning in true secret agent style. I am like a stealth, female James Bond."

"You should keep it, it looks good on you," Henry said, coming to stand by the foot of the bed and reaching out to run his hands over the soft material of his tee-shirt, fascinated with how the fabric appeared to glide over my body.

"Henry?"

"Mmmm?" he murmured distractedly, fingers perusing the hemline, grazing my skin, the touch so searing it was like being branded.

"I have a confession to make."

"Oh yes, and what is that?" Slowly, carefully, Henry was pushing the grey cotton up my legs, inching the bottom of the shirt higher and exposing more of my legs to his heated gaze.

With my arms balanced on his shoulders, I leant down and whispered in his ear, "I lied to you when we were in the lab."

"Lied about what?" His right hand had slipped around the back of my other leg and was following the same motion as his left, creeping upwards in a tortuously relaxed fashion.

"About how I feel about Jon Bon Jovi." I practically moaned at the feel of his hands on me, the material now bunched up almost to my hips.

"You have feelings for Jon Bon Jovi?"

"I do. And they are not what I originally led you to believe, Henry."

"Is he another man that I have to put on my list of people to kill in a jealous rage?"

I laughed huskily. "Maybe."

"I don't like the sound of this."

The hem of the tee shirt was now past the junction of my thighs and Henry blew out a little huff of air. "Nice knickers, Clara."

"So, about Jon Bon Jovi…"

"I don't want to talk about him," he grumbled, bending his head to plant a soft kiss on my lace-clad hip bone.

"But we really should."

"Why?"

"Because he is a god amongst men?" I murmured.

"You finally realised." Henry's lips quirked with a smile.

"Yes, and I need you to know that when I was alone in the lab, I used to listen to his greatest hits album on a loop," I whispered dramatically, placing my hands on either side of his face. "I'm sorry I abused our friendship by taking the piss out of your taste in music, but mostly I am sorry for how I treated

Jon Bon Jovi, belittling and degrading him when in actual fact I have a huge crush on him."

"He's definitely going on the list," Henry muttered, his eyes drifting back down my body again.

"I have another confession."

"I'm not sure that this is the time and place for Reverend Henry's confessional, Clara, I am looking at a very sexy pair of pants, on a very sexy woman and I have *other things* on my mind."

"Just one more confession, then we can talk about my underwear and do *other things*," I promised.

"Ok," he agreed begrudgingly, pouting in an adorable way.

"There was someone else that I had a huge crush on in the lab, back in the day."

"This hit list is going to get pretty long, I can see it now."

"He was really good-looking, maybe even better looking than Jon Bon Jovi."

"I am not sure that is possible," Henry said, "he's a god amongst men, Clara."

I laughed. "Maybe it's you with the crush on Jon Bon Jovi?"

"Undeniably."

"Anyway, this other guy who was *almost* as good looking as Jon Bon Jovi. Well, he was also really funny, which is a huge turn on."

"Is it?"

"Oh yes, even sexier than Clark Kent glasses."

"Clark Kent glasses are sexy?" Henry looked up into my face in surprise.

"Hell yes."

"Good to know."

"Anyway, back to this guy."

"Do we have to?"

"Mmm hmmm. Because he was also really sweet and thoughtful. And smart, really good at maths. Ooh and tall, really tall. The sort of person who must have won some kind of genetic lottery."

"Ok, I get the picture." Henry exhaled and leant his head against my sternum, continuing to bunch the cotton of the T-shirt, exposing my stomach and spreading one hand around my ribcage, thumb now lazily exploring the underside of my breast.

"He was a bit odd sometimes though, he had a favourite ruler, which was bizarre, but we shouldn't hold that against him," I whispered, feeling Henry chuckle against my chest. "With hindsight, I think I should have probably propositioned him in the lab supplies cupboard, or maybe dragged him behind the stacks in the bottom of the medical library for some snogging and *other things*."

"I think he would have probably liked that rather a lot, Clara." Henry's other hand was now cupping my backside and it tightened a fraction.

"Yeah, well the thing is, when I say I had a crush on him it was a bit more than that. In fact, he is the love of my life, the only man I'll ever love, someone who was made just for me," I added quietly. Placing a finger under Henry's chin, I lifted his face so I could look down into his eyes, our mouths now achingly close, his hot, toothpaste-scented breath caressing my lips.

"Is that right? Did you ever tell him this, to his face, without the need for sticky notes?" A faint twinkle of amusement was lighting up his features.

"I'm telling him now."

Acknowledgments

Well, this has been quite a rollercoaster of a ride and actually mad bonkers from start to finish. But I'll be brief, because I'm not sure anyone other than my mum will read this bit (thanks mum, by the way).

I will be forever grateful to Anne Perry and Meg Davis from the Ki Agency for holding my hand, answering my questions, and taking a punt on this middle-aged scientist from Devon. I'm sorry I've been like a rabbit in the headlights most of the time. A huge thank you to Jennie and all the team at One More Chapter, I love that you love this story as much as me. I still can't believe it's an actual book. Amazeballs. Also, massive thanks to the Twitter writing community (it will always be Twitter, sorry Elon), and the team at MoodPitch for the advice and opportunities to get my writing out of my head and in front of people; without you this book would not be here. There are some enormously talented writers out there, whose books need to be read by lots and lots of people, and I hope each of you get the opportunities you deserve. Thanks to everyone I've met online who have championed me along the way, some of you are lovely, funny, and genuine, and some of you are so downright brilliant that we hit it off instantly (you know who you are). Don't change.

Thanks to my family, particularly my mum (the original creative genius in the family) and Papa Stu for being so supportive and proud. Thanks also to the few friends I've told about this (especially Dr Sarah for being my inspiration for Professor Jo, you are a legend). To those of you just finding out now – surprise!

All the thanks to the Smallest Chalice, you are my inspiration every day and the reason why there will be a cat in every book. Thank you for your help with character names and for not being too embarrassed by my attempts at the Macarena in the kitchen. Now, you're not allowed to read this book until you are 35, so put it back on the shelf. Thanks also to Alex, for being so supportive despite your constant disbelief, sorry to spring this entirely new side of my personality on you, I promise you do still know who I am. Don't get your hopes up about a boat though.

Thank you to the cast of imaginary people who live in my head, who tell me stories, make me laugh and cry, and let me live another life through them. Here's to many more adventures yet to come.

Finally, special mention to the various traumas from my own personal life, and academic and professional career, I really am fairly disastrous a lot of the time. I'm just glad I can laugh about it all now. Mostly.

———

In loving memory of Duncan, a truly brilliant and special person, a fantastic doctor, and a hugely influential presence in my life. We all miss you every day.

ONE MORE CHAPTER

The author and One More Chapter would like to thank everyone who contributed to the publication of this story...

Analytics
Abigail Fryer
Maria Osa

Audio
Fionnuala Barrett
Ciara Briggs

Contracts
Sasha Duszynska
Lewis

Design
Lucy Bennett
Fiona Greenway
Liane Payne
Dean Russell

Digital Sales
Hannah Lismore
Emily Scorer

Editorial
Kathryn Cheshire
Kate Elton
Simon Fox
Arsalan Isa
Charlotte Ledger
Bonnie Macleod
Lydia Mason
Jennie Rothwell

Harper360
Emily Gerbner
Jean Marie Kelly
Emma Sullivan
Sophia Walker

International Sales
Bethan Moore

Marketing & Publicity
Chloe Cummings
Emma Petfield

Operations
Melissa Okusanya
Hannah Stamp

Production
Emily Chan
Denis Manson
Simon Moore
Francesca Tuzzeo

Rights
Rachel McCarron
Hany Sheikh
Mohamed
Zoe Shine

**The HarperCollins
Distribution Team**

**The HarperCollins
Finance & Royalties
Team**

**The HarperCollins
Legal Team**

**The HarperCollins
Technology Team**

Trade Marketing
Ben Hurd

UK Sales
Laura Carpenter
Isabel Coburn
Jay Cochrane
Sabina Lewis
Holly Martin
Erin White
Harriet Williams
Leah Woods

**And every other
essential link in the
chain from delivery
drivers to booksellers
to librarians and
beyond!**

LUCY CHALICE

Fundamentals in Flirting

Dr Hannah Havens is successful, independent, and as prickly as a hedgehog in a blackberry bush. When she ends back in her small home town, the last person she expects to crash into is Teddy Fraser, the irritatingly gorgeous guy she once kissed. But despite her best intentions, he keeps popping up. With his charismatic personality, surely Hannah can't avoid Teddy's charm forever...

Available to pre-order now

YOUR NUMBER ONE STOP

ONE MORE CHAPTER

FOR PAGETURNING BOOKS

One More Chapter is an
award-winning global
division of HarperCollins.

Sign up to our newsletter to get our
latest eBook deals and stay up to date
with our weekly Book Club!
<u>Subscribe here.</u>

Meet the team at
<u>www.onemorechapter.com</u>

Follow us!

🐦 <u>@OneMoreChapter_</u>
f <u>@0neMoreChapter</u>
📷 <u>@onemorechapterhc</u>

Do you write unputdownable fiction?
We love to hear from new voices.
Find out how to submit your novel at
<u>www.onemorechapter.com/submissions</u>